A FAMILY FOR THE RECLUSIVE BARON

Carol Arens

MILLS & BOON

First published in Great Britain 2022
by Mills & Boon, an imprint of HarperCollins*Publishers* Ltd,
1 London Bridge Street, London, SE1 9GF

www.harpercollins.co.uk

HarperCollins*Publishers*
1st Floor, Watermarque Building,
Ringsend Road, Dublin 4, Ireland

ISBN: 978-0-263-30202-8

11/22

This book is produced from independently certified FSC™ paper
to ensure responsible forest management.
For more information visit: www.harpercollins.co.uk/green.

Printed and Bound in Spain using 100% Renewable Electricity
at CPI Black Print, Barcelona

Dedicated to you, dear reader,
with many thanks for reading my stories.

Carol Arens delights in tossing fictional characters into hot water, watching them steam, and then giving them a happily-ever-after. When she's not writing she enjoys spending time with her family, beach camping or lounging about in a mountain cabin. At home, she enjoys playing with her grandchildren and gardening. During rare spare moments you will find her snuggled up with a good book. Carol enjoys hearing from readers at carolarens@yahoo.com or on Facebook.

Also by Carol Arens

The Earl's American Heiress
Rescued by the Viscount's Ring
The Making of Baron Haversmere
The Viscount's Yuletide Bride
To Wed a Wallflower
A Victorian Family Christmas
'A Kiss Under the Mistletoe'
The Viscount's Christmas Proposal

The Rivenhall Weddings miniseries

Inherited as the Gentleman's Bride
In Search of a Viscountess

Discover more at millsandboon.co.uk.

Chapter One

London, August 1889

Although his brother had been Baron Elmstone, only a handful of people had attended his funeral.

In a sense, Harrison was not there either. He stood by the graveside hearing the minister's voice reciting his brother's good deeds...none of which Harrison recalled...seeing the coffin covered with flowers and shifting shadows, and yet it was another image more vivid than this one which occupied his mind.

It was an occasion nine years ago in the Elmstone garden. Not an appropriate memory for the moment, perhaps, but it played in his memory as fresh as if it were yesterday.

Harrison's hand had ached that night. Not his heart, though. That had felt unnaturally numb... dead, even.

That was what came of punching one's older brother on the chin.

Juliette Huddleston had screeched, taking shelter behind Stewart's back.

Trusting Stewart to protect her had been unwise—the very last thing she ought to have done.

'You always were a fool.' His brother had rubbed his chin, laughed as if the blow meant nothing, as if Harrison's righteous anger was impotent, childish even. 'Did you honestly believe a woman like this one would be interested in someone like you?'

He had, in fact, because she'd said so. Only two nights before she'd vowed her everlasting love and told him she couldn't wait to announce their engagement.

Said fool had been sitting in an alcove, feeling the night breeze soft against his face, imagining the joy of a marriage based on trust, not betrayal. A union which was as unlike his parents' marriage as day was to night.

What an outright shock it had been to hear Juliette's voice coming from a short distance away, declaring her love to Stewart. She'd used the same words she had said to him, spoken with the same inflection in her voice.

It had been as if the words he had taken to heart were simply rehearsed. How many other fellows had she tricked with them?

Seeing her peeking around Stewart's shoulder, not a shred of remorse in her pale blinking eyes, he'd itched to hit his brother again. If his feelings meant nothing to Stewart, maybe his fists would.

He'd raised his hands, but Juliette had taken that moment to step out from behind his brother, then dash from the garden.

For the first time Harrison had noticed that the buttons of her blouse were undone, her shift exposed.

Seeing it had sucked the fight out of him. The woman who until seconds ago had been everything to him was nothing to his brother but one more conquest.

No doubt she'd expected to become the next Baroness. She would not have been the first of Stewart's conquests to think so. A trail of hard-wept tears led away from the Elmstone estate.

Harrison had thumped down on a bench, thinking that it would feel good to hit his brother again, but that Stewart was probably so used to being punched by cuckolded gentlemen he wouldn't take it as an insult. Would certainly feel no sorrow for what he'd done.

'Given your outburst…'

Stewart's expression had been unreadable in the darkness. Not that Harrison had needed to read it. He had seen the lack of remorse too many times not to know what it looked like.

'I wonder if you really are the boy your nanny used to say you were.'

'Mrs Glass? You do know she's the one who ruined our parents' marriage?'

'Her and Father together.' Stewart had given a careless shrug. 'Men will be men…and nannies are usually convenient.'

Convenient?

Harrison would never forget the first time that hell had visited Elmstone. Prayed he'd never feel as callous about it as his brother clearly had. Even now he recalled his mother screaming, heartbroken after finding Harrison's nanny in Father's chamber.

Having been woken by the noise, Harrison had crept into the corridor, hidden behind a curtain, and watched while Mother had wept, pulling in despair at her own hair. Father had simply laughed at her, much as Stewart had done to Harrison over Juliette that night years later.

The nanny hadn't run from the room, ashamed in the face of Mother's grief, but remained brazenly in Father's bed. In a rage, his mother had stormed out of the chamber, then spotted Harrison peeking around the curtain. She'd gripped his shoulders, bent close to his face.

'You'd better not grow up to be a monster like him!'

He'd tried to promise her he would not, but tears had locked his throat.

That moment was burned into his memory because he'd never seen his mother again. Not the mother he'd known, at least. She'd become another person, bitter and angry with everyone. She'd got back at his father by becoming more faithless to him than he was to her.

'Mrs Glass claimed you were a scrapper,' Stewart had said, absently rubbing the blooming bruise on his chin. 'A bad seed, she said, who liked to hit people. I wonder now if she had the right of it.'

Harrison had gone through a few nannies in his tender years, but not because he had been ill behaved. It was because Father had used them up.

A new nanny arriving in the household—or any other woman servant for that matter—had always meant an escalation of tension between his parents. He'd been able to count on their fights ringing off the walls for days on end.

To this day he had an aversion to nannies. Over the years his father had taken many lovers, selected both from his staff and willing society ladies, but it had been the nannies who'd wounded Harrison the most. Perhaps because he had been so young and vulnerable.

'Only that one time when I was four,' he'd pointed out to Stewart. 'Mrs Glass was gossiping about our mother. I've never hit anyone else until now, and you deserved it.'

'Don't look so wounded. You're twenty years old, for pity's sake. You need to understand how it is between men and women. You must admit I did you a favour.'

He had known full well a favour was not what

his brother had had in mind when he'd dallied with Juliette's virtue. In the event that she'd even had some, which now seemed unlikely.

Arguing with his brother would have been pointless. Stewart had been who he was, and nothing Harrison had said would ever have changed that.

With the flush of anger fading, he had known there would not be much point in slugging his brother again either—except that it would make him feel marginally better.

Harrison had sat in the garden that night, well after Stewart had returned to the house, whistling as if he had not just dashed the hope out of Harrison's future…

The steady thump-thump of earth hitting the coffin lid brought him back to the present.

He blinked back a tear. The only one to be shed here today, he feared. But Stewart had been young and innocent once. It was that boy he mourned.

Glancing about, he settled his gaze on his parents' tombstones on the other side of the narrow path.

Bad seed? It was nonsense, of course—simply something his brother had spouted to excuse his own behaviour. No, Harrison did not believe one could be born immoral. One could learn to be, though, and pass it on to a new generation.

Luckily, Stewart had left no seeds to go bad.

A dark thought came to him, but a true one.

It would be for the best if the Elmstone line died with Harrison.

It would not be so difficult for that to happen. He did not intend to wed—to take the risk of falling in love and ending up as miserable as his parents had been.

Even though he was a faithful sort, his former, if short-lived, fiancée was a reminder that love was not ever to be trusted.

Nothing was worth that kind of pain.

Late summer, 1890, Rivenhall House

'Let me just tame that one curl, miss.'

Minerva Grant's maid glowered at the offending lock springing from her temple. Then she cast a sidelong glance at her image in the dressing table's mirror. Despite the culprit, she looked properly proper—as a lady going to her place of employment ought to.

Not, she thought ruefully, that a viscount's daughter going to any place of employment was in any way 'proper'. But she did at least present a dignified image.

'Dottie, you know very well that it is futile to even attempt it.'

Ever since Minerva had been of an age where her hair was expected to be contained in a fashionable style, that curl had been the bane of every maid who'd attempted to make it behave.

For all that it stuck out from her temple like a

fuzzy corkscrew, Minerva rather liked it. Her late mother's hair had been curly all over. It had used to tickle Minerva's cheek when she was little. Seeing the curl reminded her of that.

It had been such a long time since her mother died. Minerva had only been seven years old, so she didn't remember everything about her. But she did recall her to have been adventurous. A woman to be admired and emulated.

'Still, I ought to give it a go. There is a gentleman downstairs. Your father is eager for you to make his acquaintance.'

Heaven help the fellow, then. Life was lovely as it was and she had no intention of changing it.

Why, she had been discouraging suitors even before she'd made her debut.

The men her father presented to her were high in society—gentlemen used to having everyone dash about to do their bidding. The only bidding Minerva wished to do was her own.

'At this time of the morning?' she asked.

She didn't know why she should be surprised. Father tended to spring hopeful suitors upon her without much notice.

'You might not wish to avoid this one, miss. I got a peek at him and he is quite handsome…if you don't mind me speaking freely.'

'You know I do not, Dottie, or you would not have spoken.'

Dottie's opinion notwithstanding, it was unlikely that this fellow was any different from the others Father had set in her path. Society had an abundance of handsome gentlemen. Which did not mean she was willing to give up her freedom to any of them.

This man might believe he was here on business—and perhaps he was. Only he did not know all of it. He was a candidate…chosen by her father with great care. Father could be very determined in getting what he wanted.

But not as determined as she was in avoiding what she did not want, she thought with a touch of satisfaction.

Thanks to Berthie, the widowed governess her father had engaged after her mother died, Minerva understood that a woman might enjoy life beyond a marriage prescribed by society.

Berthie had been much like Mother, having a merry, sportive spirit. Because of it, she'd managed to bring a grieving child from sorrow to joy. With tales of her adventures before she'd wed, Berthie had taught her to see the joy of each day, to be like her mother and embrace all the excitement she could find.

Sadly, she and her father had been at odds as to what made for contentment.

Really, though, what sensible woman would choose contentment when she could choose excitement?

'Father is persistent. I will give him that,' she muttered.

She had no time this morning to reject another suitor. She must get to the orphanage.

'Let me just make that curl neat and tidy before you go down.'

Dottie reached for it, but Minerva shook her head, tugging another strand of hair free. This one was merely wavy and hung past her chin. Judging by Dottie's frown, she looked absurd.

As acts of rebellion went, this was not much of one, and Father was not likely to take note of it, but it was all she had to hand in the moment.

'I have no time to speak with one of Father's hopefuls. As it is I will need to hurry to get to the orphanage on time.'

'You might not wish to mention you are employed, or you will frighten the gentleman away.'

'I shall bear it in mind.'

Most members of her social circle already knew of her rash behaviour in working for a wage. Although she had outgrown setting birds free and rescuing pink poodles, as she had done in the past, she still managed to set tongues wagging.

If the man downstairs did not already know of it, news of her gainful employment might very well send him on his way.

Plucking a pair of peppermint sticks from her writing desk, she put them in her embroidered purse. With a quick nod of goodbye, she hurried down the corridor, taking the stairs down as silently as she could manage, the sweet minty scent wafting out of her purse at each step.

While she was tempted to indulge in one, they were meant for the two orphans who had been delivered to London Cradle last night.

Last time she'd seen them, the poor children had been distraught. She'd felt horrid about leaving them, but her shift had been over. If she did not return to Rivenhall on time Father would send half the staff to fetch her home. She knew this because it had happened in her first week of working at the orphanage.

She had been embarrassed beyond words. How was a woman to appear responsible and independent with an army of servants at her back?

At the bottom of the stairs, she tiptoed across the hall, careful to make sure her father did not notice her leaving.

The footman opened the front door.

Escape was but a step away.

She lifted her foot and stepped over the threshold.

'Minerva, my dear. There is someone I wish for you to meet.'

'I haven't time now, Father,' she called over her shoulder.

Oh, drat! The fellow—who was indeed handsome—and Father were striding her way. She could hardly ignore them now.

With no way out, she exchanged a few polite words with Father's visitor. What he could not see was her toe, tapping impatiently under her skirt. Moments were ticking by.

Truly, she hated being late. Employees were expected to arrive on time, no matter what their father's rank was… Although, to be fair, she was the only employee whose father had a title.

That aside, there were children waiting to be comforted with peppermints and hugs.

At the first break in conversation she declared what a pleasure it had been to meet him.

Apparently he did not recognise that she was excusing herself from the conversation, because he began to discuss the weather, which he said was lovely, but usual for the time of year.

There was nothing for it now but to cut in… 'I fear I must be on my way to London Cradle Orphanage—where I work.'

She did not need to look at her father to know a red flush had crept past his collar. She had seen it enough times in the past to know it was there.

'Oh, you volunteer? How admirable.' The fellow beamed. 'It is a fine thing for a lady to keep herself occupied in noble pursuits.'

What would this man do if he was her husband? She strongly suspected he would forbid her to earn a wage.

'More noble than embroidering doilies, certainly,' she said. 'But I do not volunteer. I receive a wage.'

'I beg your pardon?'

'It still comes down to an act of charity, Lord Malden,' Father put in quickly. 'Since Minerva donates her wages back to the orphanage.'

'Oh, I am certain that a reasonable man such as yourself, Lord Malden, must agree that a woman who is employed deserves to earn a wage as much as a man does.'

If the fellow had a response, it died on his lips. His stunned gaze swung to her father.

'I must be on my way,' she said brightly. 'I do not wish to be late.'

Seeing her father's consternation, she did feel some remorse for saying what she had—even if it was the truth. Her father loved her, and wanted what was best for her...or what he thought was best, anyway. For her to be married to a nobleman, with a clutch of children.

As far as she was concerned, marriage for the sake of fulfilling society's expectations was not what made for a satisfying life.

No matter how handsome or wealthy the gentlemen Father presented to her, she would follow a path of her own choosing.

Which in that moment carried her out through the front door into the carriage.

A breeze caught the carriage door. Had the

footman not been quick of reflex, it would have slammed closed on her.

The lovely morning was quickly dissolving. Wind soon rocked the carriage, growing more turbulent as it travelled the short distance to the orphanage.

Since the children would not be playing outside in the garden today, she would pay a visit to the charming shop only a street away from London Cradle. She would purchase books and puzzles. Perhaps more peppermint sticks.

She signalled for the carriage to stop.

'Are you certain, miss? The wind is a beast this morning.' The footman closed his fist tightly around the door handle.

'I shall be quite all right.'

He did not appear convinced of it, but offered her a hand down. She hurried towards the front door of the shop.

Halfway there a great gust caught her skirt, twisting it around her ankles. She hugged her purse tightly to her side, pressed her hat to her head, then looked down, leaning into the wind.

All of a sudden a boot, long, black and shiny, intruded on her field of vision. A great bulk ploughed into her.

'Uff!' the voice attached to the person wearing the boot exclaimed.

Her balance shifted. She threw up her arms

and heard her purse hit the ground. The pavement rushed towards her face.

She reached out to catch herself, but something snagged the back of her skirt, slowed her descent, and then—

Then…impossibly…an arm grasped her about the waist, dragging her backwards in the second before her nose lightly grazed the pavement. A large, firm hand on her shoulder steadied her, drew her upright.

'I beg your pardon.'

Her assailant/rescuer had a deep, rich-sounding voice. In another circumstance it would have sounded quite agreeable.

His eyes, peering at her through black-rimmed glasses, might have been appealing too, if she had met him in another way.

But, given he had nearly maimed her, she was not disposed to look at him in a charitable light. No matter how attractively his dark lashes curled up at the ends, she would not give them a second glance.

Nor would she take special note of how interesting his smile was. She couldn't say she had ever seen one quite like it…flat, serious-looking, except at the corners. There, they tipped up congenially, giving the impression that he was expressing two moods at one time.

Surely her heart was fluttering madly for some other reason than the fact she was watching his interesting lips? The odd sensation must be a reaction to nearly taking a fall.

All of a sudden he clapped one hand on his head. A lock of black hair fell across his forehead, dangling between his eyes.

The dark strand caught her attention so thoroughly she had to take a deep breath, blinking away an urge to get lost in how green his eyes were…how very intense his gaze seemed as he looked down at her.

She felt half under a spell…or at least in a trance.

'My hat,' he muttered, casting a glance about and completely breaking the strange sensation that briefly held her.

My word, but that had been interesting. Not necessarily interesting in a comfortable way, though.

Why, she had to ask herself, did a man she did not know leave her nerves so unsettled? What were those little tingles dancing about her waist in the exact spot where he had caught her, then drawn her back from disaster?

Nature's trap, she supposed. A way of confusing a woman until she willingly gave her freedom away to a man who might take it from her.

Not that her sisters-in-law seemed to regret it… But that was neither here nor there at the moment.

'I imagine it is streets away by now,' she pointed out needlessly—because where else could it be?

'I was looking down and trying to keep it on

when we ran into one another. I do apologise. I ought to have been paying attention.'

Even now he was not paying attention.

Any other gentleman would notice his hand remained on her shoulder, even though the danger was past.

Since it was a large hand, she was well aware of it. She could not recall any other time when a man's thumb had pressed lightly on her collarbone.

This situation was completely inappropriate. Yet was there a little adventure in it? a quiet inner voice prodded.

She shook her head and tried to step backwards, to subtly remind him of where his hand was, but a hard gust tipped her forward.

He locked his elbow, which was a lucky thing. Had he not, she would have found herself right up against his chest.

Oh, dear…that would not have done.

Would it?

Now that she'd had a moment to examine what had happened, she knew it would be fair to say it had not been completely his fault.

They had both been looking down, after all. And while he had been struggling with his hat, she had been contending with her hat skirts tangling every which way, all while trying to hold on to her purse.

Not that blame mattered. There was no blame.

What did matter was that if she did not hurry she would be late for work.

Glancing down, she saw the peppermint sticks which had fallen out of her purse lying broken on the ground.

Dash it!

Rolling her shoulder, she dislodged his hand, then bent to gather her purse and the sweets before they went the way of his errant hat.

For a tall, lanky fellow, he was quick. He stooped, snatched up the purse and the peppermints. He looped the purse over her arm, then glanced at the ruined confectionery and put it in his pocket.

'Please do forgive me. And allow me to replace it.'

She thought this was a sincere apology. However, she might be misreading him. Perhaps his dark lashes and the interesting tug of his smile was confusing her.

It was uncommon for her to be confused by a man. It was not a pleasant sensation, yet not a wicked one either—which made the situation even more bewildering.

'There's no need. I bid you good day.'

She nodded, taking a step towards the front door of the Gift Emporium. The sooner she was away from him the sooner she could put this odd, off-kilter sensation behind her.

Great glory, men did *not* put her off-kilter.

It must be the wind.

She had only made it half a step away before an even greater gust caught her, pushing her sideways.

Off-kilter again…

Good. It was definitely the wind, then.

The man caught her elbow to steady her. My word he was stronger than his slim stature suggested, and tall…quite tall.

Feeling the grip of his fingers keeping her upright, so firm and manly… Oh, dear…perhaps it was not all the wind.

'Allow me to escort you inside,' he shouted, over the screeching and howling that swirled between them.

Since she did not wish to be seen blowing away in an embarrassing tumble of petticoats, she latched on to his arm.

Once they were inside, the gentleman nodded, tight-lipped. He let go of her elbow and approached the counter. He and the shopkeeper made comments about the weather.

She wondered about re-pinning her hat, but what was the point when her hair was such a hopeless tangle?

Brushing her skirts back into order, she could not help but wonder what the man's full smile would look like…

After setting herself as much to rights as was possible, she thought she might yet get to London Cradle on time.

As long as she did not linger to chat.

Not that she wished to. She had spent too much time peeking at the man's engaging eyes already. His smile, though, she would not mind looking at that for a while longer, but he was keeping it to himself.

No matter... She did not have time to be caught up in conversation if the opportunity presented.

'Good morning, Miss Grant,' the shopkeeper said, glancing around the tall fellow's shoulder.

Mr Jones was a pleasant man, who had helped her choose special treats for the orphans on many occasions.

'How is Viscount Rivenhall this blustery day?'

'My father is quite well, thank you.'

Her assailant/hero...how else was she to think of him?...cast her a quick glance over his shoulder. He smiled as he purchased a full bag of sweets, then carried it across the room and handed it to her.

'To replace the ones which were broken.'

The children would be thrilled. Surely there was time for a few words of thanks?

'They are for the orphans next door. I thank you on behalf of every sticky smiling face.'

'You volunteer there? What lucky children.'

'I work for a wage.' If she pointed it out often enough, perhaps the idea of a lady being employed would become more acceptable?

'Ah, well... I'm sure you earn it.'

While she got over the surprise that a gentleman should think so, he gave her a studied glance.

He made an odd gesture with his fingers, indicating the space in front of her nose.

'Is something wrong?' she asked. Clearly there was, but—

'Not wrong… It's only…' He wiped his thumb on the tip of her nose, held it up for her to see a smudge of dirt.

What could be more embarrassing? She must have got dirty when her nose had brushed the pavement.

It had taken him rather a long time to point it out.

And it was impolite, anyway, to point out dirt on a lady's nose!

And to be smiling about it too.

'Good day, miss.'

Why, oh, why did that smile make her feel so odd? It was almost as if she did not regret having dirt on her nose so he could wipe it away and she could see his smile.

It lit his eyes as well as his lips…

Never mind. She would probably never see him again.

She watched him go out, closing the door behind him. Through the window she saw him set his shoulders against the gale, hurrying on his way.

Where was he going? Who was he?

Why did she care?

Minerva Grant was not a romance-minded lady…and even if she had been—

Oh, bother! She was in a hurry and had no time to dwell on such nonsense.

The man was tall and…and probably clumsy, given how he had ploughed into her. The odds of her giving him a second thought were remote.

And if she accidentally did, she certainly wouldn't give him a third.

'Welcome to St Austell, sir,' the train porter nodded, offering a smile which genuinely did indicate welcome.

Harrison Wesley Tremayne, Baron Elmstone, stepped onto the platform, a frisson of anticipation racing from his boots to his new hat.

With a nod back at the porter, he took determined steps towards his fresh start in life—beginning with the carriage waiting for him outside.

Inhaling a breath of air, rich with the scents of the ocean and the warm bread in the bakery he was driving by, he rolled his shoulders to ease their stiffness after the ride from London. With one finger he pressed his spectacles higher on his nose.

He grinned.

The man who had disembarked the train was a different one from the one who had boarded it in London. Not literally, of course, but that was how he felt.

In London, he was Lord Elmstone. And the taint

of his family name shadowed him always. Even though he had done nothing worthy of scorn, he felt the stares of resentment. His family's notoriety followed him about, as noxious as the fog in London.

But he was finished with being gazed at as if he were a rake, out to wreak mayhem on innocent families. He was not his brother or his father…and not his mother either.

It was for the best that he'd decided to let the family name end with him. A child of his blood would ever be an outcast.

Did he not have good reason to know it?

Here in St Austell life would be different. He would earn the respectable reputation he had always longed for.

While he would occasionally need to return to London, to see to the needs of the Baronetcy—which he could not let go because people relied upon it for their livelihoods—his true life would be here.

At last he would have the quiet, peaceful life he had long dreamed of.

Feeling amazingly good, he drove past shopfronts, whistling. It occurred to him that he had not whistled since he was a boy.

He was going to be happier living as a common man than as a baron—there was no doubt about it. He looked forward to doing things for himself.

He was a born tinkerer. And when one had a

full staff to do everything for one, there was nothing really left to tinker with.

Except… He pulled his horses to a stop and stared into a shop window… Clocks.

Suddenly his breath caught, drying the whistle on his puckered lips. Gesturing to a boy on the pavement to come over and hold his horses, he jumped out of the driver's seat and strode over to the window. He bent at the waist, his nose nearly pressing against the glass, to get a closer look at the item on the other side of the pane.

Settling his spectacles on his nose, he narrowed his eyes to see it more clearly.

What a treasure! A fascinating ormolu clock. Not terribly old—probably only forty or fifty years. But it was an interesting piece. The bronze figure of a female…not quite mermaid but not quite human either…reclined on a snowflake. She clutched a bunch of sunflowers to her bosom, while lifting her face to whatever weather one imagined her to be enjoying.

Best of all, the inner workings of the clock lay beside it.

The timepiece was in need of repair.

Having purchased his new home without seeing it, there was no telling whether or not there was a mantel over the fireplace. If there was, it would need a clock.

Repairing this one would be a fine way to

spend his first night within the walls of Cockleshell Cottage.

Entering the shop, he paused to listen to dozens of clocks, tick-tick-ticking all at once.

A lullaby. That was what it was. Clocks ticked merrily on, never judging, never caring if their owners had a sterling reputation or a dull one. And a watch hummed happily along, no matter whose wrist it resided on.

He had been thirteen years old when he'd repaired his first clock. It had been broken and lying on the floor, a victim of his mother's anger. He'd taken it to a quiet room in the house. The peace he'd found there, tucked away and deep in the workings of the timepiece, had been incredible. Ever since then, he'd found no greater peace in any activity.

He hoped to find the same sort of peace in rebuilding his new home. That was why he'd purchased one in need of repair. He wished to do some large-scale tinkering.

He had a fine chat with the shop owner, and then purchased the clock.

Happier than he had been since that day of the big wind, he tipped the boy and climbed back aboard his new carriage, which contained some of the goods he needed to set up housekeeping.

He enjoyed driving himself. With no one he had to make polite conversation with, he was free to reflect on that windy day, and the encounter with the lady he had nearly knocked over on the street.

It didn't matter that he had spent only moments with her; he'd had a hard time putting her out of his mind.

She had been a lovely lady—charming, even while being somewhat annoyed.

Which she'd had every right to be. He had nearly bowled her over. Not to mention he had lost himself for a moment, and failed to remove his hand from her shoulder as promptly as he should have. In his defence, he had been taken off-guard by her. No one had ever looked at him the way she had, with an intriguing mix of annoyance and relief.

He had not allowed himself to be caught off-guard by a woman since being duped by Juliette. He had been stunned to find it was even possible.

Stunned, too, at finding that she popped unbidden into his mind at odd times…like this.

It wasn't as if he was likely to encounter her again. He would spend very little time in London. Just as long as it took to take care of the Baronetcy and the people he employed. The last thing he would do while in town was court a lady.

He wouldn't do that here either. Marriage might be well and good for some men, but they had not seen the side of it he had. Whatever joy might come of having a wife wasn't worth the risk.

Deliberately, he turned his mind away from Miss Grant's pretty face and directed it towards

Cockleshell Cottage. His home by the seaside was his future. A woman had no place in it.

Whistling, he drove along. Hopefully he would arrive at Cockleshell Cottage before dark, so that he could put some of his belongings in order.

According to the description he had of the place, which he was confident had been presented accurately, it was a large house with the charm of a cottage. Also according to the description, only two of the sleeping chambers were as yet inhabitable. Not that it mattered since he only required one.

Cockleshell Cottage was in need of tender care—which he was anxious to give with his own two hands.

Repairing a clock and repairing a home had something in common, he thought. He'd be taking what was broken and fixing it.

There was nothing quite like the predictability of repairing objects.

Unlike a reputation, if one put parts together in an orderly way the thing would become as new. Whether it was repaired or not was not up to anyone's opinion. It worked or it did not.

He looked forward to the challenge of making a home out of a hovel—although he did hope it was not quite as bad as that. Either way, he was dedicated to making the cottage his home in a way the London house had never been.

Travelling south from St Austell, it took an hour to reach his new home. By the time he drew his team of horses to a halt in the yard it was twilight. The scene from the front garden made it look as if the sun was melting into the ocean.

After settling the horses into the stables, which seemed in better condition than the house, he saw that the stars were out, dotting the sky all the way down to where the sea met the horizon.

He needed to unload his goods from the carriage, but that could wait a moment.

As of this day, time was his own…to use as he pleased.

The view, which he had been assured was spectacular, was that and more…at least by starlight. From the porch he saw the shadowed outline of a cliff that he knew ought to have a path leading down to the beach.

It would not hurt to unpack in the morning.

For now, even before he had a bite to eat or gave the house a look, he would sit on the cliff, breathe in the scents of a summer night, listen to the surf breaking below, all the while watching the stars glide across the sky.

He could not say how long he sat—hours, perhaps. The sense of time passing slipped from him as if it had no meaning.

It was the rumble of his stomach that brought him back to the world.

Standing, stretching, he walked back to the house. Had it not been for his appetite making itself known he might have gone on sitting there… perhaps until daylight.

One night he was going to do that…spend the night on the cliff, sleep under the heavens until daylight.

Halfway to the house he turned, watching the moon cast a streak of light across the water. It seemed to point a finger at Cockleshell Cottage—at the home he already loved, even though he had yet to cross the threshold.

A thought hit him hard, seeming to come out of nowhere. It was a shame no one would ever share this with him.

He dismissed it as quickly as it had come, because this was the life he'd chosen. Solitary…uncomplicated. He didn't regret it.

Well, then, it had been a long day and he was weary to the bone. But tomorrow he would rise refreshed and discover what repairs needed to be done.

He expected it would be the most fulfilling day he'd had since…well…ever.

Stopping beside the carriage, he rooted about in it for the ormolu clock. Finding it, he tucked it under his arm and went inside.

'Welcome home,' he muttered, setting the clock on the parlour mantelpiece.

He might be speaking to an inanimate object… but he thought rather he was speaking to himself, too…to the quiet, peaceful future he envisaged.

Chapter Two

It had been three weeks since the great wind. Since then, the days of late summer sunshine had been balmy and lovely. And Minerva meant to savour each moment.

The two children who had been so utterly distraught when they'd first come to London Cradle were beginning to adjust.

Abby was only two and a half years old, so it was hard for Minerva to know where the little girl's heart was when it came to dealing with her grief. She was too young to express it in words.

But James was seven and able to look ahead to life without his parents in a way his sister could not. Minerva knew this because she had been the same age when her mother had died. She felt his pain acutely.

Sometimes he would play with the other children as if he were not broken. But there were also times when she'd find him hiding behind sofas or chairs, sniffling into his sleeve.

All she could do was hold these two children close when they cried, and then encourage them to laugh and play when it seemed right.

While all the children who came through London Cradle held a piece of her heart, Abby and James held a bit more than usual.

She could not begin to understand why in any logical sense. There was something about them… but what?

At times, Minerva had the strongest feeling that the spirit of a woman hovered over the children… the spirit of a mother.

The oddest thing was, she knew it was not *their* mother's spirit she felt near them, but her own mother's.

This was far from the first time she'd felt her mother close by, so she recognised the sensation.

She cared for all the children in her care equally, but still that something drew her to James and Abby. She could not define it, but thought it might have to do with James being seven and with Abby's smile having the same saucy turn she remembered her mother's smile having.

A moment ago she'd called the children to her and sat them down under a tree. Now James's head lay on her lap and Abby snuggled against her breast. And in that moment she felt something… like a hand gently brushing her hair. A second later

Abby's hair lifted, and a curl shifted on James's forehead.

There was no breeze, and Minerva was not breathing upon them.

There were many things she had forgotten about Mama, but the brush of her fingers across her hair was not one of them.

Some people would believe this was not possible—was only Minerva wishing for her mother, the same way the orphans wished for theirs.

'Some people' would be wrong. Although she had no idea why her mother would single these children out for attention and not any of the others.

She certainly could not talk to her about it—nor to anyone. Perhaps it was simply that the needs of these children went particularly deep.

Many of the younger children were napping at this hour, but Minerva had decided it was not the best thing for James. Lying in bed with nothing to distract him might intensify his worry over how his world was changing, making him feel helpless to do anything about it.

But he did need to deal with it. She only hoped she could lead him safely to the other side of his grief.

'Shall we read a book?' She withdrew the small one she kept in her pocket.

'The one about the black dog?'

Oh, good. A spark of interest had flared in James's eyes.

'Wike Spotty. Spotty bwack,' Abby said.

Spotty was the dog who lived at the orphanage. A wagging tail was even better at coaxing a smile from a troubled child than a peppermint stick.

'No, Abby, Spotty is brown.' James narrowed his eyes at his sister.

'Bwack.' As young as she was, Abby delighted in bedevilling her brother as much as she adored trailing after him.

'Regardless,' Minerva said. 'The dog in the book is a very good dog—just like our Spotty.'

Abby gave a great yawn, and rubbed her eyes. 'I sweepy, Mama-Min.'

Minerva's heart lurched, then melted.

Both children had taken to calling her Mama-Min. The last thing Minerva had the heart to do was correct her.

Abby snuggled her cheek into the hollow of Minerva's shoulder. Her breathing grew shallow, indicating she was asleep.

'Naps are for babies,' James declared.

'Did your mother make you take them?'

She thought it was better to mention his mother than not. Helping him remember her and his life before would be more healthy than encouraging him to forget. Which he would do in time, anyway. She knew that vivid memories of his mother would fade and he wouldn't even be aware of it happening.

And yet…sometimes he might feel his hair stirring when there was no breeze.

He shrugged. 'Maybe…'

Apparently it was beginning already…the fog between then and now. It would increase, of course, since children tended to live in the moment.

'Do you like being here?' she asked, ruffling his hair. It sifted through her fingers, fine strands of brown and gold caught in the light of shifting leaves.

'Mostly.'

'Mostly? Is there something you don't like, sweetheart? Maybe I can make it better.'

'I don't like peas.'

'Hmm… I suppose before I go home tonight I can ask for you to be given some other vegetable at dinner. But is that all?'

There was something, and she could see he was troubled by it.

'What is it?' she asked. 'You can tell me.'

'I don't like it when you go home, Mama-Min. I get sad.' He wiped his nose on his sleeve. 'And Abby cries lots.'

Oh, dear… This was not something she had any control over. For one thing, her father would never allow her to spend the night away from Rivenhall House. For another, the night staff at London Cradle were very competent. She could hardly act as if they were not, which remaining there overnight herself might suggest.

'If you are sad in the night, tell Mrs Brown. She will keep you company until I come back in the morning.'

Mrs Brown was in charge of the orphanage. She was so devoted to the foundlings that she lived there, in the upstairs rooms.

'I get too sad for Mrs Brown.'

'I imagine you get too sad for me, too, sometimes. But, James, I promise you, it will not always be this way.'

'I want my mama.'

'Yes, sweetling, I know you do. I want my mama too.' She hugged him a little tighter, brushed the top of his head with a kiss. 'May I tell you something?'

She felt him nod jerkily.

'When I was the same age as you, my mother died too. It took a while for me to not be sad all the time. I missed her so terribly. And I still do—but not the same as I did then. I promise you, one of these days you will not be so sad. Before you know it you will smile when you think of your beautiful mama.'

'I don't remember my papa at all. He went to live in Heaven before Abby was even born.'

It was brought home to Minerva—and not for the first time—that she had been more fortunate than the children at the orphanage.

When her mother had died, she hadn't been cast adrift with no one to love her. Father, Thomas and William had filled Mama's place as best they could.

Not so for the children here at London Cradle. Here there were a dozen small broken hearts just waiting for someone to love them.

While earning a wage of her own was important, that was not the reason she came to work every day.

'I'm sleepy now, Mama-Min,' James murmured, snuggling into her side.

Within seconds he'd drifted away.

'Rest your head, little man. Mama-Min is here.'

Harrison sat on an overturned barrel, a nail pressed between his lips while he studied a broken shutter.

It had come off a window last night, during a storm which had blown in off the ocean, wild and fierce.

At least the roof was intact and none of the window panes broken.

The house was sound. He'd checked for leaks this morning and hadn't found any. In spite of being in need of repair...a great deal of it, to be honest... Cockleshell Cottage was solidly built.

Straightening the shutter frame, he considered it from all angles. He plucked the nail from his mouth, then hammered it into the corner.

He grinned, feeling pleased.

After three weeks of practice, he could wield

a hammer without smashing his thumb. Most of the time.

Last night's bluster had blown away before dawn, leaving the day bright and sunny. He had chosen a spot of sunshine to work in, and warmth touched his shoulders through his thin shirt.

He sighed aloud at the blissful feeling. He rolled one shoulder, then the other savouring the sensation.

Savouring life.

Here at Cockleshell Cottage, if he abandoned a task to take a stroll along the seashore, it didn't matter. He could simply continue with it the next day…or the day after.

There were still only two habitable sleeping chambers, but with no overnight visitors it hardly mattered.

He would finish the repairs leisurely, taking his time and enjoying the process.

When he was finished with the renovations there would be five bedrooms, a library, and a spacious drawing room. There was a room he thought might have been a dining room at one time, and it would be again—even though he preferred taking his meals in front of the hearth. One could not do better than dining in front of a toasty fire.

The kitchen had a small room off it. He could not imagine what its purpose had been, only what it was going to be. A bathing chamber. It would make life more convenient to have the tub close to where the bathwater would be heated.

It was something to consider when one did not have staff to haul pails up and down the stairs.

Not having staff was fine for now. Although he did greatly miss having someone to prepare his meals.

He was better at hammering nails than cooking. That was why he'd directed most of his efforts to restoring the kitchen. Still, it needed a great deal more work before he would be able to employ someone to use it. For now he must be content with cheese, bread, cold meat—and wine, naturally.

And, as much as he enjoyed his busy days, he enjoyed the nights as much.

Those delightful hours were spent with his clocks…researching treasured antiques…studying new innovations in timepieces…as well as repairing the broken ones he'd been lucky enough to come across.

All things considered, he wouldn't trade Cockleshell Cottage for the most well-staffed home in London.

At the seaside, life was all sunshine—even when it stormed.

In London life was shadow even on the loveliest day…especially when people stared and whispered about him.

He was done with all that.

He could only imagine what polite society

would say if he did wed. No doubt they thought he was like the rest of his family.

Although his brother had never married, he had been every bit the same as their parents had. Sometimes Harrison wondered how two brothers could be so different. Same parents…same example shown. It was a puzzle. All he could think was that he'd inherited the traits of his grandfather, who was said to have been a good man for the short time he had been alive.

Thoughts of Stewart inevitably led him to thoughts of Juliette. Thinking of her did not pain him the way it had used to, but still he wondered more than was healthy how he could have been so mistaken in her feelings for him. How blind he had been, thinking he'd loved her while she had been busy giving her virtue away to his brother…

Love was not to be trusted. He'd seen it go bad until all that was left was anger, and hatred, and families being wickedly hurt. It resulted in children cowering in their beds at night while their parents raged at one another. While nannies pranced boldly into their father's room and gardeners climbed through their mother's window.

It resulted in children being whispered about… being shunned by society.

But thankfully here he was, with all that finally behind him. The reputation he would build here would be beyond reproach.

Even spending time in London would be easier, knowing he had his seaside home to return to.

Wherever he went, he would always come home to Cockleshell Cottage—to the place where he was free in a way he'd never imagined he could be.

For instance, with his nearest neighbour a fair distance away, he could take his shirt off if he wished to. He could work bare-chested, with the sweat of good, hard labour rolling down his chest and his back.

And he did wish to do so—right now.

Unbuttoning his shirt, he shrugged it off and hung it on a bush.

Ah... Sunny warmth caressed his skin.

He pounded another nail into the shutter… grinned.

If he wished to, he could also remove his trousers, run down the path to the shore naked, and splash about as merrily as a seal.

He could…and he had, only two nights ago. The water had been nearly too cold, but he liked it that way. Brisk and invigorating. It had pebbled his skin and made him feel alive all over. Perhaps he would do it again tonight.

There was nothing keeping him from prancing about all day naked and free. He could dance in the moonlight bare, or dressed in a dinner jacket and top hat… It would all be the same to the moon.

'Good day, my lord!'

Harrison jerked, yanked suddenly from his musings.

A man on horseback was trotting down the long path leading from the main road to his house.

Harrison snatched his shirt off the shrub and shrugged into it, tucked the tails neatly and properly into his trousers. He hurriedly cleaned the lenses of his glasses against his sleeve.

He approached the fellow.

'Mr Goodhew?' He recognised who it was, now that his glasses were clean.

He was beginning to make some acquaintances in St Austell. Mr Goodhew worked at the post office.

'It's a letter, sir. From London,' he said, while dismounting his horse.

He handed over the missive.

The red wax seal was his own, which meant the letter would be from his solicitor. Business, then. He hoped whatever it was would not require him to return to London.

'It was kind of you to come all this way,' he said.

'It seemed important, with that red seal. We thought you ought to have it as soon as possible, rather than wait for your postman.'

Since Goodhew had travelled an hour to deliver the letter, it seemed only right for Harrison to sit and converse with him for a while, to share some bread and cheese.

He tucked the letter in his pocket. Whatever it relayed could wait until his visitor had left.

As it turned out, it was after dark when he thought again about the letter. In the bustle of afternoon activity he'd forgotten about it altogether. And it had been late when he'd finished the day's chores.

He looked through the pantry to discover what there was to eat. Leftover bread and cheese.

Adding a glass of wine, he sat by the hearth and called it a meal.

Having eaten, and with his toes nicely warmed, he drew the letter from his pocket…

Midnight, and he was still standing on the cliff.

Stunned by the news from his solicitor, he could do nothing but stare at the stars crossing the sky… listen to the waves wash on the shore one after another.

How was this possible? He could not wrap his brain around it…

But the truth remained, nonetheless. A few written lines had brought his idyllic life crashing about his feet.

Children? Orphans?

His?

By obligation—not by blood. Not close blood, at any rate.

He shook his head.

But there was a young boy and his even younger

sister who were left helpless in the world. They belonged to a distant cousin who had apparently passed away three years ago. He'd spent time with the cousin once, when they were children, and not heard anything of him since.

This letter had brought him the first thought he'd had of Harlow Evans in more than twenty years. From what his solicitor had written, he gathered the mother of the children had died recently, and a family friend had delivered them to the London Cradle Orphanage with instructions to contact Baron Elmstone.

Reportedly, the mother had no relatives.

These children had Harrison or they had no one.

To his shame, there was a part of him that wished to ignore the letter. Someone would probably adopt them shortly. Someone far more qualified to be a parent than he was.

The cat in the stables was a better parent than he would be.

He had never been around children. Did not know the first thing about raising them.

Perhaps he could settle a sum of money on them? To be given to anyone wishing to adopt them?

But, no…that would not do. It would be like selling them. If someone took them it had to be for love, not money.

There was only one honourable thing to do and that was to claim them himself.

But did he really have to give up the peaceful life he had here? There was the London townhouse. He might install them there…hire someone to see to their needs.

He could do that…

Except that he could not.

In London they would be subject to the same unkind stares he had grown up with.

The thought of someone belonging to him… and there was no pretending that they did not… becoming the fodder of society gossip… No, he would not have it.

No matter what he might have to say about it, people would not believe the truth. What they would more likely believe was that his brother had sired them, begotten them out of wedlock, and now they were shamed by simply existing.

Or they'd believe that he had sired them.

If the children were raised in London they would be gossiped about…outcasts. He would not leave them there and return to his paradise while allowing them to be raised by a…a nanny.

He ought to be over his revulsion at members of that occupation by now, but no…he did not think he ever would be.

If the children grew up here they would not be subject to society's scorn.

Children should never feel judged—not for any reason. Even if they misbehaved. Disciplined, perhaps, but never resented or judged.

He was not quite sure how to accomplish raising them on his own. Was there an instruction book of some sort? An experienced matron he could consult?

He did not know. What he did know was that he would bring them here.

If he ever meant to stand on this cliff again and gaze out with a peaceful heart he would need a clear conscience.

When he'd decided he would be the last of the Elmstone line, he had not anticipated the line continuing on another branch.

His hope was that they were far enough removed that they did not share his own family's traits.

Tomorrow he would travel to St Austell and send a telegram to the orphanage to inform them he was coming to London and collect the children.

While he was there he would purchase beds, and whatever else he could think of that children might need, and have them delivered to the cottage.

Hearing the waves below, he realised what a long drop it was down to the beach. He would need a fence and a gate for the children's safety. He would employ builders to see to it while he was away.

And a cook. He would need to feed them. There was a widow living with her brother on the property next to his. On his way out he would ask if she would bring them meals. The kitchen was not ready for a proper cook, but if the lady wished to make extra money by bringing food for them, that might work.

As unbelievable as it seemed, Harrison Tremayne had children.

Abby and James.

Gazing past the stars, as if such a thing were even possible, he prayed that the Good Lord would help him deal with the turn his life had taken.

Minerva knelt to hug Lilly Winston goodbye.

The little girl had been adopted by a wonderful couple who owned a jewellery shop in Mayfair. Clearly the child was going to be as much a blessing to her new parents as they were to her.

Watching Lilly walk out through the front door of London Cradle, her new mother clutching one of her hands and her new father gripping the other, Minerva felt her heart glow.

This was why London Cradle existed. Although not all children were as lucky as Lilly. To find shelter in a reputable orphanage and then to find a home of her own was fortunate indeed.

But why was Abby hiding in the folds of her skirt?

Why were James's hands clenched into fists?

Minerva knelt between the children. 'What is it? Aren't you happy that your friend Lilly is going to her new home?'

'No.' Abby's fair brows drew down over the

sombre expression in her brown eyes. 'She going to cry.'

James wrapped his arms around her neck, pressed his cheek to hers. 'I don't want to go.'

A small, worried voice in Minerva's heart feared the day they might be taken in. There was a possibility that in gaining new parents Abby and James would be separated.

It wasn't as if she could keep them herself. She was not married. Even she was not so independent-minded as to think she could. It was simply not done.

Perhaps she should ask her father to take them in? But would he? He might think doing so would make her even less likely to marry. Why would she tie herself to a man when she could become a mother, of sorts, without doing so?

Oh, but the idea of losing them nearly brought her to tears. She had bonded so deeply with Abby and James. They had moved right into her heart.

A part of her—a fanciful part—wondered if it might be because of her mother's heavenly urging.

It could not hurt to bring the matter up with her father…

'Well…' She wiped James's cheek with her thumb, then stood. 'I imagine that Spotty would like to play fetch before dinner, don't you? Run along and I will find you later.'

Mrs Brown closed the front door on the three people going home for the first time as a family.

'Miss Grant, may I have a private word?'

Judging by the width of her grin, Mrs Brown was overjoyed about something.

Perhaps the orphanage had received a generous donation.

Minerva followed Mrs Brown into her office. The lady's smile was infectious. Minerva gave an answering smile in anticipation of whatever good thing it was that had befallen London Cradle.

'I have the most marvellous news!' Mrs Brown grasped Minerva's fingers. 'We have heard from Abby and James's guardian. He is a distant cousin on their mother's side and is coming to collect them in a week. We had hoped, of course, but—'

'I was not aware they had one.'

A guardian! It felt as if a fist had grabbed Minerva's heart, squeezed it hard.

'No, you would not be. I didn't make it known because I had my doubts that the man would take them. I couldn't get anyone's hopes up.'

It seemed worth a mention to Minerva! She might have been carefully preparing the children had she known. Preparing herself!

'I'm afraid they won't be pleased to hear it. They were upset seeing Lilly leave.'

'Yes, the poor things have only just settled here and now they'll need to adjust to a new life all over again. It's not easy for our little ones, is it? But for the children to be taken in by a member of their family is the answer to our prayers, is it not? If only all the other children were as fortunate.'

'Of course… This is a great blessing.' Truly it was. 'We could not ask for more. Who *is* their guardian?'

Great blessing notwithstanding, Minerva felt as if she had been dumped in a puddle and was now floundering in mud.

Please let him be someone stable, financially sound, and of a loving heart.

'He is a baron from right here in London,' Mrs Brown said brightly, but then for some reason her smile slipped. 'It's just…he is Baron Elmstone.'

Chapter Three

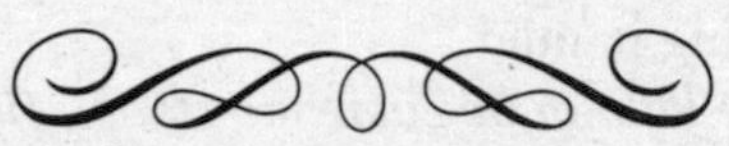

It was early in the morning when Harrison walked up the steps of the London Cradle Orphanage. Seven steps in all, each one carrying him towards a different sort of life than the one he'd envisaged for himself.

No one answered his knock. He still had time to retreat, suggested a small voice in his head. It sounded like his brother's voice. Had Stewart still been Baron, Abby and James would have remained orphans, at the mercy of the workhouse or…worse…the streets. Of that he had no doubt.

If nothing else, they would be safe with him.

He knocked again, more determined this time. Reviled or not, he was a man of position, and he meant to give these children as good a home as he knew how to.

Was no one about?

He pounded a third time.

He'd thought children were early risers—but

what did he know about it, really, except that he had been an early riser when he was young.

At last a woman drew open the big oak door.

She appeared annoyed at his early visit—until he introduced himself.

'How wonderful of you to come, Lord Rivenhall. I am Mrs Brown.'

Seeing her smile put him at ease. If she disapproved of his plan to raise the children on his own, she hid it.

He knew not everyone would approve, and that they would not hide their feelings.

An unmarried man becoming a father was not terribly common. Perhaps if he had a wife people would gossip less.

But he did not have one.

Let society's tongues wag—he and the children would not hear a word of it at the seaside.

He followed Mrs Brown down a corridor, up a flight of stairs. At the first room on the right she opened the door.

She pressed a finger to her lips, indicating that he should enter quietly.

'Abby is under the weather but has finally fallen asleep,' she whispered.

Under the weather? How was he to deal with that?

'What is the matter with her?'

'A high fever. Minerva has been sitting with her

all night long. It is a shame they must be woken now, but… Well, here you are.'

'Shall I return later?'

'Do not trouble yourself, my lord. We shall have the children ready to travel in no time at all. I will bring James.'

With that she spun on her heel and went out of the room.

The sleeping woman who was holding Abby in a rocking chair murmured in her sleep, then shifted the child, laid her cheek against the top of the little girl's head. She did all this without waking up. To Harrison it looked as if caring for children came so naturally to her that she did not need to be awake to do it.

He could not see the lady well because her dark hair was undone, hiding most of her face.

However, it was not the woman he wished to get a look at but the child.

His child now.

It made him quake inside, wondering what to do with her. And she was ill…her cheeks red with fever.

Approaching the sleeping pair as lightly as he could, he bent down, peered at Abby.

The girl was small, fair-skinned, with hair that circled her head in a blonde wreath. What colour were her eyes? he wondered.

He bent closer, settled his glasses on his nose

for a sharper peek. It troubled him to see her fevered cheeks.

Abby squirmed…moaned.

The woman patted her back, made a cooing, comforting sound. Then the lady's eyes drifted open, settled blurrily on him.

She sat up with a jerk. Her hair slid back from her face.

'You!' she gasped.

'You!'

He was not likely to forget such a lovely face. He had pictured it in his mind so many times since their brief meeting. Brief, but memorable, it had to be said.

His ward started to cry—a small, pitiful sound that twisted his heart.

Minerva stared at the man bent over her, peering down through dark-rimmed spectacles.

This was not the first time she had seen those eyes.

Oh, not at all.

Why, this was the very man whose eyes she had become so fascinated by after he had run into her in front the Gift Emporium!

Waking to see him looming over her was startling in the extreme.

Praise everything good that the surprise had not made her screech, jump to her feet and drop Abby on the floor.

Even without that ignominy, Abby was sobbing.

'Look what you've done. Have you no more sense than to hover over a sleeping child?'

He jerked upright, looking alarmed.

What on earth was he doing here? She would have demanded to know if her attention had not been focused on quieting Abby. In her condition, weeping would make her feel so much worse.

In between rocking Abby and crooning to her, she did manage to think of a word—several words—to direct at the intruder.

It was a shame she could not deliver them in the appropriate tone without further upsetting the little one.

'Who are you?' she murmured, trying to speak soothingly. 'There now, sweetling, he's not a bad man... You aren't, are you? Don't cry, love, it will be all right. If you *are* a bad man you should know I have older brothers...hush now, baby...and they've shown me a thing or two.'

She directed a severe glance at the spot on his body that her brothers had indicated, where a blow would immediately disable a male assailant.

Prudently, he backed away.

'I am Lord Elmstone. I have come to take my wards home. And I assure you I am not a bad man.'

He seemed even taller than she remembered. Which might have something to do with her sitting in a chair and being forced to look up.

'Please forgive me for behaving in a forward manner, Miss Grant. I did not mean to startle you.'

'Surely you cannot imagine Abby and I would be anything *but* startled to wake and find you gawking at us. And how do you know my name, sir?'

A second or two passed in which she had time to notice that his eyes, and the dark curly lashes accentuating them, were just as handsome as she recalled.

Which was an absurd thing to remember in that moment.

'When we met before…it is what the shopkeeper called you.'

Had he? Perhaps… She hadn't noticed because she had been preoccupied in wondering how a man with such a lanky build could be strong enough to pluck her from disaster, as he had. Most men she knew would have toppled over along with her.

But this was no time to think about that—or to wonder why he'd remembered her name after such a brief meeting several weeks ago.

Not any of that mattered.

Only James and Abby mattered.

So this was Lord Elmstone. What kind of a guardian would this fellow…this maligned baron… make?

Ever since she'd discovered he was coming for the children she'd been worried. Ordinarily she paid no attention to gossip, having been the subject of it herself often enough. But what she did know was that it was not always misplaced.

In his case? She couldn't be sure. The things she'd heard had to do with his parents and his brother. This baron tended to keep to himself—which was why she hadn't recognised him that day.

'May I speak to her?' he asked now.

She nodded. He was the one in charge of Abby's future—her guardian. Minerva only loved her. Which gave her no rights whatsoever.

A situation which seemed incredibly unjust.

'Would you like to hold her?' Minerva asked, because she must, but tightened her grip on Abby.

'I…no. I would not know how. But I would like to say something to her.'

'Very well, but speak softly. I don't wish her to begin crying again.'

'Thank you.'

He knelt down in front of the rocking chair. The front of his coat brushed Minerva's skirt. That was a bit too close for comfort, but he could hardly speak softly to Abby from far away.

All right, then, she would allow it.

For a few more moments she had some authority over what happened to her children… But they were not hers—not really.

Once they left London Cradle she would have no say at all.

If it was in her power to do so she would keep Abby and James…become their guardian herself.

Knowing very well she could not, she'd allow Elmstone's coat to press against her skirt.

'Abby, sweetling, there is someone here to see you. Can you open your eyes and greet him?'

Abby turned her face into Minerva's bosom.

'It's all right,' the Baron said, in a low, kind voice.

He reached his hand towards Abby's hair, but then snatched it back. Abby's head did rest upon her bosom, after all. Perhaps this Lord Elmstone was more respectful of women than his brother and father had been.

She really had no way of knowing, since they'd only met that one time. He had grabbed her skirt then, and snagged her about the waist with his arm. There had been good reason for it, she knew. But then he'd also kept his hand on her shoulder longer than he ought to have.

In all, though, she'd come away from the meeting believing him to be a gentleman—a rather strong one who'd kept her from being injured.

'I just want to tell you not to be afraid, Abby.' His voice was so gentle it even soothed Minerva. 'You will be safe. I promise you will.'

Abby turned her face away from Minerva's chest, pinning her guardian with a fevered glare.

'I onwy want Mama-Min.'

The Baron looked up, giving Minerva a worried look.

'Are you Mama-Min?'

She nodded. 'I'm going to put you in your bed, for a moment, Abby.'

'No!' Abby grasped her clothes, clung tightly to her.

'Just for a moment, darling.'

For all that Abby was not happy to be put in bed, she didn't resist in the end.

Minerva stood, taking a moment to stretch her back and roll her shoulders. She'd sat on the chair for so many hours her joints were stiff.

She took several paces away from the bed. The Baron followed.

'Abby calls me Mama-Min because she's put me in place of her mother. She understands I am not her, of course, but she needs the love her mother used to give her. So she calls me Mama and then adds part of my name… Minerva…so it's Mama-Min.'

He dipped his head close to her ear. His whisper brushed the wayward curl at her temple, causing a shiver to pebble her neck. He smelled nice, but many men did. None of *them* had ever given her a shiver. How very odd.

'The thing is, I am not very experienced with children.'

She had not expected him to be, naturally. His family wasn't known for being nurturing. It was one of the many things she'd worried about last night, especially after Abby had taken ill. Ordinarily children recovered from fevers, but not always. Abby needed someone who knew how to care for her.

She needed Minerva.

Mrs Brown entered the room at that moment, leading James by the hand.

James yanked his hand out of Mrs Brown's, dashed for Minerva and then wrapped his arms about her skirt. He looked sleepy-eyed, his brown hair rumpled.

The Baron bent at the waist and offered his hand in greeting. 'It's a pleasure to meet you, James.'

Looking down at the man's dark head, at the waves of soft hair on the back of his neck, Minerva felt an echo of her recent shiver.

The only sense this made was nonsense. Only last month Harold Bunnt had whispered in her ear, and all she'd done was chuckle politely at his joke.

'Don't want to go away from Mama-Min.' James stuck out his lower lip, as if a petulant stance would help.

How could she blame him? He was only seven years old and not accomplished at hiding his emotions.

'Shake His Lordship's hand, James,' Mrs Brown urged.

He buried himself deeper in Minerva's skirt.

Minerva rooted about for his hand, found it, and then guided it towards the Baron's long fingers.

'Go ahead, James. It is quite all right.'

But it wasn't. This was not something a child

should have to go through. Go through *again*, she thought. He had lost his mother and now he was losing Minerva.

'It is also quite all right if you don't wish to. I understand.' Lord Elmstone withdrew his hand, then straightened up. 'Perhaps later, once we have become better acquainted. Do you enjoy the seaside, James?'

'Don't know, sir,' he mumbled.

'James has lived in a city all his life. I doubt if he has ever seen the seaside,' Mrs Brown explained.

'It is where we shall live. I think you'll enjoy it.'

'You and your sister are very lucky children, James. Now, say goodbye to Miss Grant. I imagine the Baron is anxious to be on his way.'

Was he? The apprehensive glance he slid Minerva's way said otherwise.

To her way of seeing it, the Baron looked as nervous as a man facing the gallows. Not that she had ever seen one, but her vivid imagination supplied the image.

'I could come with you,' she said quietly, because it was evident that the Baron needed help.

Had Abby not been so ill she might have remained silent, but she couldn't just hand the poorly child over to a stranger. Almost a stranger. Their brief encounter from a few weeks ago hardly counted as being acquainted.

Simply because she'd had an interesting reaction to seeing him again, and his eyes were still as appealing now as then, it did not make them friends. For them to be acquainted there must be more between them than her recollection of how wonderful his smile had been when he'd finally relaxed enough to give one.

Evidently Mrs Brown had no reservations about bidding the children goodbye, because she said, 'Nonsense, Minerva. The sooner the children adjust to their new life the easier it will be for them. And you, my dear, have been up all night. I'm very grateful your father allowed you to stay, under the circumstances, but I insist that you go home and get some rest.'

The Baron glanced at Abby, who was now no more than a small heap hiding under the blanket, and then at James, who still clung desperately to her skirt.

Of them all, she did not know who was most worried.

It might even be Baron Elmstone.

'Miss Grant, would you like to carry Abby to His Lordship's carriage, or shall I call someone else?'

This might be the single most difficult thing Minerva had ever had to do, but she went to the bed, tucked a blanket around Abby, then carried her out of the room, walking a few steps behind the Baron.

James dragged his feet, winding his fingers into the tail of the blanket.

Once they were at the kerb, the footman opened the carriage door, but it was the Baron who scooped James up and placed him on the seat.

Then he reached out his arms to take Abby.

Minerva's heart cracked right down the middle, flooding her throat with tears which she felt she must release or choke on.

Choking it would be, since she was not going to let the children see her cry.

Taking a great gulp, she set Abby in his arms and put on the bravest smile of her life.

Clutching the child to his chest, the Baron climbed into the coach. If Abby's weight caused him strain, it did not show.

She suspected he was putting on the bravest smile of his life as well.

Somehow, she felt admiration for him…but grudging admiration, owing to the fact that he was taking the children away from her.

It was clear that he was taking on this obligation and acting for their good, not his own.

That spoke of a decent heart…a brave one too.

He leaned out of the window, gazing down at her. 'I promise you I will not leave for the coast until Abby is well enough to travel. You may come to the Elmstone townhouse and visit if you wish.'

Mrs Brown would advise her not to. The new

family would bond more easily without her there to confuse the children.

She wanted to say she would visit…felt her voice twisting in her throat because she wanted so badly to say so. But perhaps Mrs Brown was right. She had far more experience in these matters than Minerva did.

Except that it was not just a 'matter' to Minerva…it was as if her very heart was about to ride away in the carriage.

'The truth is, I would greatly appreciate it if you did, Miss Grant,' he added.

'Perhaps, then.'

Watching the carriage jostle down the street, she thought perhaps being chained to a post might keep her from doing it, but she rather believed not.

Minerva's chamber door opened. Her sister-in-law Evie stepped inside, carrying a tray of food.

'Why weren't you at dinner tonight?' she asked.

'Father would have wanted to know why I had no appetite.'

In a flounce of skirts, Evie sat down on the bed beside her, placing the tray on Minerva's lap.

'I want to know why, too.'

'You recall Abby and James?'

'How can I not when you speak of them so often?'

'Their guardian came for them today and I

feel…' she glanced at the slice of buttered bread on the plate. 'Bereft.'

'I know you love them, but there will be other orphans who need you.'

There would be, of course, as there had been many before them, too…and yet a lump was growing uncomfortably large in her throat.

'Why have you become attached to this pair more than the others?'

'You will think me daft if I say.'

'I already think you are daft, so you might as well tell me.'

Minerva set the dinner tray aside and got up from the bed. Going to the window, she stared across the garden, thinking that the conservatory roof looked lovely in the moonlight. Why, just look how—

What was she doing? Hiding from her own thoughts and emotions. That was what. In that moment she didn't care a fig what the conservatory roof looked like.

She spun about, leaned against the windowsill.

'I think it has to do with my mother. Sometimes I have a sense of her hovering about them, loving them. It's the strangest sensation, but I am convinced I'm not imagining it.'

'I felt my mother's presence when I gave birth to the twins. It's like you just said…her love hovered over them.'

'I can understand that, Evie. But they are your

children. Abby and James are not mine. So why would I feel it?'

Evie cocked her head. 'I wonder if she was giving you a message of some sort.'

'What sort?'

'That you ought to have babies of your own. It might be her way of suggesting it. You do want babies, don't you?'

'I want them. I've always seen myself with children. It's only the father I've not seen myself with.'

'He is a rather important part of the equation, I believe.'

'That does put me in a spot, I suppose.'

'Come back here and eat your dinner.'

'I don't think that will help with my dilemma.'

'I suppose not, but it will keep me from having carried a tray all the way up from the kitchen for no reason…and in my delicate condition.'

Evie patted her swelling belly, smiling tenderly at it.

Minerva did want to smile in that maternal way one day, but unless she changed her mind about having Father appoint her a husband she knew she would never have it.

When the butler announced that Miss Grant had come to call, Harrison's relief was so great he nearly collapsed backwards into a chair in the small parlour which was serving as a temporary nursery.

He could not recall passing a worse day or night in his life.

No matter how he tried to copy the manner in which he had seen Miss Grant interact with the children, he was simply inept at it.

His voice was too deep to be comforting. His hands too big and clumsy to be soothing.

Simply put, he was not a woman. He was coming to suspect there was a difference between man and woman when it came to caring for children—especially when one of them was sick and the other one distrustful.

All things considered, who could blame them for rejecting him?

In their eyes he must be no more than a hulking stranger who'd ripped them from the woman who stood in place of their mother.

The question playing over and over in his mind was, would a time come when they put him in the place of their father? A man neither of them remembered?

There was one thing he had done right. Although it hadn't taken a great deal of fatherly wisdom to know that calling a physician was in order. He'd paid the doctor a great deal of money to remain all night and sit up with Abby.

Unfortunately, Abby hadn't taken to the doctor either—perhaps even less than she'd taken to him. Probably because the doctor had poked and prodded her, peered into her mouth.

And even with dedicated professional care, Abby had seemed to grow worse, not better.

After a long day and an eternal night, he wished for nothing more than to fall at Miss Grant's feet and beg her to spend the day…or the week…until Abby felt well enough to travel to their new home.

Which was not here in London.

Having spent time at the seaside, he realised that it would be a far healthier place for them to grow up.

He had spoken a bit to James about Cockleshell Cottage, and had managed to coax a half-smile from him. A brief one, to be sure, but a smile nonetheless.

Perhaps there was some hope of winning James over.

Not so when it came to Abby. All he had to do was look at her and she drew the blanket over her head.

But now Miss Grant was here. Striding down the corridor on his way to greet her, he reminded himself not to gather her up in a great hug of relief. Not to weep upon her shoulder in thanks for her delivering him from whatever he had got himself into.

Delivering him for an hour or two, at any rate.

Minerva walked a pace ahead of the Baron, even though it was his house and he was supposed to be leading the way.

It was rude, but she was impatient to see how Abby had done overnight.

Better than she had, Minerva hoped. Twice she had put on her shoes and coat with the intention of coming to check on her. Luckily, by the time she'd reached the hall, good sense and the locked front door had reminded her that even though the Baron did not know how to care for children he did have servants. Someone must know what to do for a sick child.

No one would be better off for her dashing through the streets of London in the wee hours.

'Miss Grant.'

She spun about. Lord Elmstone stood still, staring at her, his brows arched over the rims of his glasses.

'I appreciate that you are anxious to see how the children fared last night, but if you continue the way you are going you will end up in the garden.' He nodded towards a corridor which cut across this one. 'They are his way.'

'Oh…of course.' She must seem a perfect idiot, charging through his home not even knowing where she was going. And if something dire had happened overnight he would have told her already.

Containing her urge to run, she walked beside him at the pace he set.

'I understand that you are worried about Abby.

Her condition has not changed overnight. Neither Dr Hume nor I got any sleep.'

'You sent for a doctor?'

'I may not know anything about raising children, but I do know when a physician is needed.'

It was well and good that he'd acted responsibly in this situation. But how would he handle the next crisis? Children did tend to come with them, after all.

'Has the doctor made a diagnosis?'

'Her throat is inflamed. He thinks she will be better soon, as long as she rests and is not overwrought by anything.'

'Anything such as her whole life being upended?'

Oh, dear, she'd meant to keep that thought to herself.

'Do you blame me for that, Miss Grant?'

Did she? Possibly.

'I'm sure you will do the best you can for them.'

He would try to. She did believe that.

Coming into the room he indicated, she spotted James. He sat on the floor, inspecting the hull of a toy boat.

She didn't see Abby. Her breath hitched…her heart pounded.

'Mama-Min!' James dropped the boat, leapt up from the rug, then dashed for her. He hugged her, clinging tightly.

Abby's head suddenly poked out from under a

blanket. She looked pale and weak. Still, she tried to get off the bed.

'No, little lady.' Dr Hume shook his head. 'You have a way to go before you can be up and about.'

Abby sniffled, then wailed, 'Want Mama-Min.'

'This is the Honourable Miss Minerva Grant, Dr Hume,' the Baron said.

'May I hold her, Dr Hume?' she asked.

'It's possible that what she has is contagious.'

'I'm willing to take the risk.'

Really, could she do less than the doctor was doing? Less even than Baron Elmstone was doing?

'Very well.' Dr Hume lifted Abby and handed her to Minerva. 'It will do her good to be with you. His Lordship tells me the children are quite attached to you, Miss Grant.'

Abby's skin was still too hot, her cheeks dry and flushed.

She reminded herself that the Baron had told her the doctor expected Abby to recover…as long as she was not overwrought.

James returned to his spot on the floor. 'Look, Mama-Min. His Lordship has let me play with his sailing boat.'

'It looks like a fine boat,' she said, while stroking Abby's hot cheek.

'The Baron made it when he was a boy.'

'It is kind of him to let you play with it. Make sure you treat it gently.'

Now that James had a guardian, was it even her

place to advise him of proper behaviour? She still felt responsible for him.

Walking in a circle, she rocked Abby, crooned soothing sounds to her. She went towards the window, where the Baron had sat down on a chair.

The man looked done in. He'd rested his head on the back of the chair, his eyes were closed and his hands were crossed over his flat stomach.

She had to step over his long legs, crossed at the ankle, to get to the window, but she didn't think he noticed.

From where she stood, his garden looked as lovely as any she had ever seen. It would be a wonderful place to explore if circumstances were different.

'Miss Grant.' He opened one eye, peering up at her. 'In case I did not say so first thing, I am grateful that you came…more than you can imagine.'

She could imagine quite a bit, though. This was a huge responsibility he was taking on. One which he was unprepared for.

Stepping over his legs again, she approached the doctor, who had also taken her arrival as a chance to close his eyes.

It must have been a difficult night.

'Doctor,' she murmured quietly, reluctant to interrupt him but needing to. 'Abby's fever has not improved since yesterday.'

He opened his eyes, nodded, and gave her a weary smile.

'It is not unusual, my dear. But try not to worry. I have reason to believe she will recover.'

'Only reason?' What she wanted to hear was that nothing would prevent Abby from recovering fully.

'She will recover as long as there are no setbacks.'

'Yes, that's what His Lordship said. I only—'

'You're worried he's not up to what he is taking on? Because his reputation hardly suggests he will make the best guardian for them?'

She shrugged, not willing to say so aloud. But, yes, the thought had crossed her mind... She'd obsessed over it—that was more accurate.

'It's my opinion, after observing him last night, that the children might do far worse. The Baron has every intention of doing his best for them.'

'But he doesn't know how to care for a child, let alone a sick one.'

'Nor does any woman after giving birth to her first one. He will learn, the same as they do.'

She only hoped Abby and James didn't suffer while he did.

If only there was something she could do... Very soon he would be taking the children to the seaside and she might never see them again.

Footsteps tapped in the hallway. A woman came in, carrying a tray of food. She set it down on a table, nodded, then went back out.

Someone else walked by the door, then another

person. This was a busy household. The Baron possessed a large staff.

She assumed he would employ a nanny to take care of the children.

She could not possibly fill that position, could she?

For one thing, she already held a position she adored. There was also the fact that her father might not recover from the ignominy of it. His plan for her future was that she would become the lady of a great household, not a servant.

Oh, but Abby lay so limp in her arms. The doctor's words played over and over in her mind. Abby would recover...as long as she suffered no setbacks.

There were other women who could take her place at London Cradle.

Father would be upset if she became a nanny, but Abby was worth more than her father's sensibilities. And this would not be a position she held for ever. Only until the children were adjusted to their new life and Lord Elmstone was more confident in his care of them.

Once Abby had fallen deeply asleep, Minerva put her back in her bed.

She crossed the room and poked the sleeping Baron's shoulder. While she did hate to disturb him, what she had to say would benefit him as well as her.

Most of all it would benefit the children, and nothing mattered more than that.

'Baron Elmstone, may I have a private word with you?'

A walk in the walled garden was just the activity Harrison needed to clear the trials of last night from his mind...and from his muscles and bones.

He'd tried his best to comfort Abby, but his efforts had only upset the child more.

What a relief it had been when Miss Grant arrived. Abby had settled quickly once that lady had picked her up.

'You will learn how to care for them in time,' Miss Grant said, as though understanding his anxiety. 'I'm certain of it.'

'I must, mustn't I? I only hope they don't suffer while I'm reading the book.'

'The book? You're learning childcare from a book?' Her frown indicated that such a thing wasn't possible.

'It came highly recommended. It was written by a mother of six children...boys, mostly.'

'I see... Well, the most important thing is that you're willing to try. It speaks highly of your character, in my opinion.'

'I thank you for that, Miss Grant. I cannot recall anyone else ever saying so.'

'One should never listen to gossip. I know it quite well.'

She *would* know it, he thought. Viscount Rivenhall's daughter was known for being…well, a lively sort.

Lively and lovely. That was what he thought. What he had not heard was how loving she was too. At least when it came to his wards.

After strolling past blooming rosebushes and a bed of lavender, all abuzz with bees, near the entrance to a small maze, he asked, 'What is it that you wish to speak with me about, Miss Grant?'

'Let me begin by saying that if you believe you can learn how to bring up a child by reading a book, you're sure to fail.'

'That's hardly encouraging.'

'I don't mean to criticise. I admire you for what you're doing. It would have been easier for you to ignore the needs of children so distantly related to you.'

'The fact is, they *are* related to me, and I cannot in good conscience abandon them.'

'But you will need help—and I can give it to you.'

'Whatever help you can give me while we are in London I will be grateful for.'

'I am happy to help, naturally. You must know how attached I am to Abby and James.'

'It is easy to see. And they are equally attached to you.'

'So, yes, I will do what I can while you are here. But after that? What will you do when you move to the coast?'

'That is the very thought keeping me awake at night.'

'Oh, excellent.'

Excellent? It did not seem so to him. It felt overwhelming!

'Being inadequate at something so important does not feel "excellent" to me, Miss Grant.'

'Naturally not. I only meant that it is excellent that I am in a position to help you.'

Her smile was bright and confident. Very pretty too. There was a funny curlicue of hair at her temple that half distracted him from their conversation. He had not really noticed it on their first or second meeting, but now that he had, how was he to concentrate on anything serious?

'I believe you do not yet have a nanny for the children. I am applying for the position.'

'Nanny?' Nothing could have snapped him back to the here and now more fully than hearing that word. Nausea churned in his stomach, and his palms broke out in a sweat.

It was an unreasonable reaction, he knew, but real, nonetheless.

'Your father would never allow it.'

'He didn't allow me to work at London Cradle either, and yet I am doing so.'

'You would need to leave that job if you worked for me. You would need to leave your home.'

'I have considered that. Still, I am applying for the position.'

'My house is not fit for you to live in.'

'If it is fit for the children it will be fit for me.'

It would not—not with only two habitable bedchambers.

No…employing a nanny would be impossible—even if it did make sense. He simply could not have an unmarried lady living under his roof. It might be different if he had even a small staff, but it would be some time before he had even that.

Besides…a nanny? He simply could not agree.

'It is kind of you to offer, but I must turn you down.' Her disappointed expression made him feel like a heel, but he had no choice but to refuse. 'Shall we return to the children?'

Harrison Tremayne turned his back on her as if to say their conversation was at an end. Just like that, he strode towards the house.

This would not do! Not for an instant. Their conversation was *not* at an end.

Minerva stood for a moment, feeling her temper begin to buzz and steam inside her.

Looking up, she could no longer see him.

She dashed in the direction they had come from, but grew confused about where she was. She turned right at a path lined by tall hedges.

No, this wasn't the way. In fact, she found that she had dashed into a maze. She detested mazes. What was the point of wandering about lost, after all?

After a few more turns, she decided that was exactly what she was.

Minerva was not one to be easily embarrassed, but she knew she would be if she were forced to call out to him and admit it.

There had to be a way out of here.

After ten minutes she decided that either there was not or it was skilfully hidden.

Moments later she heard footsteps on the other side of the hedge from her. She made a small noise which couldn't possibly be interpreted as a cry for help.

She heard the Baron's footsteps turn back the way they had come, and then his throat being cleared as he stepped up behind her.

'This maze is a hazard to womankind,' she declared crossly. She couldn't be the only hapless visitor to have wandered into it.

'So it's been said.' His gaze on her looked dark, stricken. 'However, you are quite safe.'

Oh, that was not what she'd meant. Only that the twists and turns were not easy to make one's way out of.

'Follow me,' he said, then spun on his heel and walked quickly out of the maze. 'Please forgive me for rushing ahead and leaving you to become lost. I ought to have the wicked thing cut down.'

'It doesn't seem the safest place for a child.'

'No, that's not what I… Well, never mind. Once again, I apologise.'

Poor man. No doubt he thought she was judging him for the sins of his family. If he'd been anything like his father and brother she likely wouldn't have come out of the maze unscathed.

'I cannot possibly accept a misplaced apology, Baron Elmstone. It wasn't your fault that I went charging into the maze. Besides, no harm was done except to my pride. You must recant your apology.'

'Very well, I take it back.'

She had the oddest urge to reach up and smooth away the frown lines between his eyes. She smiled at him instead—because how wrong would it be to reach out and touch a man she barely knew?

Adventurous, yes, but even she was not quite that bold.

He answered with the funny half-smile he had given her on their first meeting. It was as compelling now as it had been then.

'You are right, though, about the maze being a danger for the children. I have a great deal to learn about parenthood, I'm afraid.'

She was glad to hear him say so, because this gave her the chance to press her point.

'You really must see what a great help I would be as their nanny. It is an ideal solution.'

'It is a kind offer that you present, Miss Grant. I do regret that I cannot accept it. My life would be a great deal easier if I could.'

'I'd like to know what you'll do when James misbehaves—as at seven years old he is bound to.

And what will you do when Abby bedevils him, as little sisters will do?'

'Honestly, I do not know.'

'If you truly believe a book will be a better help to you than I will, I'll withdraw my offer. But surely you see the sense in it.'

'I cannot say that. But please understand that I can't have you living alone with me. Your reputation would be ruined and mine would be beyond repair—if it isn't already. For the children's sakes I must do what I can to live above reproach. I will not have them living under the condemnation I did as a child.'

It all made perfect sense. As much as she wished it did not.

The scandal would be insurmountable… Father did not deserve to be ruined.

As for the Baron, it would be the last nail in the Elmstone coffin…symbolically speaking.

If he did have any hope of restoring his family name he couldn't employ her.

Which left him to learn about children from a book, by trial and error.

There was no argument she could present, so she gave a great sigh and stepped around him. She wasn't used to being defeated, to not finding her way around a difficult situation.

'I shall continue to visit the children until Abby no longer has a fever, if you don't mind.'

'I wish circumstances were not what they are.'

But they were, and there was nothing she could do to change them.

Hurrying away, she realised how foolish she was to have presented him with such a plan. That was what came of following her heart.

She was nearly up the patio steps when she heard him catching up with her.

She pressed her eyes with her fingertips, desperate to keep the tears from spurting hotly down her cheeks. She could not recall ever being so disappointed about anything in her life.

'Miss Grant! One moment, please!'

'I don't know what else we can have to say to one another, my lord.' If she'd been able to think of something she would have already said it.

He was breathing unusually hard. But, really, he had not run all that far to catch her.

'What if we changed our circumstances?'

'I don't know how that is possible.'

'It's entirely possible, if you wish it.'

'Abracadabra…all is changed.' She fluttered her fingers between his nose and hers. 'I have wished and yet nothing is changed.'

'Perhaps I ought to have said it differently…'

'I really have no idea what you're talking about.'

'Circumstances would change…if you married me.'

She blinked, her mouth falling open.

The man was mad!

'I think the stress of suddenly becoming a parent has unhinged you, my lord.'

She dearly hoped that was the reason.

'I'm sorry—that was inelegantly said. But I am asking for your hand in marriage.'

'And I am turning you down.'

Firmly. Steadfastly.

'If you take a moment to think about it you will surely see the wisdom. It is a sensible solution to our dilemma.'

Unflinching and unwavering!

'*Your* dilemma,' she said bluntly—because how else was she to deal with a man who had lost his mind? But he wasn't completely wrong. It was her dilemma too. 'I have no intention of marrying.'

'I will admit until a moment ago I had no intention of it either. But don't you see how it will help us both? More, it will help the children.'

It would...and yet, no!

'Do you perhaps recall quite a few years ago,' she said, arching one brow, 'when there was some gossip about me swinging from a tree in front of Rivenhall House while wearing—?'

He grinned... Oh, dear. Perhaps she shouldn't have—

'Wearing something fetching? All of us gathered in your front garden were enchanted. We were not a bit put off by the banner you'd hung over the front door, declaring that all suitors would be turned away. To a man, we were intrigued rather than repelled.'

'You were there?'

'I was. It is not something a fellow easily forgets. As soon as the shopkeeper addressed you as "Miss Grant" the whole scene came back to me.'

He had the nerve to look amused.

'I only mentioned it to remind you that from a young age I've never been interested in being just another debutante, longing to marry as soon as I could. But I see I was unwise in recalling it to your memory. Perhaps it would be for the best if I did not come back to visit the children after all.'

She spun about and snapped her skirt, looking as put out as she could manage.

'Best for who, Miss Grant? For you? For me? Certainly not for Abby or James.'

Nothing could have sliced her soul as sharply as those words.

But marriage? She simply couldn't do it.

'Good day to you, my lord.'

She continued on her way, through the house and out onto the pavement.

The Rivenhall carriage waited at the kerb. But it was such a short distance from here to her home. She would rather walk, and shake off the sensation of bees buzzing in her head.

Naturally, it was forbidden for a lady to walk anywhere alone…

She was so weary of the constraints that being a lady of society put upon her.

When the footman opened the carriage door she climbed inside. At least here was a bit of privacy, where she could weep freely.

But was Abby weeping too?

The carriage moved and the horses' hooves clopped along the same as any other day. Leather creaked and harnesses jingled. It all sounded so normal, even though her life seemed to be crashing down about her.

Of course Abby was weeping.

Would she suffer a setback?

And all because Minerva was set on not marrying?

Baron Elmstone had sacrificed what he'd intended for his future. And why? Because Abby and James needed him.

Could she, who loved them, do any less?

Halfway down the street, she signalled for the driver to stop.

She must be as mad as the Baron.

Without waiting for the driver to open the door or lower the steps, she leapt down to the road. Gathering her skirts, she dashed back towards Elmstone House.

The Baron still stood on the porch. He hurried down the front path and met her at the gate.

'I am willing to discuss it,' she gasped, out of breath.

She could not believe those words had come out of her mouth. This was very last thing she had imagined happening when she rose this morning.

Considering a proposal of marriage? Or something like it.

She would wager that Lord Elmstone hadn't risen that morning thinking he'd be offering for her hand in marriage either. Although he hadn't actually risen, had he, having been up all night with Abby?

He nodded, his lips pressed thin, his gaze subdued.

'I will ring for tea and we shall discuss it.'

While she thought tea was the last thing she could stomach, the simple commonness of the act might keep her grounded.

It was as clear as water that he didn't wish to wed any more than she did. Perhaps with that understanding between them they could find a way to go forward.

Once inside, Lord Elmstone had a word with the butler, then indicated that Minerva should follow him.

She obeyed, walking behind him into a small parlour at the front of the house, with a large window overlooking the street. She left the door open to observe the proprieties.

But where to begin a conversation like this? For once in her life she had no idea what to say.

So she did not speak, but sat quietly waiting for him to do so.

This was his grand idea, after all.

'Miss Grant, I do not wish to wed—not any more than you do. Trust me, I hadn't considered it until you suggested becoming Abby and James's nanny. Since that would be impossible, it only makes sense that instead we should get married.'

Minerva sighed. To her, being the children's nanny had sounded like a perfectly reasonable idea—until he'd pointed out the shortcomings.

'Abby and James need a mother, not a nanny,' he continued. 'Do you not agree that, given what they have been through, they should have someone of their own? Someone who loves them and isn't there just for her wages?'

Put that way…yes, she did agree. But still…

'But what would that mean to you?' she asked. 'How do you see our sensible marriage? In the event that I consent to it, that is.'

A maid entered, set down a tray with tea and small sandwiches.

What Harrison wanted was to go on with his life as it had been a few weeks ago. And that was something she ought to know from the start. Surely she felt the same way?

'Given a choice, I would carry on with my life as it was. But there isn't a choice for me. Abandoning James and Abby to an unknown fate has never been a possibility for me. Not for you, either, I imagine, or you would not be sitting here.'

Sitting here looking even lovelier than she had years ago, swinging from that tree in front of Rivenhall House. Given that he shared her opinion on marriage, he had silently applauded her.

It felt completely impossible that they were now looking at each other over a teapot and discussing the very thing each of them had always rejected.

Miss Grant poured them both tea. Her hand trembled ever so slightly, which he thought was probably uncommon for her.

He really had no idea how to put her at ease. There was no comfort in what they were contemplating.

There was nothing for it but for each of them to present their expectations.

'As I see it, Miss Grant, we will simply carry on our lives in St Austell as if you are the children's nanny.' Although he would do his best not to see her as such. 'Marriage is the cover that will save our reputations.'

Hearing the words, he knew how cold they sounded.

'In the process we might become friends,' he added, to soften his statement.

In spite of the situation they found themselves in, he thought he would enjoy getting to know this woman.

'We might at that,' she said. 'But there is one thing I should mention…'

Just then he learned something new about her. She had a very lovely blush.

'Surely you wish for children of your own?' she asked. 'An heir to carry on the Elmstone title?'

'It is the very thing I do not wish for. The Elmstone title is not worthy of being continued. Any heir of mine would only suffer for bearing it.'

Miss Grant set down the sandwich she had been about to take a bite of and slid her glance away.

Perhaps she wanted children of her own? But she didn't want a husband, and the two did tend to go together, so perhaps not.

Still, he had to ask…

'Will Abby and James be enough for you? I'll understand if you wish to refuse my offer.'

And what *was* it that he was offering? A loveless but friendly marriage…none of the comforts she had at Rivenhall…separation from her family and society…

She must love the children a great deal in order to sit across from him and even discuss it.

'What would *you* ask of our marriage, Miss Grant?'

While she seemed to consider her thoughts, one occurred to him. It came from the area of his heart rather than his brain. That little spring of hair was giving his heart a tickle. But he could not allow his heart to be affected. Only misery could come of it.

He would need be on his guard in the event she accepted him.

'I ask to be a true mother to Abby and James, rather than a nanny. I will not be treated as an employee. We'll act as a family. But as to what will be between us…'

Her reappearing blush indicated that she was embarrassed to be discussing this, but her gaze on him was steady, nonetheless.

'I don't require that we share a bed, but we will share our lives. And, as you say, perhaps in time we'll become friends.'

'Will you marry me, then?'

She folded her hands on her lap and stared at them. The house was quiet except for the ticking of the three clocks in the room and quick footsteps approaching from the hall.

What more could he say to convince her?

The housekeeper appeared in the open doorway. 'I'm sorry to disturb you, my lord, but the doctor's asking for you. Miss Abby is crying her poor little lungs out and he fears—'

Before he could take a step out of the parlour Miss Grant had raced past him. When he arrived in what was serving as the nursery Abby was already snuggled in her Mama-Min's arms, her sobs reduced to hiccups.

The sight was incredibly tender. His heart went soft. It was unlikely that his mother had ever looked at him that way.

'You may call upon my father in the morning,' she murmured.

It struck him that he was making a love match.

Minerva Grant's love for his wards.

Families had been founded on a lot less.

Chapter Four

Leaving Father's study, Minerva found Evie hurriedly straightening up from the keyhole.

'That went well,' Evie said, her tone dripping sarcasm and laughter. 'Has your father risen from the floor yet?'

He had not actually toppled over when she'd informed him she was getting married, but it had been a near thing.

'You can hardly blame him for being stunned.'

'No, I suppose not. But don't you think that since he's always wanted me to wed he'd be pleased?' Minerva asked as they walked away.

'Except that he had his mind set on a viscount or higher for you.'

'Nonsense. It's not as if I'm eloping with the stableman.'

'At least that would be romantic, in its way.'

Evie slipped her arm into Minerva's as they entered the garden.

'You only talk about romance since you and my brother have it in spades.'

'Elmstone, though… Are you certain about him, Minerva?'

'He's not like the rest of his family.'

'You haven't known him long enough to know for certain. Oh, Minerva, are you really going to leave London? I will miss you dreadfully.'

'I suppose I must leave home at some point. At least this way I am choosing my husband, not having him appointed for me.'

'You are not choosing him…you're choosing the orphans. Besides, you barely know him.'

For all the day's upheaval, Minerva could not help laughing because… 'I'm a Grant, aren't I? We tend to wed people we barely know. It's worked out well for both of my brothers.'

'Still, Minerva, I think you might take your time, given his family history. One day you'll have children together.'

No, apparently that was not to be. But she would have Abby and James. They would be enough.

And one never knew what the future held…

But, no, she wouldn't allow herself to think it.

She might not ever have the secret glow that Evie had as she came downstairs some mornings, but many women did not. And at least she wasn't going into marriage with stars in her eyes.

Why did she need them? Abby and James were her stars.

'What I think is that when you meet him tomorrow morning you'll find him to be a decent fellow.'

Walking past the conservatory, Minerva watched their shadows stretch before them, long with the coming sunset.

'I wish you every happiness, sister, you know I do.'

'I am not saying my marriage will be like yours and my brother's is. But it will be enough. I have a feeling that Lord Elmstone and I will get along well.'

'Minerva Grant, there is much more to marriage than getting along well. I hope you will not settle for so little. You might find marriage to be exciting in a…well, in a uniquely delightful way if you but give it a chance.'

'If by "exciting" you mean adventurous, then moving to a seaside cottage, living without staff or the company of society, should suit nicely.'

'That is not at all what I mean. Just… Don't close yourself off to the possibility of the delightful.'

'Only a moment ago you warned me to be wary of him.'

'But since you decline to be, then stay open to the prospect of…' Evie patted the swell of her belly, grinned.

What she would actually do was close herself off to it and be content with the children she was blessed with.

* * *

Harrison could not recall ever being as nervous as he was striding up to the front door of Rivenhall House. The Elmstone shadow hovered over his every step.

There was no reason the Viscount should give his daughter's hand to a Tremayne in marriage. Surely higher-ranked men of sterling reputations had come this way before him.

With his foot poised on the first step, he sent up a quick prayer for success. If Minerva's father refused his suit he wouldn't know what to do.

The children needed Minerva. Having lost their mother in a tragic carriage accident, he was determined to do what he could to make sure they did not lose their Mama-Min as well.

It would be too much sorrow for them. And, as their guardian, it was up to him to make sure they had the best life he could possibly give them.

Looking at the closed door, he felt his collar grow tight, damp. If only he could loosen it…take a steadying breath.

He would need to convince the Viscount that he would be a proper husband to his only daughter. Which he did intend to be.

Rivenhall might not think so, though. There was every chance he would refuse Harrison's suit.

When the day came for him to give Abby's hand to someone, it wouldn't be to a man like he was perceived to be.

'Press on,' he murmured.

The front door opened before he knocked. It was Miss Grant taking his coat, not a footman.

'You look pale, my lord.'

'I feel pale.' He tried to give her a smile, but it sat rather flat on his lips. 'In the event your father consents to our marriage, will you call me Harrison?'

'I shall call you that now if you will call me Minerva.'

'But are you certain about all this? Can you be content living so far from London, from your family? And it will be a while before we have any servants, so we must fend for ourselves in the meantime.' He felt compelled to point this out one more time.

'We did discuss all this yesterday afternoon. If I miss such things I can return to London for a visit. It is not as if we will be living on the moon.'

'But you could marry higher. Carry on with life as you are accustomed to.'

'I don't want to live as I am accustomed to… nor as I am expected to by society. I'm not and never have been comfortable obeying every one of their narrow rules of behaviour. You should know this about me…in the event you have not already guessed it.'

How could he not have guessed it? The lady swung from trees…she worked for a wage. Quite honestly, she fascinated him.

'But don't worry about Father. I imagine he's relieved I've consented to marry anyone at all.'

'Yes, well…so am I.'

'Truly? Because you also have time to change your mind, Harrison.'

Should he? Marriage was a risk…

In fact, he'd had a nightmare last night. Not a new one, but a recurring dream which had to do with his parents' marriage and the misery it had caused.

No doubt he'd woken in the wee hours, drenched in sweat and breathing hard at the reminder of the evil which had gone on behind his mother's closed chamber door. At the warning that he should not risk that fate.

Dreams, he reminded himself, were not real.

Minerva's smile was real—and lovely.

He dismissed the lingering ugliness of his dream in favour of the nice feeling it gave him when she uttered his name. The sound whispered into his heart…made it feel lighter.

An indication of what living with Minerva Grant would be like?

He didn't know whether to hope it was or not. A safe marriage was all he wanted—a friendly one, not vulnerable to the whims of passion that loving someone caused.

'I will not change my mind,' he said.

'Nor will I. However, I should point out that if

your intention is to avoid a scandal, our marriage is probably going to create one,' she said.

'My intention is to give Abby and James a mother…to give them you. I am used to scandal.'

'Good, then. Because our sudden vows are going to invite rumours, not prevent them.'

'People will likely believe that I've compromised you. Why else would we wed in haste?' he said, though he didn't like even implying such a thing. 'I understand if you don't wish to have people think that of you.'

Then she laughed—and it nearly cut him off at the knees.

'Truly, Harrison, wagging tongues are not something I'm overly troubled by. Did you know that once I followed my brother to his club and then sneaked inside? It was a great scandal for a time. I only brought up the subject of gossip because I understand how it troubles you.'

'You invaded your brother's club?'

'I did—and it was great fun. Not for William, though. Father blamed him for it.'

'I'm looking forward to meeting your brothers… I hope.'

She laughed again, and this time he laughed with her.

When was the last time he'd laughed like that?

Maybe sharing his home with a friend would be better than living in solitude, after all.

It surprised him that suddenly he hoped for her

father's consent to the marriage for more than just giving the children security and a mother.

'I believe you had a great deal more fun growing up than I did,' he said.

Well, it was the truth. While both families had been troubled with scandal, her family was founded in love for one another. His was not.

It really did make a great deal of difference.

'And our children will have fun too… Abby and James, I mean,' she added quickly.

In a lady of such daring he would not have expected a blush. It was a dozen shades of lovely, though…

'Well, shall we go to Father's study?' she asked.

He straightened his shoulders, drew himself to his full height. 'Escort me to the lion's den, my dear. I shall try not to flinch under attack.'

And then the most magnificent thing happened. Something that had never happened to him before.

Minerva stretched high up on her toes and kissed his cheek.

The day before the wedding Abby was feeling better. The morning was fine and sunny, so Minerva decided a walk would be the very thing to help her get her strength back.

James walked close beside her, gripping her skirt. And she held Abby's hand because the street, with its parade of carts and carriages, was only feet away and she couldn't be too careful.

The stroll began pleasantly, with birds singing and squirrels chattering at the children. It would have ended that way too, had it not been for Myrtle Smythe and her daughter Jane walking towards them.

The pair were among the worst of society's gossips. If they cast the children judgmental glances like the ones Harrison had told her he'd used to get… Well, she would not be held responsible for what might happen.

Baroness Elmstone might not have cared enough to protect her children from gossip, but Minerva would protect Abby and James.

But no, they were looking at *her*…at her waistline. She could see the speculation in their expressions even from a house length away.

'Good day, Minerva,' said Mrs Smythe.

It had been.

'Allow us to congratulate you on your engagement. You have quite surprised us all.'

Myrtle Smythe had the snarkiest smile of anyone she had ever met—and Minerva had encountered her share of them.

What she ought to do was hurry the children along and not engage with these women. Who cared what went on in their uncharitable, shrivelled hearts?

Very well—*she* cared! And the impish side of her nature wanted to engage with them.

'It's all very sudden. I am to be a mother.' She

pressed her hand to her waist, because there were times when the imp could not be repressed.

Jane's mouth dropped nearly to her bosom.

Myrtle's lips pressed so thin they disappeared.

'Being a mother yourself, Mrs Smythe, you can imagine how delighted I am.'

She should not let the moment stretch, but how could she not? It was time they choked a little on the gossip they so adored.

Both children were clinging to her skirt and gazing up at the women.

'My Mama-Min,' Abby announced.

Mrs Smythe looked satisfyingly confused.

'But perhaps you have not heard?' Who knew what they had heard? But they were about to hear the truth now. 'Baron Elmstone recently found himself guardian to Abby and James. It is wonderful how he has taken them into his heart and home right away, don't you think?'

'They do have that look about them...' Mrs Smythe narrowed her eyes at James, then at Abby, her lips taking on a nasty curl.

'What look is that?'

Every nerve Minerva had was spitting hot. She couldn't express her anger the way she wished to, because of the children. Still, there were other ways.

'Elmstone.' Jane sniffed, as if the name had an unpleasant odour.

'Yes, well...they would. They are the orphans

of the Baron's cousin. His Lordship is such a good and noble man. Abby and James are very lucky—and so am I.'

'Indeed,' said Myrtle, staring at Minerva's belly and lifting her nose in the air at the same time.

How did the old besom do that?

'Oh, my goodness! Do you think I am pregnant?'

The blunt word Minerva used for the condition was bound to make the woman faint back into her daughter's arms.

'I am not. The truth of it is… You will recall that I work at London Cradle? Well, that's where I met Abby and James. I fell desperately in love with them—because who would not? And then the Baron, having the best heart of any man you can imagine, offered for my hand so that I wouldn't have to be parted from them. Oh, Jane! My position at London Cradle is available, if you are interested in earning some money of your own.'

'How…very…' Jane spluttered, casting a desperate glance at her mother.

Dreadful was what she meant, of course.

'I'm James Evans.'

James had extended his small hand in greeting. Minerva only hoped his mother was looking down upon him and seeing the well-mannered child she had raised.

These genteel ladies of society didn't express half the good manners this little boy did.

Jane simply stared, looking as if by returning the greeting she might be infected with immorality.

Minerva couldn't recall ever being so angry in her life. It was all she could do not to hiss, strike like a snake and spew poisonous words.

'Take care, James. Miss Brown cannot shake your hand, although I'm sure she would like to. But she has some sort of fungus on her fingers and so she cannot.'

'She a meanie,' Abby declared, as clearly as she had ever declared anything.

'What sort of fungus? Like mushrooms or mould?' James asked, staring at Jane's fingers in amazement.

Minerva led the children away—but not too quickly.

'Where did it come from?' James asked curiously.

'From a very dark place…in her heart.'

Minerva cast a glance over her shoulder. Good. They'd heard.

If this was anything like what Harrison had endured as a child… Well, she wanted to weep for him. He'd only been a small boy, with no one to defend him.

But her children had someone…*two* someones.

'Is it the kind of mushroom we can eat?' James asked.

'Oh, no, it would make us very sick.'

* * *

Minerva had not expected to leave her family so soon. Harrison's plan had been to wait two weeks and then travel to Cockleshell Cottage.

But once she'd told him what had happened on their walk, and asked if they could leave for the shore the day after the wedding, he'd agreed nearly at once.

Nearly…because he'd had to warn her that the house was still in rough condition.

Before he'd had a chance to explain how rough, she had declared that she didn't care—that the less time they spent in town, the better.

By concocting an outrageous story about fungus on fingers she'd managed to direct the children's attention away from those women's nasty attitude. Next time she might not be able to.

The only thing to do was to take them away from London as soon as possible.

And so here she was—wed one day and boarding the train to St Austell the next.

Taking a seat by the window, she held Abby on her lap, watching London slide swiftly past the glass.

Although her life had changed in almost every way it could, it was this moment which made it seem real.

Leaving everything she knew and everyone she loved behind her was bound to make a person feel that way. Was bound to make her wonder if she'd got herself into a situation she could never undo.

'I wuv you, Mama-Min.' Abby kissed her cheek.

Well, then, she hadn't left everyone she loved behind, had she? Love was the very reason she was here.

If she'd left anyone behind it was Minerva Grant. That was what a married lady did. Left the carefree girl behind and became a woman who cared for others.

The wedding had been accomplished quickly and privately. Which was fine. It wasn't as if they were in love and wanted to celebrate their grand romance, after all.

All her family had been there, along with Abby and James. Even William and Elizabeth had managed to travel south to attend. Having everyone together had been wonderful…nothing could have made her wedding nicer.

William and Elizabeth, Thomas and Evie… those happy couples had provided all the love a wedding needed. It didn't have to be the bride and groom casting lovey-dovey eyes at each other, did it?

She glanced at Harrison, sitting on the bench across from her. At James kneeling beside him and gazing in fascination at the scenery rushing by.

Her husband of a day smiled at her. She smiled back.

There was a sense of strain between them which

hadn't been there in the beginning. Perhaps it was because they were now on their own.

Although she had spent a great deal of time at Elmstone House with the children in the week before her wedding, she hadn't seen Harrison all that often. He had been busy taking care of business and accounts, meeting with the staff, his accountants and his solicitor in preparation for his absence.

When Minerva had not been with the children she and Evie had spent their time getting ready for the wedding.

Now, here she sat… Baroness Elmstone. Wife to the man sitting across from her, who was probably feeling as awkward as she was.

Not only had she become a wife, but also a mother. That, at least, felt as natural as breathing. Now that it was done, and they were on their way to a new life, she was glad Harrison had turned down her offer to become the children's nanny.

As their mother she would be free to love them with all she had. A nanny would have been temporary. A mother was for ever.

She wondered if her own mother was looking down at her now. If she was, what would she think? Minerva was convinced that Mama had singled out Abby and James over the other orphans at London Cradle. Was this why? So that she would end up on this train, speeding towards St Austell?

Had Mama, knowing that Minerva would not marry of her own accord, played matchmaker?

It would be a comfort if that was so, because right now her husband seemed a stranger.

One to whom she had given her future.

Minerva Grant no longer. She was Minerva Tremayne… Baroness Elmstone.

She had garnered her fair share of sidelong looks in the past week. Did people think that she had become suddenly wanton?

Perhaps so. Even to someone who was accustomed to encountering raised brows, the sly glances cast at her had felt like an itch between her shoulder blades.

If one more proper lady had darted a glance at her waistline, she might have done something to cast even more shame on the beleaguered name of Elmstone.

After her run-in with the Smythe women, she understood how a life of isolation at the seaside must appeal to her husband. He had suffered a great deal in society.

With each mile away from London the train chugged, she imagined the weight of being judged falling off him.

For herself, she was torn. On the one hand she did look forward to the adventure of a living in a new place, of learning to live in a new way. On the other hand she had never lived without servants to look after her. Not only would she need to see to her own needs, but to the children's as well.

Was she capable of it?

'Are you worried, Minerva?'

A smile picked up the corners of his mouth indicating that he wasn't nervous or worried.

Of course he wasn't. He knew where they were going, while she did not. Seeing his confidence encouraged her.

'Nervous more than worried. I trust that you wouldn't take us anywhere we need to be worried about.'

'Once you get a look at Cockleshell Cottage you'll feel better. There's something about living at the seaside that changes a person.'

'Will there be seals?' James pressed his nose to the glass, bouncing about in anticipation.

'Want to see, too!' Abby scrambled down, climbed on the other bench and tried to push James out of the way.

'Abby, stop it!' James complained.

Harrison lifted her off her brother and passed her back to Minerva.

He must not have learned how to settle disputes from his book!

Abby pressed her own small nose to the glass, copying James.

'It will be some time before we see a seal,' Harrison explained, with the slightest furrow to his brow.

It was an endearing furrow, she thought. She looked forward to getting to know all of his gestures, and learning the emotions behind them.

'I couldn't do this on my own, Minerva,' he said. 'I cannot say how grateful I am for you being here.'

What did it mean when his smile was flat? When the one corner tipped up and the other down? It had intrigued her from the first, and was only one of the things she wanted to learn about him.

'I don't know all there is to know—far from it. But I probably know more than your book.'

'And I thought you knew everything in regard to children,' he teased.

'I will admit they can be puzzling at times.'

He cast a glance at James, bouncing about on the bench. And it was a good thing he did, because at that moment James took a tumble. Harrison caught him by the back of his trousers before his head hit the floor.

'Well done,' she said.

'I suppose between the two of us they'll survive.'

Yes, they would.

Moments ago she'd felt apart...alone. With those four words 'the two of us' something shifted inside her.

Settling into the bench cushions, she relaxed.

Within hours they would arrive in St Austell

and then their new home. Time would tell if she continued to feel hopeful.

As they chugged along through the afternoon, Abby fell asleep in her arms. James crossed over to her bench, laid his head on her lap and fell asleep too.

Harrison gazed out of the window. In profile, she saw his long lashes nearly touched the lenses of his glasses.

What was he thinking?

About marriage? About parenthood?

About what unknown future the train was speeding them all towards?

If he was wondering about those things, so was she. With both of them dwelling on it, they were united.

It could be that she was not as alone as she'd imagined she was when she'd boarded this train.

Harrison turned the team from the main road to the winding path which led to Cockleshell Cottage.

The builders he'd employed to construct the fence on the cliff had finished it, even painted it white. It looked good and sturdy.

Surf broke on the shore below. The rush of water on sand seemed to call *Welcome home*. Cool ocean air brushed his face, and to his mind it felt like freedom.

It didn't matter that he'd grown up in London

and spent such a short time at the seaside. As far as he was concerned, this place was now home.

The very first time he'd seen it he'd fallen in love with it. The cottage was all he'd ever dreamed of.

He hoped his wife—

His thoughts came to a sudden halt. It might take time for him to get used to the idea that he had one.

But he hoped she would come to feel the same sense of belonging here that he did.

Glancing over at her, he wanted to see her smiling.

It shouldn't be a surprise to find that she was not.

This remote place wouldn't be anything that a gently bred young lady would be used to.

No servants. No chamber of her own. Nothing that would suggest luxury.

He glanced at the cottage again, this time through Minerva's eyes.

It looked tattered. Not as bad as it had been before he'd begun repairs, but now that he was seeing it as she must be…it could only be described as ragged.

Had he been more forthcoming about the condition of her new home her jaw might not have dropped.

She hadn't seemed to mind when she'd told him they ought to come here the day after the wedding.

Now that she was looking at it, she might be reconsidering.

'I suppose I should have fully prepared you.'

In his defence, until this moment Cockleshell Cottage had been nothing but a paradise to him. Making the repairs was a delight, not a challenge.

'It will do nicely,' she said, but he wasn't sure he believed her—neither her words nor her brave smile.

'The truth, Minerva. How do you feel about living here?'

He needed to know if his gently bred wife felt that she had landed in a hovel.

'I can understand why you love it here. The view from the upstairs windows must be stunning.'

It wasn't the answer he'd hoped for. She'd only stated the obvious without telling him how she felt about it.

'But can you be happy here, do you think?'

Shifting her gaze away from him towards the cottage, she looked it over, from roofline to front door. He couldn't breathe, waiting for her answer.

'If you tell me my chamber has a view of the ocean I will be.'

Her chamber? One more thing he had failed to reveal… They would be sharing a chamber for now.

At least they wouldn't have to share a bed.

He'd ordered an extra bed to be delivered and set up. Hopefully it had come early.

'It has. A glorious view.'

'I'm anxious to see it.'

'We want to see seals!' James declared.

'And fishies,' Abby added.

'Soon, children,' Minerva said warmly. 'First we have some things to carry inside. Isn't this the grandest adventure?'

He helped Minerva down from the seat, and then the children.

She handed each of them a small package.

He in turn gave a package to her.

'Is this for my chamber? Which room shall I take it to?'

He pointed to a dormer. 'That one on the right.'

Turning, she went after the children.

'Minerva…there is something I must tell you first. About the house.'

'Don't worry. We'll make it a lovely home in no time at all.'

She cast him a smile over her shoulder. At least, he thought it was a smile, but it might have been a grimace. He didn't know her well enough to be certain.

But wait… It *was* a smile—a warm and genuine one. It gave his insides the oddest flicker. A warm frizzle that he didn't understand.

He admired his bride. That must be why. Most society misses wouldn't even have alighted from the carriage, but would have insisted on being taken back to London within a heartbeat.

She was not a society miss, though, was she? Minerva was a wife…his baroness.

He caught up with her, touched her arm.

A baroness who was courageously walking up the path to an unfamiliar life…

Perhaps she was putting on a brave front for him with that smile. If she was… Well, it made him flicker and frizzle all the more. No one had ever gone out of their way to make him feel at ease.

The only time he'd ever felt something like this before was when she'd kissed his cheek before he'd faced her father.

'The thing of it is, Minerva, there are only two habitable sleeping chambers. One is for the children…'

'And one is for us? You and I together in the same room?'

'Only until I complete your chamber. We need not share a bed, though. You'll have one of your own.'

He was sure something was buzzing about in her mind. He only wished he knew what. He swore he'd had a dozen heart seizures wondering what she'd say about the shared quarters.

'Oh, then…that will do. I'm certain we can accommodate one another.'

He wasn't convinced she was certain, because now she was frowning at the left dormer.

'I can sleep in the stables until we complete your chamber,' he said.

She took a long time to answer, glancing between the house and the stables, which could be seen a little distance inland, behind and to the left of the house.

He didn't truly wish to sleep with the horses, but he would if it came to it.

'I really don't mind,' he added.

Hopefully she'd think it was the truth. He didn't wish to make her feel guilty for putting him out.

'I will take my things over as soon as we are settled inside.'

With a nod, she continued to the front door. Reaching the top step, she turned and looked down at him with a sincere little frown cutting her forehead.

'I'll be comfortable there,' he said.

'I completely understand that you don't wish to share a chamber with me,' she replied. 'But if you don't mind too terribly I'd rather have you in the house. Everything is so different from what I'm used to, it would be a comfort to have you close by.'

Him? A comfort? Hearing her say so made him want to wrap her up, keep her safe from every fear and doubt. It made him feel like a husband.

'As you wish, Lady Elmstone.'

He nodded, when what he really wanted to do was kiss her.

Not that he was going to. He must resist feeling anything but friendship for her. Behaving any other way would be foolish.

Except…maybe he would kiss her on the cheek… the same as she had done to him.

Before he could act on that impulse, she said, 'I don't know about you, but I'm famished—and I'm certain the children are too.'

Turning, she walked ahead of him to the front door.

One day he might kiss her cheek, but clearly not now. Not when people were hungry.

'I don't suppose you know how to cook?' he asked. 'I have a lady who brings food in, but she will not be expecting us today.'

She stopped, turned, arched a slender brow at him. 'This *is* going to be an adventure, isn't it?'

Stepping into the bedchamber, Minerva walked about it in a circle. It was a large space, rather plain-looking.

Perhaps Harrison believed the view of the ocean was all the decoration it needed.

Passing the window, she paused to gaze out.

She could only agree. Not a frill known to mankind could equal the spectacular view. She wondered how far away the horizon was. Her eyes had to be scanning miles upon miles of ocean…farther than she'd ever seen before.

From where she stood she could hear the children playing in the adjoining chamber. It would be reassuring to have them so close by in the night.

And when her bedroom was completed it would be on the other side of theirs.

It was a comfort to think of them tucked between her and Harrison.

Footsteps thumped in the corridor. Harrison entered the room, his arms piled so high with firewood it was a wonder he could see where to walk.

He knelt in front of the hearth, which spanned half of one wall. He dumped the wood on it, then went about the business of adding kindling and logs.

This was not a task a baron usually performed, and it had to be said…or thought…that it showed off his masculinity exceedingly well.

His arms stretched and the muscles of his back flexed. Sometimes there was an awkwardness about Harrison Tremayne. Not now. He was delightful to watch.

And why shouldn't she watch? There were some things she would forego in their marriage, but looking at him wasn't one of them.

'The nights are getting chilly this time of year, but this will keep us warm until morning.'

She didn't miss the note of pride in his tone.

Her husband was a man of society and yet he was not useless, as some were.

How interesting that, until this moment, she'd never seen society gentlemen as being of much use. Perhaps because she'd never seen them on their knees building a fire.

It seemed to her that setting logs afire was manly in a way that playing cards at one's club was not.

'I imagine it will keep us warm.'

Why did she feel the need to fan her face?

She went over to the window to do it, so he wouldn't see and wonder what she was about. She didn't even know why she was suddenly blushing, but it seemed something she ought to keep to herself.

The darkness beyond the window was deep in a way she'd never seen before. In London it was never completely dark, given there were lamps on all the street corners.

She wasn't yet over the loneliness she'd felt upon leaving home. It was so quiet here. So different.

Then she became aware of Harrison standing beside her. She glanced up to see him smiling. In a small way it eased the aching spot in her heart.

'The darkness grows on you. And when the moon comes up, you won't believe how beautiful the view is.'

'I'm anxious to see it, then.'

She returned his smile. This was the life she'd chosen and she meant to embrace it.

She crossed the room to her bed, which was against the wall closest to the children. She bounced two or three times, testing the mattress.

'This is very nice. Thank you for thinking of it.'

Not only had he purchased a bed, but a pretty set of bedding to go with it.

'Do you like it?'

'What woman would not adore bouquets of pink rosebuds to sleep beneath?'

'Oh, good. I wasn't sure of your taste.'

How could he be? They did not yet know all the little things about one another. It touched her that he'd gone to the trouble to choose something pretty.

'I'm sorry there's no dressing room,' he said, glancing about as if he'd only just noticed there wasn't one.

'I suppose it will not be terribly difficult to make some adjustments,' she said. 'A curtain might be placed down the middle, which will create two rooms, in a sense. It will be homely, I think.'

He went to the hearth, stooped to gather an armload of leftover wood. Pivoting on the balls of his feet, he glanced up at her.

'I hope you come to feel that this is your home, Minerva. Although I realise it's far from what you're accustomed to.'

Rising, he carried the wood to the door adjoining the children's room, leaned against the doorframe.

'Whatever I can do to make this easier for you, please, just tell me.'

'I will admit it is different. But at the same time I'm not accustomed to being able to see all the way to the edge of the earth from my window, or to hearing waves on the shore instead of carriage wheels on the road.'

Or to sharing a bedchamber with a man.

Some things would be lovely here, but there would be things she missed.

Since she would not be sure what, exactly, those things might be until she was missing them, she didn't bring it up. Rather, she would look forward to the things she would enjoy.

'I would much rather walk on the shore with the children tomorrow morning than spend an hour being dressed to make social calls,' she admitted.

'From the look of the sky this evening, the morning is going to be spectacular. Look at all those stars.'

Because the land was so dark, the sky was alive and sparkling.

Even though his words were encouraging, his gaze at her seemed puzzled. Perhaps he didn't know what else to say to a woman sitting on a bed in his chamber. The notion must be foreign to him—something akin to finding her fallen from the moon and landed here.

'I'll just light the fire in the children's room. I wonder, after they're asleep, will you come with me to the cliff? I can't tell you how much I've missed sitting out there and watching the stars.'

'I'd like that. But can we leave them unattended?'

'We won't be long. The cliff is not so far that we cannot hear them if they wake up if we leave the window open.'

Several hours later, when the children were deeply asleep, they went to the cliff and sat down. She wore a heavy coat against the chill. Sitting on a blanket with her new husband, she saw the world stretch away for ever.

Now that the moon was up the landscape was not as desolate. Rather, it was enchanting in its way.

A breeze lifted the hair away from her face. She inhaled a lungful of moist air. Sticking out her tongue, she tasted the ocean.

If her former nurse, Berthie, were here she would agree that simply sitting in this spot was an adventure.

Back in London Minerva had watched the stars while sitting in Rivenhall's garden. They had been lovely, of course, but not majestic, obscured as they had been by the lights of London.

It was an easy thing to imagine herself on a giant trapeze, swinging from one star to another, merrily and magically flying across the heavens.

What better time was there to begin learning more about her husband than right now?

Who was he at the heart of him?

She thought she knew some of him, but she wanted to know much more.

'May I ask you something?'

She shuffled a little closer to him, because it was chilly and he radiated warmth.

'Of course.'

He lifted the end of the blanket wrapped around his shoulders.

'You don't mind?' she asked.

He laid it across her back, moved an inch closer. 'It's beautiful out here, but cold.'

'I believe that married people may share warmth,' he said, and nodded, smiling in that curious way he had, his lips half up, half down. 'What is it you wish to ask me?'

'It is rather personal, so you may refuse to answer, but we did say we wished to become friends… Have you ever been in love?'

His eyes went round, blinked once. Clearly this wasn't the question he'd expected.

'Once, I was. When I was twenty. I was betrothed for a short time.'

'Oh? Then why didn't you marry her?'

'She chose my brother, Stewart, instead.'

How horrid! Poor Harrison must have been devastated.

'I don't recall that your brother ever married.'

'He didn't. To him, taking my fiancée was another game to be played.'

'What an awful thing to do to you. No wonder you didn't wish to ever marry after that.'

What would he think if she hugged him? It

was only natural to give one's husband comfort, wasn't it?

Natural for another wife, perhaps…not for her.

The new bed in his chamber only reaffirmed the fact that she was not a wife who could comfort her husband with intimate, loving touches.

Down below them waves crashed upon the shore. In the moonlight she saw the high tide nearly covering the beach with water. Only a narrow sliver of sand kept it from disappearing altogether.

He let out a long, slow breath. White vapor swirled in front of his face.

'I still have nightmares. Not so much about her but about my parents. I don't know what your parents' marriage was like, but mine were at war with each other. My brother and I were the battleground.'

He leaned a little closer, until his shoulder brushed hers.

'When I told you I wouldn't employ a nanny, I said it was because the children needed a mother. It was the truth—they do. It was clear from the start that they needed you. Only, that's not all of the truth. I never had a nanny that my father didn't dally with. I always saw them as my father's weapons against my mother. My mother had her own weapons as well. She took lovers—many of them. I saw all of it as a child. Still do occasionally, in my nightmares. I understand there are many fine nannies. Only, for me, employing a woman to care for the children was out of the question.'

She wouldn't hug him, but she did pat his hand. That was friendly without overstepping the mark.

'It must have been terribly lonely for you, growing up.'

'I was used to being lonely. And I decided that remaining unmarried seemed better than taking the risk of becoming like them.'

'I cannot imagine you would ever become like them.'

She only realised that she'd left her hand on his when he gave it a squeeze, then released it.

'And what about you? Have you ever been in love?'

'I have been infatuated before. Quite lovely interludes. But I have avoided being genuinely in love.'

'You know why I've avoided love, but why have you? Surely you've had many men competing for your hand?'

The warmth of her fingers lingered on Harrison's hand. He was tempted to respond by leaning over and kissing her cheek. He'd been thinking about it. But, no, the gentle press of her hand was enough…it was better that he did not do it.

'It isn't because of my parents' marriage,' she said at last. 'As much as I recall it, it was loving.

I was only seven when Mother died. Ever since I was small I have wished to be like her.'

Minerva was quiet for a moment, gazing out at the moonlit sea.

'I've always felt her presence, you see. My adventures were hers too, in a sense. But I imagine that sounds odd.'

'It sounds nice. I, on the other hand, would not want my mother's presence hovering about. But why did you never marry?'

'My father would say that it's because I dislike being told what to do. It's true, in a sense, I suppose. When he said my future was to wed a duke, I decided to become a trapeze artist… Oh, but you are already aware of that! Don't worry—I was young and have outgrown the idea.'

'I confess I'm much relieved to hear it.'

'It seemed a glamorous life at the time, but I learned better.'

'If you want a glamorous life, Minerva, I fear you'll be unhappy here.'

She shrugged, glanced away from the vista and held his gaze.

'Well, there is true glamour—like this view we're looking at—and then there is the false glamour I used to dream of. But as for my reason for avoiding marriage… I've always believed a woman should not be obligated to wed…that she should have a choice about her future.'

'But you did marry out of obligation, did you not? Obligation to Abby and James.'

'But *I* made the decision. It makes all the difference.' She tapped the bodice of her coat with her fingertips. 'And I do love the children.'

'Why the two of them, though? Why were you willing to give up the life you had for them and not any of the other orphans you cared for?'

'For one thing, the others didn't seem to need me in quite the same way. And for another… Well, it might sound odd, but I feel my mother gave them to me.'

'Yes, it does sound a little odd. But it also sounds wonderful.'

'I've never told anyone that before.'

'Your secret is safe with me.'

Her smile gripped him around the heart, wrapped him in a sort of tenderness he had never felt before. It must come from sharing a secret, he supposed. He had never done such a thing before.

'You are safe with me,' he added.

'How did you know that's exactly what I need to hear?'

'Because none of this is what you're used to. Because you've left everyone you love behind, and every comfort. You smile, and put on a brave face, but I think this cannot be easy for you. You must feel vulnerable. I do mean it, though. You're safe with me.'

And then, all of a sudden, it seemed right more

than wrong, so he leaned sideways and kissed her cheek.

She touched the spot. 'You're right. I am feeling a little lost. But not so much as I was a moment ago.'

'Good, then. I want you to feel that this is your home.'

She lifted her hair from under the blanket, spreading it across her back. It brought to Harrison's mind a vision of dark waves rushing onshore.

'When we agreed to marry we hoped to become friends, do you recall us saying so?' she asked.

He nodded. 'And I believe we will.'

A breeze came up, caught the scent of her hair. It wafted towards him. Roses…and something else…lemon?

'Are you ready to go back inside?' he asked.

'Not quite. But we mustn't leave the children for much longer.'

He wasn't ready to go either, but he stood and reached a hand down to her.

'What is your favourite colour?' she asked, taking his hand and rising.

'Colour? I never gave it a thought. But…perhaps it is green.'

Green was the colour of the ocean. The colour of spring leaves and emeralds. He liked all those things.

Green was the shade of Minerva's eyes.

'What is yours?' he asked.

'I can never decide on only one. They all have their moments.'

Walking slowly towards the house, he felt the brush of her skirt against his leg. How could something so simple feel so special? Intimate, even, in a friendly way.

'Then what is your favourite smell?' he asked.

'Baking bread…a puppy's breath… No, wait! It's the way Evie's babies smelled when they were first born. What's yours?'

Roses and lemon…

'I've never smelled a baby, so I cannot compare, but I agree with puppy breath…also kitten fur. And the very thought of baking bread is making me hungry.'

'Truly? You have never smelled a baby?'

'It's not so surprising. I never had a younger sibling. Babies were not a part of my world.'

She pursed her lips, cocking her head at him. Did she find him lacking for not having smelled a baby before?

'I'm certain Evie will allow you to smell her baby when it comes. But puppy breath evokes something of the same good feeling.' All at once she smiled, looking as if a brilliant thought had come to her. 'Tell me, what's the worst thing you've ever tasted?'

They reached the house way too soon. He hadn't learned nearly enough about her. But they were wed. He had time to learn everything about her.

What he hoped was that, going back inside, she didn't feel as lonely as she had coming out.

He didn't.

Minerva lay flat on the bed, patted the rosebuds on the quilt. She turned on her side and stared at the wall.

'You may come into the room now,' she called.

This was an inconvenient way to prepare for bed, with Harrison waiting in the corridor while she dressed for bed, and then her having to stare at the wall and listen to the clocks ticking while he changed.

Tomorrow night would be easier, since they were going to St Austell in the morning to purchase some sort of barrier for their privacy.

She listened to him shuffling about, then heard the bedsprings squeak when he lay down on his bed.

'I'm so tired I could sleep on a rock,' he said with a long sigh.

Flopping onto her back, she turned her head to look at him. 'Your blanket is too short.' His long toes stuck out of the end. 'Your feet are going to get cold.'

'I'm used to blankets being too short.'

'You could put on socks.'

'I'll be fine. Goodnight, Minerva.'

He closed his eyes.

'Shall I wake you if you snore?' she asked.

Harrison opened his eyes again and sent her a glower. 'I don't snore. Shall I wake you if you do?'

'I have no way of knowing whether I snore or not.'

'Goodnight, Minerva.' He flipped onto his side.

'Are you always this grumpy at bedtime?'

'Are you always this talkative?'

She sat up, drawing the blanket under her chin for modesty. 'How could I be when I've never shared a chamber with anyone?'

'I haven't either, but I do not feel the need for conversation!'

'You haven't?'

'I've not been a complete monk, but share my own chamber with anyone? No, I haven't.'

'Oh… I thought perhaps a childhood friend or a cousin or… At any rate, goodnight.'

'Are you nervous? Is that why you're chattering away?'

She might be. There was a man not ten feet away from her and she was in her nightshift. It made her feel strange…not in an altogether unpleasant way.

'You probably are. My name might be Elmstone, but you have no reason to fear falling asleep.'

'I don't! I only meant that this is my first night in a new place. I'll hear every sound.'

'You'll soon grow used to them. Sleep well.'

'Sleep well,' she answered.

Humph. She might get used to sounds, but the

fact remained that lying a short distance away from a handsome man did cause in her a certain amount of tension.

Had they not agreed to the sort of marriage they had, their first night alone together might have been quite different.

It wasn't something she could ignore.

He was a man and she was a woman.

A fact which didn't seem to keep him awake!

It must be because he didn't want an heir, and therefore didn't look at her in a way that might lead to one.

It was a shame. He showed every promise of being a brilliant father to Abby and James.

Perhaps once he held Evie's baby…got a good whiff of that magical newborn scent…he would change his mind…

But even if he didn't she still had Abby and James. They would be enough. She had settled it in her mind and…well…her sisters-in-law would have plenty of babies for her to smell and cuddle.

She turned onto her right side. Then her left. She flopped onto her back and stared at the ceiling.

'You do snore,' she mumbled, and then squeezed her eyes shut.

It was only a shame she couldn't do the same with her mind and her ears!

Even believing that a chaste marriage was what was best for his family, as well as for himself, last night Harrison had slept as if his mattress was stone and his blanket woven of thorns.

He had claimed he could sleep on a rock, but it hadn't been the truth.

What else could he have expected, spending the night within touching distance of a greatly desirable woman?

A woman he was married to.

A woman he could not now take his eyes off as she walked with the children along the shore.

Having just returned from St Austell, with a swath of fabric to serve as divider for their bedchamber, he now stood on the cliff, enjoying the sight below him of the children dashing towards the surf and then running away from it.

All under the watchful eye of Minerva, who had taken off her shoes and stockings, tucked the hem of her skirt and petticoats into the crook of her arm and was dashing about with them.

How was it possible that he had a family? This was not the life he'd envisaged for himself. Clearly his life was now destined to be something else, belong to someone else…three someone-elses.

If he could somehow go back and change things, would he do it?

Hearing the children's laughter wafting up to him on the breeze, knowing that as a child he'd never laughed in that carefree way, he thought, no. He would not change this. Abby and James would have what he'd never had.

Only, he would need to be careful where his bride was concerned. A mistake with her could lead to heartbreak for them all.

The curtain hanging over his arm ought to help. He supposed he should take it to their chamber.

Instead, he laid it across a fence post, which still smelled like new paint, and hurried down the path to the beach.

It had been weeks since he'd walked in the surf. The water would be cold today, but that was how he liked it best.

James dashed across the sand, lifting his arms.

What did he want?

'He'd like you to swing him about…'

Minerva had leaned close to his ear to whisper. The scent of the sea clung to her.

The boy was dancing about on his bare toes. Catching him under his arms, Harrison flew him around in a circle.

Apparently this was something children liked, because James screeched with laughter. He lifted the boy up, high then low, to make it more thrilling.

'Fwy me too, Uncle-Papa!' Abby lifted her arms impatiently.

Uncle-Papa? *Him?*

Touched to the heart to have that title, he set James down, then caught the little girl up. This moment was special, because it was the first time she'd come to him of her own accord.

He'd accepted that the children would be more attached to Minerva than to him. She had a natural way with the children, while he was still rather awkward with them. But he wanted to be the best father he knew how to be for them. Only he didn't know how to accomplish that.

Now that he knew they liked to be lifted and swung about, he took heart. Later he would get advice from Minerva on what other ways he might please them.

'You're just in time to join us for afternoon tea,' Minerva said, her face blushed with sunshine.

'Tea?' He glanced about, but didn't see a teapot. Did he even have one at the cottage? On his next visit to town he would ask Minerva to purchase a tea set. It was something a proper home ought to have.

'Only cheese and crackers,' she explained. 'But it is teatime so we shall make do.'

'On my way home I stopped to speak with the lady who prepares my dinner. I let her know that there'll be four of us from now on. I'm afraid she wasn't prepared, since she didn't expect to see me for a while longer. But tomorrow she'll come.'

Minerva wore her hair loose today. Tossed by the sea breeze, it blew across her cheeks and lips. She whisked it away with the back of her hand.

Once he'd stopped thinking about how pretty she was, he wondered what more she'd have to 'make do' with. It wasn't right that she should lack for anything just because she'd married him.

Except for one thing. But she'd known before she married him that he didn't wish to carry on his line and she'd accepted that.

He was putting a great deal of faith in a curtain to help him get some rest tonight. He was a man, after all, and being so near a beautiful woman… *his* beautiful woman…was incredibly tempting. He knew there were ways to indulge in intimacy without a child resulting from it. However, they were risky and could fail.

The risk wasn't worth it.

'We shall manage for one more meal.' She indicated the blanket on the sand, with a basket placed upon it.

The children raced for it, plopped down, rolled about laughing.

Looking at them now, he could scarcely believe they were the same tearful orphans he had taken from London Cradle.

He didn't believe it had anything to do with him. The only reason they now resembled a pair of boisterous puppies was because of Minerva and the loving care she gave them.

'There's nothing quite like having sand squished between one's toes,' he observed as he strolled towards the blanket, breathing in the sea air, feeling it fresh on his face.

'It's wonderful.' She flicked some sand up with her toes.

They sat on the blanket. His knee skimmed her ankle.

She didn't flinch from his touch, which must be an indication that their friendship was growing quickly.

The time they'd spent last night on the beach had brought them closer. For him it had, anyway. Hopefully it had for her too. It was important for the children that their parents liked each other.

Abby gobbled down a cracker. Minerva gently brushed crumbs from the corners of her mouth. The tenderness in the gesture twisted his heart, because he wasn't used to tenderness. And the more he saw of Minerva with the children, the more he realised what he'd missed out on as a child.

'Perhaps I can catch us a fish for dinner,' he said.

Minerva gave the children tenderness; he would give them dinner. He had seen men having great success further down the shore.

'Or purchase one from that fisherman over there.'

'What will we do with it if you do?'

'I have no idea. But it will be worth discovering, I think. Fish for dinner would be delicious.'

He would wager that until today his gently bred wife had never considered the necessity of learning to cook a fish. Neither had he.

If necessary he would triple what he should pay his neighbour for a fish, and it would be well worth the cost.

Settled on the blanket, they all ate crackers and cheese. Pleasant company on a leisurely afternoon made a few grains of sand in his cheese worth it.

'Seal!' James bolted to his feet, pointing at an outcropping of rock near a cave, where the creature lounged in a bath of sunshine.

'Go see!' Abby jumped up and started to run towards it.

Quick as a seabird rushing for the ebbing tide, Minerva hopped up and scooped Abby into her arms.

'We must walk very slowly, or it will swim away before we get a good look at it.'

They made it to within a stone's toss of the creature before it slid into the sea.

'I think it lives in that cave,' James said. 'Let's find him.'

That was a bad idea. Harrison had explored the cave and found it to be a dangerous place, which flooded when the tide came in.

He knelt beside James, motioning for Abby to come over too. He wanted to make it clear that they were never to go near the rocky cave.

Abby hurried over and bumped her brother sideways. Her eager, trusting face made him feel soft in a way he never had before.

Fatherhood, he was learning, was not all duty

to be fulfilled. Children, like kittens and puppies, could steal a person's heart.

But this moment was about duty.

'That cave is a very dangerous place,' he told them.

'Is it magic?' James asked, his expression bright and hopeful.

'It is not. It fills with water. And heaven help anyone who's inside when it does. They will be carried out to sea.'

'I would ride a seal back to shore. It must be magic, sir.'

James had been calling him 'sir', but all of a sudden it seemed too formal. He much preferred the title Abby had given him.

'Me don't wike magic cave. Me wike Mama-Min.' Abby dashed for Minerva.

It was no surprise that the little girl felt safe with Minerva. He shouldn't feel disappointed that she didn't feel so with him. Perhaps one day she would.

In that moment he was most concerned with James. Would that the boy appeared even a little cautious of the cave…

'We shall establish a rule.' He bent at the waist, giving James a stern glance in order to lend the edict proper authority. 'Neither you nor your sister will come down to the beach without me or Mama-Min coming with you.'

The boy frowned, but his sister said, 'Bad cave. Don't wike it.'

'That is so clever of you Abby,' Minerva announced. 'And I bet your brother is clever too.'

'You will not let your little sister come here without one of us, will you, James?' Harrison asked.

'No, sir, I won't.'

He was certain it wasn't what the boy wished to say.

'Good lad. Now, I would wager you're a good runner. Shall we race back to the blanket?'

'Quick, Abby!' Minerva snatched the child up. 'Let's not let them beat us!'

His wife was quick—he would give her that—but she was handicapped by having to carry Abby.

James got to the blanket first.

Harrison pretended to step on a shell, slowing down enough to be overtaken by the ladies.

A short distance from the blanket Minerva set Abby down. 'Run, baby, run!'

Abby dashed across the blanket. 'I win, Uncle-Papa!'

Chapter Five

Minerva stood at the kitchen table, staring at the large fish. It would make a filling meal for her family. She poked it gingerly with her finger. It looked slick, but in fact the scales were rough. And at the same time oddly smooth. If it were not for the dead eye staring up at her the fish would be pretty.

'Did the fisherman tell you what to do with it?'

'He began to, but then it started to rain and he was anxious to get his catch home to his wife.'

'I suppose that good woman knows what to do with it.' All Minerva knew was that they were going to have it for dinner…somehow.

Harrison bent, peering intently at it. 'It's pretty in the candlelight. Do you see the rainbow colours on the scales?'

'It will be prettier on the dinner table with a fork in it.'

There was one thing to be said for it. This would

be an adventure to tell Evie about. Not exactly a delightful one. She could only imagine what her father would think if he could see her picking up a kitchen knife and poking a dead creature with it.

This was hardly the elegant life he'd envisaged for his only daughter.

Here she was, though. There was nothing to do but carry bravely on.

'What did the fisherman say before it began to rain?'

'To slit open the belly longwise.' He grinned. 'And clean out the guts.'

All of a sudden she wasn't certain she'd be able to eat the fish, even if she did manage to cook it.

She glanced up at Harrison. He extended his hand and waggled his fingers, gesturing for her to give him the knife.

He did have nice fingers. Long, callused with hard work, and manly in the extreme. But now was not the time to imagine how they would feel if she handed him the knife ever so slowly and those fingers caressed her skin…

Never mind that. Now was not the time—and it never would be the time. The challenge before her was enough for the moment.

'Perhaps we should just slice some more cheese for dinner.' Cheese didn't have guts.

'It's a chilly, wet night. The children should have something warm to eat.'

He winked, then smiled, nodding at the knife.

The wink surprised her. It revealed a side of him she hadn't yet seen. Wouldn't it be nice if she discovered a way to bring that out in him more often? She'd enjoy being married to a man who winked.

'I will do it,' she told him.

She no longer lived in a grand home, with servants to do everything for her. If only she'd gone to the Rivenhall kitchen more often and watched what the cooking staff did.

'Give me the knife. I'll do it.'

'And take all the fun for yourself?' She tapped the fish's pale belly with the tip of the blade. 'Not on your life.'

'You look green.'

Not quite touching her, but nearly so, he traced the outline of her face with his finger.

'No more than you do,' she pointed out. 'If only our acquaintances could see us now. Some of them would faint.'

'And you are certain you won't?'

'Reasonably certain.'

'We'll do it together, then.'

Since feeding the family was becoming urgent, she was relieved to hand over the knife to his waiting hand. Again, she was struck by how strong and capable it looked.

'Place your fingers around mine and we will slay this beast together.'

'The beast is already slain...it's the innards

which— Oh, they're going to be nasty, aren't they?'

He placed one hand at her waist. 'Just in case, Min. I don't wish to have to go out in this weather to fetch a doctor if you do faint.'

Min? That was an endearment, was it not?

Endearments were used when people shared intimate bonds with one another.

Although in this case the bond was probably only due to them facing an obstacle together.

Too bad he wasn't likely to use it again. *Min...* It gave her a nice feeling. Warm and…

Never mind. She had a fish to clean…to gut.

When the moment came, she closed her eyes. Harrison's hand flexing underneath hers felt competent, so really there was no reason she needed to watch the gutting happen.

'It's done.'

His breath brushed her ear, stirred her curlicue hair.

'That wasn't so bad after all,' she murmured.

'Are you ready for the next step, then?'

Probably not. 'Yes.'

'The head will need to be cut off. Unless you wish to have it looking at us while we eat?'

She had seen fish served that way, but now… Well…no.

Extending the knife to her, he arched his dark brows.

He meant for her to do it?

Having never chopped the head off anything, she found the prospect daunting. However, a challenge was a challenge and meant to be overcome.

'I wouldn't wish for the children to be disturbed by the sight of cooked eyes…' she said.

'Just give it a solid whack,' he advised, looking sage and experienced in such matters—which she was pretty sure he wasn't.

One… She lifted her arm high. Two… She focused on her target. Three… *Whack!* The knife blade got stuck in the cutting board, but the head was neatly separated from the body.

She picked up the body and rinsed it in a bucket of clean, cold water.

'I'm glad that's over.' She wiped her brow with the apron she was wearing.

'Not quite over. The fish must be scraped of its scales.'

This was growing ever more gruesome. She could hardly wait to tell Evie about it.

'I think I hear the children arguing.'

Taking off the apron, she fled the kitchen.

Beheading was all the challenge she could manage for the day.

But he had called her Min. She might behead a dozen fish to hear that again.

In a sense, Harrison thought that sharing a chamber with his wife had been easier before the curtain had gone up, separating her space from his.

It had taken him four days to find the opportunity to hang it in place. During that time they had fallen into a way of doing things which protected each other's modesty.

She changed into her nightclothes before he entered the chamber. By the time he came in she was in her bed, with her face to the wall, which gave him the chance to change.

It was a polite, respectful arrangement.

This had become his favourite time—when, in the quiet of the night, the children at last asleep, they turned on their separate beds to face each other. In quiet conversation they passed an hour, sometimes more, speaking of the day, of the children, and of the progress of the cottage's restoration.

It was surprising how quickly he'd grown comfortable with having a wife. He'd never had a friend like her…or a friend at all, he had to admit. Visitors had rarely called at the Elmstone home during his childhood. When they had they hadn't brought children with them.

The curtain shifted in a draught of air hissing down the chimney.

He had half a mind to take the flimsy barrier down again. It made life less comfortable, not more.

Because what he had failed to anticipate when he'd tacked it up were the silhouettes against the firelight.

When his wife went about the business of preparing for bed, he was witness to her every movement.

If she bent over the basin and splashed water on her face, he saw it. When she dropped her petticoats and stepped out of them, he saw that too. When she raised her arms to slip into her sleeping gown…

Which was what she was doing now.

Fighting the urge to watch, he sat on the edge of his bed, staring instead at his bare toes, flexing on the rug.

It didn't help. He was hot, which made no sense since the room was very cool. Sweat made his shirt claw at his neck. He wanted nothing more than to rip it from his body, fling it and all his clothes across the room and sleep bare.

Not that he dared to. Cool air touching his skin would only make him wonder what Minerva's small smooth hands would feel like, gliding down his throat, brushing the hair on his chest, then—

Damn it.

Their marriage was getting along well enough. The last thing he wanted to do was put it in peril. He wouldn't risk the particular vulnerability that becoming intimate opened one up to.

Bedsprings creaked. Blankets rustled. How long would it take for her to fall asleep?

He changed out of his clothes, shrugged on his

nightshirt, then got into bed. Hearing her sigh, he turned towards the curtain.

In shadow, she fluffed her hair, spread it over the pillow.

Was it such a short time ago when all he'd wanted was to live here alone?

The letter from his solicitor, a trip to London Cradle and a brief, awkward wedding had changed everything.

Life was better now in every way…

Except for the curtain. It interfered with their pleasant night-time conversation.

Wind blew against the window, cold and blustery. It was appropriate for this last night of summer to be blown away with autumn's first breath.

Now, that was a poetic thought. It would be good to share it with Minerva.

He kept it to himself, though. Because it would be awkward to speak through the barrier, not being able to watch her expressions.

'Harrison?'

'Yes?'

'Oh… I was just wondering if you were still awake.'

'I was wondering the same thing about you.'

However, he knew she was, because he had been watching her touch her hair.

A pair of clocks ticked…the wind rattled the shutters. Minerva was silent again.

'It sounds like summer is blowing away,' he

said. The thought had sounded prettier in his mind. 'Do you like autumn?'

She didn't answer, but he heard her feet on the floor, padding towards the curtain.

It moved. Minerva's face peeked around the edge.

'Do you mind leaving this open just a little bit? I would rather see you while we're speaking.'

She slid the curtain open a few feet.

Did she always wear such flimsy fabric to sleep in?

She held the curtain across the upper part of her body, but the outline of her calves and knees was clear to see.

'I do like autumn,' she said, and then got back into bed and turned to smile at him.

This was much better, he decided. For the most part they had their privacy, but they were still able to see one another's faces.

'Tell me…what is your favourite thing about autumn?' he asked. It was nice, asking each other silly, mean-nothing questions.

'It used to be bundling up for carriage rides, wearing long cloaks with furry hoods and going to balls decorated in autumnal colours…seeing guests rushing into the house shaking off the rain and laughing. But I don't know what it will be now. I suspect the best thing will be holding the children by the fire, or sitting on the cliff and drinking hot soup…if our neighbour is kind enough to bring some for us. I wonder if we ought to hurry and complete the house so we can employ a cook who will live here.'

'I thought you did a rather good job of cooking the fish.'

And so the conversation went on…

While he was telling her the history of ormolu clocks, like the one on the mantel, Minerva tangled her fingers in her hair. With her lips slightly parted, she sighed and drifted off to sleep.

Ah, Min… So close to him and yet still miles away—by his own choice. Perhaps hers as well.

The gentle rise and fall of her chest made him drowsy too.

Or it made him restless.

Whichever it was, he closed his eyes, seeking sleep.

Harrison sat in a corner of the parlour at the large desk, studying the assorted clock parts spread across its surface.

The cuckoo clock he was restoring was an interesting piece.

Ordinarily he would have been so involved in what part went where that he'd be unaware of anything else.

Not this afternoon.

Right now, he was more aware of Minerva's voice, bright and animated, reading a story to the children.

They had been restive, having to remain indoors because a dense cold fog had rolled in off the ocean, which made it unfit for outdoor play.

Glancing up and seeing them cosy on Minerva's lap, he realised—again—how much he had missed out on as a child. For him a peaceful day had meant finding a place to hide where he couldn't hear his parents arguing.

He gave his attention partly back to his task, letting the voices of his family carry softly, reassuringly, across the room to his ears.

'What are you doing Uncle-Papa?'

James was peering past his shoulder at the clock parts on his desk.

'Did you break it?'

Hearing James call him Uncle-Papa, he nearly dropped the delicate mechanism he pinched between his fingers. This was the first time the boy had not referred to him as 'sir'.

'No, lad. But I'm fixing it. Would you like to watch?'

James scrambled onto a stool beside him, picking up a spring and squeezing it.

With James touching everything he knew it would make repairs more difficult, but all of a sudden this was not about repairing a clock. It was about becoming a father… Uncle-Papa…to James.

'Does the bird fly about?'

'Not quite, son. It pops in and out of that small

door, making a "cuckoo" sound on the hour and half-hour.'

'Will you put it on the wall with the others?'

'The wall is a perfect spot. Would you like to choose where it should be?'

James pointed to a place near the ceiling.

'It will need to be wound sometimes, so maybe we ought to place it lower. But I have an idea, James. How would you like to be the one to wind it?'

'I want to… It's just that my sister will break it if it's very low.'

'That is a good thought—she is rather young to wind the clock.'

'Abby likes stories better than clocks, anyway.'

'How about you? Do you like stories?'

He nodded. 'But maybe I like clocks better.'

'Clocks have stories. Perhaps I shall tell you some of them one day.'

'May I have one now?'

Harrison thought for a second. The lad did seem to like magic, if his comments on the cave were anything to go by.

'Would you like to hear the *Tale of the Ruby Fairy Watch*?'

'Is there a fairy in a watch? A tiny one? Does she have a ruby or a different treasure? Is she a good fairy or a tricky one?'

'Ah, well…she's a very good fairy, as you will

see. And she does have another treasure, and it's worth more than even a giant ruby.'

James set the spring down, his expression amazed. Harrison had the strongest urge to place a kiss on his wavy hair. Minerva did it often, but he wasn't certain it was what fathers did.

'The watch does have a small ruby, though. Even better, it has a legend attached to it, too.'

'I want to hear the legend!'

'Then so you shall. Many years ago—a hundred or more—there was a fairy from the Isle of Skye, which is known to be an excellent place for magical fairies.'

'My mama told me that too.'

Harrison gave James a pat on the head. The child must miss his mother terribly. He took a second before going on to give silent thanks that the children had Minerva.

'Well, this was a happy fairy. She wore a gown made of deep red rubies. And when someone spotted her she didn't fly away in fright, but instead offered them a flower and a smile. She gave pleasure to everyone who saw her. Then one day a great storm—bigger than any seen before—blew across the isle and swept the Ruby Fairy out to sea. She was carried by the wind for a great distance. Eventually she grew so tired her wings stopped working and she fell into the water. A young woman walking on a beach no great distance from here saw the fairy struggling in the waves. She was a brave lady… She didn't know if it was a fairy or a pixie, you see. But she waded in and saved the Ruby Fairy, who was so grateful that she created a watch and gave it to the lady as a reward.'

The legend was only fantasy, of course, but the watch itself was real. It was a much sought-after piece which hadn't been seen in thirty years or more.

Since James seemed more interested in the legend than the timepiece, Harrison went on. 'It was a beautiful thing. Made of silver and hung on a gold chain. It had an engraving of a pair of swans, with their beaks meeting at the top of the watch. At the point where the beaks met was a small ruby. It's said that whoever is in possession of the watch will have their dearest wish granted.'

'Who *is* in possession of it, Uncle-Papa?'

'No one knows. It hasn't been seen in many years.'

'Maybe I'll find it!'

He ruffled James's hair. 'I imagine someone will find it one day. It could be you.'

Well, there were treasures and there were treasures. There were the ones made of gold, silver, rubies and legends, and there was the one sitting beside Harrison with his small shoulder pressed against his arm.

'I shall always be on the lookout for it.' James's small round face showed great determination.

'Between now and then, would you like to learn to repair the cuckoo clock?'

James picked the spring up again. 'Does this make the bird pop out of the door?'

'Indeed. In a sense… Let's discover how.'

The dense fog which had lingered all day lifted sometime during the night. Dawn broke bright with sunshine.

Minerva didn't know who among them was the happiest to go outside.

While the children played with some kittens in the meadow between the house and the stables, she spotted Harrison doing some sort of work outside the cook's future quarters.

Lovely—she could help him and watch the children at the same time. Whatever she could do to hasten the employment of a cook, she was willing to do it.

For now, work on her own chamber was postponed in favour of having a full-time cook. Besides, their neighbour wouldn't appreciate having to come here in inclement weather to bring them meals.

It had been her idea to alter the construction plans. The prospect of continuing to share a bedchamber with Harrison was less grim than going hungry.

Very well, it wasn't at all grim.

She had become used to waking in the night

and hearing his steady breathing, and the creak of bedsprings when he turned over.

Knowing there was a large, dependable man only feet away was a comfort, and if she could keep it a little longer she certainly didn't mind.

'I've come to help,' she announced, glancing over her shoulder to make sure the children were within sight.

All seemed well, so she returned her attention to what Harrison was doing.

Her husband had a knack for putting things together, be it a home or a clock. There was so much she could learn from him.

He plucked a nail from between his lips. 'I won't take you home to your father with calluses on your hands. But you may watch if you like.'

'What does it matter if I get a callus from sweeping or hanging laundry or from a hammer? Father will never know the difference.'

'I do not care for my wife getting a callus of any sort.'

'I don't know…' She turned her hands this way and that. 'They'd be proof that I'm doing something worthwhile.'

'Still, I will not have you smashing a finger.'

'I might burn my finger having high tea at home…in London, I mean.' She picked up a saw. 'Show me how to use this.'

'You might cut yourself.'

'What I might do is expire from—'

He plucked the saw from her fingers, handing her a hammer instead.

If only Evie could see her now!

'You may attach this shutter to the window, as long as you allow me to help. I won't have you injured.'

'I'll do my best not to be.' She waved the hammer about, looking at it from all angles.

'Here, give me your hand. You only just missed hitting your nose.'

'You're making that up.'

He winked. Oh…she was becoming fond of that gesture…fond of all of him. In ways he might not appreciate.

What would he do if she leaned into him and let her shoulder brush his? But she wouldn't do that.

He was afraid of becoming vulnerable to betrayal. She understood that.

And yet… Well, never mind. She had come over here and she would learn how to attach a shutter to a window.

He plucked a nail from the pouch he wore slung across his chest. He put it between her fingers, then guided her hand to where the nail was to go in.

'I will hold the nail steady for the first strike or two.'

Would he? Who was going to hold *her* steady? His chest grazed her back and his lips were within an inch of her ear.

How was she to learn anything except how he

smelled like sunshine and good, clean sweat? Such a masculine scent that made any thought of hammering nails flee from her brain.

She was certain she wasn't reacting to his nearness in an appropriately friendly way. He wouldn't be happy if he knew.

'I can do this on my own,' she said, and yet he didn't let go of her hand…didn't put an inch of space between them.

'No doubt. However, we shall try it together for a time or two.'

She cast a glance at the children. They were still safely engaged with the kittens.

'First thing, we tap it lightly. Once the nail is slightly embedded in the wood, then we can give it some good whacks.'

'How many times did you hit your thumb before you learned?'

'Four times. You are gaining the benefit of my mistakes, my dear.'

My dear *friend*, he'd meant. She must not take those words to heart.

With the nail slightly embedded, she was ready to give it a good whack.

Then Abby screeched. James ran towards them.

'Uncle-Papa! Uncle-Papa! A kitten fell in a deep hole! It's crying.'

So was Abby.

'Show me where it is.'

He took the children by their hands and followed them to where the kitten had disappeared.

Minerva trailed behind. To Abby and James the hole would look deep, but in fact it was only about four feet. Narrow, though. It wouldn't be possible to climb down and rescue the kitten.

'The thing I've noticed about these kittens,' Harrison said, 'is that they like to climb.'

'On earth?' Minerva thought it unlikely.

Harrison took the pouch off his chest and threw out the nails.

'Shall we see if it will climb up this canvas?'

James wiped his nose on his sleeve. Abby hugged two of the other kittens to her cheeks.

'Here comes mama cat. She must have heard her baby crying,' Minerva said.

Harrison lowered the canvas pouch into the hole.

Mama Cat trotted across the yard, and peered down the hole. That was all the urging the kitten needed to catch its sharp little claws in the pouch.

Inch by inch, Harrison drew it out. Once the kitten was on the grass the mother cat licked it, then made a sound which caused all the kittens to follow her back into the barn.

'I not scared any more.' Abby hugged Harrison's trouser leg. 'Uncle-Papa get me out too.'

'You can't fall in that hole, Abby, you're too big,' James pointed out.

Harrison scooped her up. 'You must avoid falling in holes, certainly. But if you do I will always get you out.'

'I wuv Uncle-Papa.'

That said, Abby wriggled down to run after her brother, who was chasing a colourful bird.

'She adores you. Is that a tear in your eye?' she asked.

'Dust.' He blinked hard. 'From the hole.'

For a man who seemed to be such a natural father, it was a shame he didn't want another child.

Not that she would point it out.

He'd made his decision in that regard and she would accept it—had done so on the day she'd agreed to marry him.

Only then she hadn't understood what a fine father he would be.

Now that she did know…it should make no difference.

Only, it was beginning to.

'Where's Uncle-Papa?' Abby stood on a chair at the window, staring at the road leading towards the cottage.

'He went to town on some errands. He'll be back any moment now.'

Hopefully he would. It was getting dark. Wind swirled the leaves in circles. Huge black clouds raced in over the ocean.

She was trying her best not to appear worried in front of the children, but it was difficult.

'Come,' she said, when another hour had gone by. 'We will have dinner.'

After dinner and a story she put the children to bed, then took Abby's place at the window. Except she couldn't sit. She couldn't see anything through the rain, either.

She paced about, imagining all the dreadful things that must have happened to him.

After three hours—each one announced by a pair of chiming clocks—she was at the point of tears.

Caring for a man was far from the easiest thing she had ever done.

Then she saw a lamp go on in the stables.

Her relief was so great that she ran outside, hatless and coatless, dashing for the stable.

When she was halfway across the meadow the lamp went out and Harrison appeared in the doorway.

Seeing her, he ran through the lashing rain to meet her, nearly slipping in the mud and losing the box he was clutching to his chest.

Without considering the right or wrong of it, only needing to express her relief at seeing him home safe, she launched herself against him. She hugged his ribs fiercely. He must be aware of how her heart beat so madly.

'Min?' He leaned back from the waist, staring hard at her. 'What's happened? Is something wrong with the children?'

'The children? No, they're asleep.'

He let go of her, took a step back.

'What are you doing outside without a coat, Min?'

He set the box down, took off his coat and slung it over her shoulders. Stooping, he snatched the box off a mound of wet grass.

Delightful warmth lingered in the fabric of his coat, but it was his scent which heated her. She took a discreet sniff, feeling heat swirl through her limbs and all the way to her heart. Until Harrison, she had never known how good the natural scent of a man could be. Society gentlemen tended to douse themselves in cologne.

'You're so late home. I was worried.'

Rain dripped off the brim of his hat. He peered at her through spotted spectacles. 'I cannot recall when anyone has worried about me before. I think…it's touching.'

'Touching? It felt terrible from my end.'

'I'm sorry. Let's go inside. I think I can make it up to you.'

As long as he was home safe, nothing else mattered. It was absurd to be angry with him for it.

And by the time they'd hurried inside the house her temper had been replaced with embarrassment.

Whatever would he make of her throwing herself into his arms like that?

Going into the dining room, he placed the box

on the table, took off his hat, then shot a wet grin at her.

'What is it?' she asked.

'Open it and see.'

She lifted the lid…peeked inside.

'Cake?'

'Chocolate. Half of it is. The other half is apple. I wasn't sure which one you'd like better.'

She clapped her hands. 'You are my hero, Harrison Tremayne.'

Their neighbour was a saint to bring them dinner, but she never brought dessert.

'If all it takes is bringing home cake, I shall do it more often.'

'Go and sit by the fire and get warm.' No doubt he was freezing. 'I'll bring you a piece. Have you had anything else to eat?'

'Cheese and bread on the ride home,' she heard him say from the parlour.

When she came back, she nearly dropped the plates she carried.

Harrison was sitting on the hearth, chafing his hands, wearing nothing but his undergarments.

While not sheer, they grazed the bold shape of his limbs. It wasn't her fault if she was staring. If he didn't wish her to gawk, he shouldn't have taken off his clothes.

'I collected a telegram in town. I've had news from London,' he said, rolling his shoulders into the heat. 'We must return. Some important business with my solicitor.'

She handed him his plate of cake, one slice of each kind, then sat in her chair.

'Will you mind?' she asked.

'I won't enjoy it, but I'll get by. Besides, you will want to spent time with your family.'

What a relief that he didn't intend to leave her here alone. There was no denying how good it would be to go home…to London, she meant.

Only, she had to wonder… When they returned to Cockleshell Cottage, would she go through all the loneliness of missing her family again?

As it was now, she felt at home here. There were things she preferred about living at the seaside… and yet, in her heart, London was her home as well.

Still, this was the life she'd chosen of her own free will. If it meant she was balanced between two worlds, she would make the best of it.

No, not that. She would embrace both of them—not grieve for the one she missed.

The idea sounded brave and adventurous. Only time would tell if she could live up to the ideal.

Chapter Six

They'd arrived at Elmstone House after dark last night, each one of them weary from the trip. It had taken only an hour for all the Tremaynes to fall asleep.

This morning Minerva had been woken by a maid delivering her breakfast. She'd forgotten that married ladies were served breakfast before getting out of bed.

It seemed odd. Not at all what she was used to.

After that, another maid had dressed her and styled her hair. It felt stiff, piled on top her head and forced into curls and waves. She had come to enjoy it falling loose, where the sea breeze could catch it and flutter it about her shoulders.

Finally ready for the day, she emerged from her chamber to find that Harrison was already in meetings with his accountant.

Since he would probably be involved in business matters all day, she decided to take the children to Rivenhall.

The morning was lovely—crisp and sunny. Walking the short distance from here to her home would be just the thing. After spending most of yesterday travelling, the children needed exercise.

To Minerva's great relief, the Smythe ladies were not taking the air this morning, and within ten minutes they entered Rivenhall.

It was so good to be home. Familiar sounds and scents wrapped her up, held her like a hug.

Her father must have heard the front door opening and the footman's greeting, for he rushed out of his office, arms open wide.

She ran into his arms. He wrapped her in a great hug. No matter what she'd done, or would ever do, she would always be his little girl. His arms would always be supportive, even when he didn't understand her.

'I've missed you so much, Father.'

'I've missed you too, Minnie. We were all overjoyed to get your husband's telegram, informing us that you were coming to London.'

He released her, gave her a great smile, then glanced down at the children.

'But what is this? Have you brought me grandchildren to play with?'

Bless the man for accepting them so readily. She regretted all the grief she'd caused him over the years.

'I have. Are Evie and the twins at home? Will you be able to keep up with four?'

'Your nanny can help me.' He glanced about. 'Did she not accompany you?'

'A nanny? I don't have one. Why would I give over the care of my children to someone else?'

'Because it's the usual way it is done?' Father shrugged and smiled. 'Although I am not a bit surprised.'

'I have become an independent woman, Father. I have skills.'

'Mama-Min cooks fish,' James announced.

'Your mother never ceases to amaze me, young James.'

Father took James's hand, then held his other hand out to Abby. Minerva was surprised to see how easily she rushed forward to clasp it.

Was it that Abby sensed what a loving man her grandfather was, or was she becoming more confident now that she had a family of her own? Hopefully she was beginning to put her sorrow away.

'What do you say we go to the kitchen and see what treats Cook has prepared for your arrival?'

Treats! Minerva meant to indulge in as many as she could before they returned to Cockleshell Cottage.

'Perhaps you can tell me how you cook a fish on the way to the kitchen, Minnie.'

'The first thing to know is, do not boil it in water or it will turn to mush.'

Father laughed.

Yes, it was wonderful to be home.

* * *

By the time Harrison had finished all his business it was time for dinner. He hadn't minded the long day, since the sooner he'd finished with the affairs of Elmstone, the sooner they could go home to Cockleshell Cottage.

Coming out of the office, he wondered where his family was. What had they done with their day?

He listened, heard footsteps crossing the hall.

A maid passed by, giving him a quick curtsey.

'Maisy, do you know if my wife and children are at home?'

'Yes, sir. They're in the conservatory.'

'Thank you,' he answered, giving her a smile and a nod.

At the cottage, he didn't need to go searching for Minerva and the children. Even when he was working outside he could hear them laughing and playing.

Just now, Cockleshell Cottage seemed a world away.

And Minerva…how did she feel about Cockleshell Cottage now that she was at home, where everything was familiar and comfortable. Was she now feeling a world away? In London she had breakfast in bed, a lady's maid, housekeepers and kitchen staff.

She had her own chamber to sleep in, as a lady ought to.

Here she had friends to call on.

Her family lived only streets away.

He had taken her away from all this.

Coming to the conservatory door, he saw Minerva chasing the children, laughing and as merry as he had ever seen her.

'Uncle-Papa!' James flew at him, followed by Abby, who placed herself in front of her brother in order to get the first hug.

'We pwayed with Gwandfather!' Abby reached up to be held.

'Playing with Grandfather was fun. He let me eat three treats and hold a parrot,' James added.

Not only could Cockleshell Cottage not live up to London, he feared that he could not live up to Grandfather.

'How was your day, Minerva?'

Because he and his wife weren't lovers, if she decided to remain in London he wouldn't be broken. Sad, yes…but because he kept his heart to himself he would survive it.

And yet he found himself thinking, *Please don't let her decide to stay.* Life with Minerva was far better than life without her. He would be a fool to deny it was not so.

'Lovely. I spent it with my family. How was your day?'

Again, please let her decide to come home to the seaside!

'Father is giving a dinner party in our honour. I hope you don't mind.'

There was nothing he would dislike more. 'It sounds delightful. When is it?'

'In two days.'

Minerva had given up everything for his children.

The least he could do for her was appear happy to attend a dinner party.

'I look forward to it.'

Minerva heard a sound in the night. She sat up in bed, glancing at dark corners, feeling nervous.

As lovely as this chamber was, she had spent only one night in it so far. Nothing was familiar. She mustn't be as adventurous as she thought she was if she wasn't bold enough to sleep alone in a strange place.

If her marriage was like her brothers' she would not be sleeping in here alone.

And she had a perfectly strong husband she had become accustomed to sharing a bedroom with.

The noise did not come again, but that didn't mean she would easily fall back to sleep.

If she heard a noise at Cockleshell Cottage she simply turned over and drifted peacefully back to her dreams. Knowing that her husband was only across the room gave her the comfort to do it.

Funny, she had slept by herself all her life, and now…

Now everything was different. *She* was different.

Getting out of bed, she grabbed her robe, shrugged into it, then walked down the corridor.

Opening the door to Harrison's chamber, she stood for a moment, wondering if should step inside…approach the bed.

She shouldn't. Only she really wanted to. There was a large chair by the window. She would sleep there.

'Min?' Harrison sat up, took his glasses off the bedside table and put them on.

'I can't sleep. I heard a noise.'

'What sort of noise?'

'A strange one.'

He folded back the blanket. Did he mean she should join him or that he was getting out of the bed?

'It's a large bed. I think we shall manage.'

He patted the mattress. She dashed forward, hurrying across the room. She sat on the bed.

'Thank you. I promise not to disturb you.'

She lay down, pulling the blanket to her nose, keeping as far towards the edge of the mattress as she could.

'Goodnight, then.' He removed his glasses, set them back on the table.

'Goodnight.'

She hoped it would be.

While a strange noise wouldn't leave her sleepless, the large man beside her might.

Because it was dark, she couldn't see what he

was wearing. A proper sleeping garment or his soft underwear?

Knowing how he looked in his underwear… *Oh, my word.* She wasn't likely to sleep any better in his bed than she had in the Baroness's chamber.

But at least she wasn't lonely now…only feeling a bit prickly…all over.

She was giving far too much thought to what he was wearing.

What she was going to do was fall asleep…as quickly as she could…on her own side of the bed.

Not her side of the bed, she reminded herself. It was all his. She was only borrowing one slim edge of the mattress for this one night.

In the morning she would wake on it. Just like she woke on her side of the bedroom each morning.

That wasn't really any different from this.

Except that the bed was smaller.

Except that she could feel the heat of his long body underneath the blanket.

Except that all she could think of was what it would be like if she were free to move over and…

The plain fact of the matter was that she was not free to move over.

The only thing she was free to do was go to sleep.

So she would…quite soon. Or a bit after that.

Harrison awoke slowly, the dream he'd been having lingering in his mind.

It had been so vivid he did not wish to open his eyes. Even now he felt the imagined warmth of Minerva's leg draped across his thigh, her hand on his heart.

He didn't want to move for fear that the dream would leave him before he was able to gather her closer, relish the scent of roses and lemon.

Before he lost it, he covered her hand where it curled on his chest. He nuzzled his nose in her hair, breathed deep.

It tickled vividly for a dream.

Since it was a dream, why not kiss her? It wasn't something he'd dare to do during waking hours—wouldn't even think of it…much. But in a dream all things were possible.

Making sure to keep his eyes closed tight, so that he wouldn't awaken too soon, he traced the shape of her cheek with his thumb, drew her chin up, tasted her lips.

'Min…' he dream-whispered.

She snuggled closer, so warm. Her shoulder was smooth under his fingertips, the strap of her gown so easy to slip down her arm.

All at once the blankets erupted as Minerva flung them about. She scrambled across the mattress and leapt out of bed, her gown's strap dangling.

No dream! He rolled out of bed, staring across the mattress at her in utter shock.

What had he done? What must she think of him?

That he was an Elmstone and no gentleman, no doubt.

'I beg your pardon, Minerva. I didn't mean to—'

Mean it or not, he'd done it. It didn't matter that they were wed. They had an understanding between them. One he had just broken. And, if the truth were to be admitted, he'd relished those moments when he'd thought he was dreaming.

'Forgive me, I thought I was— I do beg your pardon for acting like a beast.'

For a long, silent moment she gazed across the bed, giving him a look he couldn't begin to interpret.

She mumbled something which sounded something like 'or a husband' but that couldn't have been it.

'Think nothing more of it,' was what she said only a heartbeat later.

How was he to do that?

Could any man not think about holding heaven in his arms? Forbidden heaven. Forbidden by his own decisions because of his past.

'Really, Harrison,' she tucked the edges of her robe about her while she backed slowly towards the chamber door. 'There's nothing untoward about a friendly hug in the morning.'

There had been a hug…of sorts. Had she missed the part where he'd kissed her?

Maybe. It was possible that she had woken after that.

Relief swept over him. If she thought the embrace had been friendly he wasn't about to tell her otherwise.

For him, holding her had slipped past friendly territory into intimacy. Into danger!

It was something he couldn't risk happening again. As soon as they got home to the seaside he was going to employ builders to hurry the construction along. He'd wanted to do it all himself, but the sooner Minerva had her own chamber to sleep in the better off they'd all be.

To give in to the way she'd felt in his arms was only to invite disaster.

He knew enough of marriage to understand that love had no place in it.

'You'll be the most beautiful woman in the room tonight,' Minerva's maid Dottie declared, while arranging the last curl of her hairstyle to her satisfaction.

Dottie had come over from Rivenhall for the week and it felt like quite a treat.

'If you don't mind me saying so, you've had a blush about you these last few days.'

And why wouldn't she? Ever since she'd awoken in her husband's embrace, experienced his unknowing kiss, she'd felt like a walking, breathing blush. Because, make no mistake about it, it had been an embrace and a kiss.

She wouldn't still be flushed if the moment had

been as platonically friendly as she'd indicated it had been.

Who, she had to wonder, had been the first to cross the bed? Not that it mattered greatly in the end. What had happened had happened—she was only curious to know how it had.

A friendly morning hug? Hardly!

Yet what else was she supposed to say?

That her heart had melted in an instant? He wouldn't appreciate knowing that.

Perhaps she was wrong about what she was feeling and it would soon pass.

She clung to that thought while descending the grand staircase.

Harrison waited for her at the bottom step.

Unless she'd missed her guess, he was feeling like a man going to the gallows rather than a gentleman attending a common dinner party.

No matter how he felt about it, he looked handsome dressed in his finest.

Seeing him this way gave her flutters in odd places. She could only hope that once they returned to the cottage everything would be as it had before.

Comfortable, appropriate…safe.

He shot her a bright smile. Clearly it was his attempt to hide the fact that he'd rather be doing anything than this.

She winced internally. What Father called a dinner party would involve a good-sized crowd…

'You look stunning, Minerva.'

She thought he meant it, because his eyes softened, and his smile was warm and genuine.

'And I shall have the most handsome husband at Rivenhall tonight.'

'People will be envious of us, don't you think?' He took her hand and placed it in the crook of his arm.

'They will want to be us,' she answered.

His smile while leading her to the carriage was completely disarming. At least to her eyes it was. There would be many present tonight who would see that smile and believe it the gesture of an utter rake. She was likely to be considered his victim. Their sudden marriage being proof of it. Mrs Smythe knew the truth, but was unlikely to have set anyone straight on the matter.

Dressing for tonight, she'd purposely chosen a gown to show off her slim waist. It was worth a bit of discomfort for people to see that she was definitely not expecting a child.

Really, anyone who truly knew her would understand that she wasn't so easily seduced.

As far as society marriages went, she would wager there were many not as satisfying as hers—even given its limitations.

What was to say a marriage must be entered into for love? Nothing at all. Duty, as her own father had used to insist, was a brilliant reason to wed.

Her marriage might not be like Evie and Thomas's marriage. And few people could expect to have what William and Elizabeth had either.

But that was an issue she'd settled in her mind from the beginning.

What she and Harrison had was enough.

Chapter Seven

Before tonight, Harrison had met Minerva's father on exactly two occasions.

The first had been when he'd asked for his daughter's hand in marriage. It had been clear that the Viscount had wished to refuse, and Harrison had understood why. No decent man wanted to give his daughter to a fellow with his reputation, and of a lower rank than he had wanted.

The second time they met had been at the wedding—a strained affair, with only her father, brothers and sisters-in-law in attendance.

But it had been only natural for it to be uncomfortable since he was a stranger to them.

Entering Rivenhall tonight had been different. He'd been warmly welcomed, treated informally, as a member of the family would be.

He could scarcely believe it. The last thing he was accustomed to from any family was warmth.

If it had only been Minerva's family in attendance he'd actually have enjoyed the evening.

That was far from the case. There had to be three dozen or more guests, invited to celebrate his and Minerva's marriage.

Whether the reason they were there was to celebrate or to indulge in curiosity, who could say?

But, given what he knew of some of them, he guessed it was the second reason.

Dinner went well enough. And Minerva made a point of showing him affection.

If she noticed the occasional sly glance sent their way, she countered it with a kiss to his check or by sliding her hand into his.

Anyone would think she was smitten with him. Only he knew it was all for show. To convince people she hadn't been coerced into marriage. That she had not, in fact, been compromised.

His new sister-in-law, Evie, must know the reason for their marriage. She and Min were close friends, so they would be privy to one another's secrets.

But even knowing the truth, Evie still accepted him as part of the family.

The Grant family was as different from his own as could be. The Tremaynes didn't welcome anyone—especially each other.

Watching Minerva moving about the large drawing room, where they had retired after dinner, chatting easily with guests, he thought she looked as happy as a little red bird in her beautiful ruby gown.

Seeing her so easy amongst these people made him wonder idly if she might even manage to change people's minds about the Tremayne family name. Transform it from sordid to being above reproach.

He shook his head at the fanciful notion. Nobody and nothing could do that.

It was still a surprise to find that he was enjoying the evening.

For the most part.

There was an element to it, however, which disturbed him.

It had to do with Minerva's beauty…her outgoing charm. And he wasn't the only man here who'd noticed it. Some dandy was flirting with her, even with him standing beside her!

But his wife was a lady of honour, who wouldn't betray her wedding vows as Juliette had so easily betrayed their engagement all those years ago.

He reminded himself of that whenever a man cast an interested gaze at her.

Which was unnervingly often.

'Minnie, I cannot tell you how happy I am that you are home,' Evie said as they walked in the garden, bundled in warm coats. 'I promise I won't take you away from your groom for long, but I must ask…are you truly happy? So far from society I wonder if you can be.'

'Life is very different, of course. But I'm learning things I never had any idea about.'

'I can see that.' Evie cast her a knowing smile. 'You have calluses on your hands and yet you have a glow about you that I don't recall seeing before.'

'Evie Grant! If I have a glow it's because I am wearing a red gown and it's reflecting on my skin. Not every marriage is like yours.'

'It's dark. There is no reflection.'

'Torchlight.'

'Really, Minnie? I see right through you. But your father says you cooked a fish. Is that true?'

'Oh, you would never believe it!'

They sat down on the bench in front of the fountain.

'I gutted it and scooped out the innards. And if you do not wish for it to be staring at you while you cook it, you must chop off the head.'

'You're making that up. I know you are.'

'You cannot eat a fish which is not cleaned before you cook it.'

For all that Evie looked at her as if she had become another person, Minerva felt proud. It was important to know how to prepare a meal…even if she knew only that one.

'And when you come to visit, Evie, I shall teach you how to hammer a nail.'

'Are you happy living that way? It's so different from what you are used to. Just look at your hands.'

Minerva held them up, turned them this way and that, feeling content with the way they looked.

'You see this?' She pointed to her palm. 'That red area is from doing the laundry.'

'Who *are* you? You should employ some help.'

'I'm still who I was—only different. Better, I think. And we will get help as soon as the house can accommodate it.'

Two young men strolled into the garden, smoking cigars and making their way towards the conservatory.

Evie arched her back, closed her eyes, then covered a yawn. 'Forgive me. The baby is making me tired.'

'You must go to your chamber and rest.'

What Evie was going through was something Minerva would never experience. And yet she did have Abby and James. Some women had no children at all, even though they desperately wanted them.

Her heart was so full of Abby and James it would seem ungrateful to mourn what would not be.

'Go on, Evie. I want to sit for a while and enjoy the garden.'

Evie stood up slowly. 'I will send your husband out. It's a romantic evening. Who knows where it might lead?'

Nowhere her friend hoped it would…

She closed her eyes, listening to the garden sounds. Water trickled from the fountain. Conversation drifted from inside the house. The conservatory door opened then closed. Footsteps crunched along the path.

Hopefully Harrison would come to her soon. She would enjoy sharing the garden with him.

The bench gave a creak as someone sat beside her. The brush of a sleeve crossed her arm. She sighed, glad that he had come so quickly.

'You look extremely fetching this evening, my lady.'

She opened her eyes to find Lord Billery sitting beside her. She slid sideways, providing a respectful distance which he immediately ignored.

'Good evening, Henry. Not nearly as fetching as your wife. Is she out here enjoying the garden with you?'

'I don't want to enjoy the garden with her. I want to enjoy it with you.' He moved closer, pinning her between his thigh and the arm of the bench. 'Do you not wish to spend some…*private* time in my company?'

'No. I do not. Keep in mind that I am a married woman and you are here tonight to celebrate that fact.'

She stood up.

'I am celebrating your new title… Baroness Elmstone.'

Oh, the cad! He had never been known for behaving in a respectful way towards women. But he was an important associate of her father's and so he'd expect to be invited.

'But not in an inappropriate way,' she told him.

It crossed her mind to wonder if he had ever dallied with the former Baroness.

He got up, closing the distance between them again.

'I'd say it's wholly appropriate,' he leered, bracing his hand on a tree trunk, the better to loom over her.

'Then I'd say you are a ninny. Are you really suggesting that by changing my name I might have changed my behaviour?'

'I might be... I wonder, when it comes to a lively woman like you...'

His tone suggested that being 'a lively woman' was somehow shameful.

He smelled of alcohol, but that by no means excused his behaviour or his twisted attitude.

'How much did you have to drink in order for you to believe it proper to say such a thing to me?'

'Kiss me, Minerva... Just one kiss and I'll go away.'

'Where *is* a lady's fish-gutting knife when she needs it?' Minerva mused.

He frowned, cocking his head in confusion.

'Or even better...' the sudden, menacing voice made her assailant flinch '...a lady's husband.'

Harrison clapped his hand on Henry's shoulder, spinning him away from her.

Tall, strong, and in a temper…her husband was magnificent.

She might have handled Henry on her own, but she was relieved that Harrison had stepped in to do it.

Besides, she wouldn't have been able to lift the cad by the back of his jacket and the seat of his trousers and then toss him into the fountain like Harrison did.

The splash was impressive.

'Are you all right, Min?'

'Quite.' Her heart pounded madly. 'But let's go inside. It's growing cold.'

He slung his arm about her shoulder, casting a glance back at Henry, who continued to splutter and flounder in the water.

'If you do not mind, Minerva, I would like to return home tomorrow. I fear that London isn't the best place for a Tremayne.'

By 'home' he meant the seaside, not the town-house.

She was going to miss her family terribly. But the thing was, she had another family to consider now.

She felt the weight of all the unkind judgement Harrison had suffered over the years. A moment ago she had experienced it too. If it could happen to her, it would likely happen to the children as well. There were too many people in society like the Smythe women and the ignoble Lord Billery.

'I'll say my goodbyes tonight and we will take the first train in the morning,' she said.

Later that night, when the rest of his family was in bed, Harrison went to the conservatory. Although it might not be the best place to go, given his mood.

Seeing that man with Minerva had been unsettling. The shock of it had shot him back in time to similar scenes. Some of which had taken place here, in this very room.

He would go somewhere else, but the whole manor was riddled with such memories.

At least the conservatory had also been the place where he and Minerva had played with the children.

This was where he needed to be in order to get his perspective back.

Just because Minerva had been too close to Billery, it didn't mean she had encouraged him.

He knew her better than to think so.

And yet his fears sat heavily upon him in that moment. Some of them reasonable and some not.

He ought to take heart that, faced with temptation, Minerva had not succumbed to it. He'd felt a flash of pride in her for threatening Billery with her fish knife. And there had been a great deal of satisfaction in tossing him into the fountain.

He wondered if he had been reacting to more than that one moment. Perhaps he had been tossing the shadows of his past into the water along with Billery.

While it had been satisfying, seeing the look in Minerva's eyes had been even more so. No one had ever gazed at him as if he were a hero—except maybe Abby, when he'd rescued the kitten out of that hole in the ground.

This was different from that. Minerva had made him feel that he could slay a dragon.

There was a large dragon breathing fire at him right now—and he didn't mean the men who'd gazed so longingly at his wife.

It was society—the lure of it.

What he had to offer Minerva couldn't compare. There was no reason for her to put on an elegant gown at Cockleshell Cottage. No occasion when she might feel like the lady she was. Her father wasn't there. Her brothers were not there. Nor her sisters-in-law either. Earlier tonight he'd seen just how many people had gathered about her. She had left many friends behind when she'd come to the seaside.

She had no friends in Cornwall. No society.

Only now did he truly appreciate how much she'd given up for the three of them.

Had it been too much?

When they returned to the seaside cottage he feared she wouldn't be fully content.

Had she married a man of society she'd have a husband far more suited to her. A man who'd freely give all of himself to her. Not even in his dreams could he risk doing that, because then he'd put his marriage at risk.

But he couldn't know what would happen tomorrow, or how Minerva would feel about leaving now that she had experienced society so briefly again.

Rising, he returned to his chamber. Where he was greeted with the memory of holding his wife.

He would strive to forget, but he wasn't sure it was possible.

The best thing he could do was be wary of it ever happening again. Be strong and protect his family.

As soon as they arrived in front of the cottage, Harrison looked at her in the oddest way. It was as if he were trying to read her mind, see her thoughts.

She might as well reveal them. Those she felt comfortable revealing.

'The children will need to run off their energy before bedtime. Will you take them down to the beach?'

He nodded, his thoughtful expression somewhat relieved.

Minerva watched the three of them from the cliff, listened to their laughter while they dashed about.

It was tempting to go down and join them, but she needed some time apart to think about what she *hadn't* revealed to Harrison.

She suspected he'd been worrying that she wouldn't be happy here once she'd experienced London again.

It was understandable. Her two worlds were as far apart as could be. Even she had wondered how she might feel.

Now she knew.

Standing here, she experienced a great sense of coming home.

Alone on the cliff, she had a moment to consider everything that made this place feel like home… to listen and absorb it into her heart.

Harrison, the children, the sound of waves rushing on the sand, the call of seabirds and the scent of salty air…

Home sweet home.

Although she detested embroidery, she thought the house might need a framed stitching of that sentiment to hang on the wall…

After a short time, her family came back up the cliff, hungry and ready for dinner.

Thinking ahead, they'd purchased meat pies in St Austell. There would have been berry pie for dessert too, but they'd eaten it on the train.

When at last the house was quiet, and Harrison was contentedly inspecting a clock, Minerva had a few more moments to herself.

What better way to spend them than bundling herself up against the autumn chill and sitting on the cliff?

While in London she'd missed watching the stars creep across the heavens and listening to the wind stirring the long grass which grew along the path down to the shore.

She thought about the trip to London, weighing in her mind what had been good and what had not.

Spending time with her family had been wonderful. She appreciated them more now than she ever had. Father especially. In spite of being unhappy at her sudden decision to wed a man he hadn't chosen for her, he had accepted her husband.

And the way he'd treated her children! Her father had welcomed them as fully as if they'd been born to her. She had felt undone by it.

Growing up, she hadn't always appreciated how wonderful her father was. Perhaps she shouldn't have caused him such turmoil! Now that she was a mother she was beginning to see life differently.

As for what had been not so good about London…

She would rather not dwell on it.

She heard footsteps, softly muffled in the grass.

'You're shivering, Minerva.'

Harrison sat down next to her, draped a blanket across her shoulders, and then shrugged the other end of it over himself.

She might have been shivering, but now…no. Any chill had vanished with him so close.

'It's good to be home,' she said, knowing he needed to hear her say so.

Harrison looked at the stars. 'Your head wasn't turned by all London had to offer?'

Lightly said, but she suspected he was anxious to hear her answer.

'I felt something as soon we turned down the lane.'

He snapped his gaze from the sky to her.

'As if the cottage was calling to you?'

'Yes, something like that.'

Enough for her to consider embroidering.

'I felt it too. From the first night. I sat in this spot for a long time before I ever went into the house…just feeling as though I were finally… home.'

'I can imagine why.' She waved her hand from one end of the horizon to the other. 'Anything London has to offer is washed out in comparison to this.'

'I haven't had a chance to explain about last night in the garden.'

'I don't know that anything needs to be explained,' she said. 'It was one of those unfortunate things which sometimes happens.'

'Was it? I've never seen anyone thrown into a fountain before. I've certainly never done it myself.'

'Don't you wish we could have seen Lord Billery trying to explain to his wife how he ended up getting wet?'

As far as unfortunate events went, this one was not completely unfortunate. Not in her eyes.

What she couldn't tell him was how she had felt her heart quiver when she saw him act so gallantly, so heroically.

Any married man acting as if he were not deserved a good dunking.

'But you must think me a heathen, behaving that way. Seeing him threaten you… I went red inside and acted in the heat of passion.'

'I like you in the heat of passion. You were splendid—my champion.'

'You think so?'

He blinked and frowned at the same time. He would make a splendid owl.

'Not a barbarian?'

'Not a heathen nor a barbarian. You are a hero and a gentleman.'

'It's unlikely that's what people in London are saying about me.'

'Oh, I imagine Henry has kept what happened to himself. But if he didn't, and people are gossiping, it hardly matters. We cannot hear them from here.'

'There will be times when we need to go back. We will hear them then.'

She pressed a little closer to him, because a

bank of fog was beginning to roll in from the ocean and it looked cold and wet. And because her husband's warmth was inviting. 'Shall I tell you what I think?'

'I'm not sure...but carry on.'

'I think that here you were, quite content to live a splendid life alone, with your privacy and your clocks—'

'And my house-building,' he put in quickly.

'Yes, and then all of a sudden you discovered that two vulnerable children needed you. So what did you do? You gave up the life you were making for yourself. And then, because those two children needed me, you took me too. You are the bravest man I know.'

'That's not exactly how I see it, Min.'

A breeze came up and he hugged the blanket tighter around them, drawing close enough for their shoulders to touch.

'You're the one who gave up everything for us.'

She shouldn't lay her head on his shoulder, but it would feel so good to do it.

Very well, she'd do it regardless.

The bank of fog crept in, enveloping them, making it seem as if they were alone in the world. The only sound was the rhythmic heartbeat of the ocean crashing on the shore.

The night called for this sort of closeness between friends. Let him wriggle away if he was uncomfortable being so close to her.

Apparently, he wasn't.

He placed his hand on her shoulder, drawing her even closer. 'I like this,' he whispered against her hair. 'We should sit here more often.'

Her answer was to sigh and nod.

No doubt these lovely magic moments would fade when morning came, bringing back all of life's common duties. But right now…with nothing beyond him and her, and the moment ripe for exploring one's heart…well, what she wondered was, what sort of friendship was this?

Different from most, to be sure. She had never snuggled next to a friend. Had never indulged in the scent of them or the strength of their arm across her shoulder.

Again, what sort of friendship was this?

She felt the pressure of his lips as they brushed the top of her head.

Was he going to kiss her lips next? It felt as if that was what the moment was leading to. How would she react if he did?

Move quickly away? Lean in and indulge in it?

This wasn't supposed to happen between them, but she had to admit to a growing excitement fizzing inside her.

'Min…' he murmured, his breath tickling her ear. 'I'm going to employ builders so that we can complete your chamber more quickly.'

Had he carried her down to the surf and tossed

her in, she couldn't have felt more thoroughly doused!

Scrambling for something to say, she straightened, moved away from him. The warm of his breath combined with what he'd just said confused her.

Her confusion confused her.

'The children might wake up. I need to return to the house.'

She shouldn't feel at such a loss. Having separate chambers was what they'd intended all along. He wasn't rejecting her by making it happen more quickly.

Wise. That was what it was.

Given how they had awoken tangled together the other morning.

Given the way she was clearly imagining feelings that weren't there or mistaking their meaning.

He did care for her in his own way. That was obvious enough.

Only, the other morning had left her confused.

The moment played over and over in her mind, making her warm and shivery by turn. Even just looking at him made her wonder about things that were forbidden between them.

It was good that he'd decided to hurry with her room.

A curtain would be a poor barrier if one wished to breach it.

That 'one' being her, not him.

An hour later she was in bed, lying on her side and watching him settle in under the covers.

'Goodnight, Minerva.'

Yes, just so.

'Goodnight.'

He turned on his side and it was a good thing he did.

How would she explain the tears that silently ran down her cheek and dampened her pillow?

She could not. Not to him, and not to herself.

Surely it was just that she liked sleeping across from him and that, in spite of the fact she'd slept alone all her life, she'd miss having him close by in the night.

Harrison wished Minerva goodnight, then rolled on his side. He tugged the blanket over his shoulder as if he intended to fall asleep.

Something he wasn't about to do.

Their relationship had changed while they were in London and thinking about it made him restless.

He felt things for his wife he'd never planned on feeling. It had begun when he had awakened with her in his arms, the two of them happily entangled.

At least he had felt happily entangled. Minerva might have felt trapped.

Then, later, when he'd waited for her at the foot of the stairs before the dinner party, he had been like a boy with a crush on the most beautiful lady in the city.

He was a man who would avoid society completely if it were possible, despite being a wealthy baron himself.

His wife had been born and raised for balls and dinner parties. As a lady of society she was lovely, polished and comfortable in her role.

What reason had she to be content with their quiet seaside cottage?

But had she not just said she was happy to be home a short time ago?

What had happened to bring her to silent tears? He'd seen them on her cheeks when he'd pretended to go to sleep. What had they meant?

Her sadness tore at him. Even feeling at home, was she unhappy?

He flipped to his other side in order to look at her again.

She was lying on her back, and he couldn't tell if her eyes were closed or if she was staring at the ceiling.

Was she trying to convince herself that she didn't miss London when she really did?

He had seen her with her family and her friends, so cheerful and happy. Indeed, she'd made him think of a lively red bird.

Now, feeling her sorrow, he wondered if he'd made a mistake when he'd offered marriage.

Had it been selfish to ask such a thing of her?

She'd given up everything for them and what had he given her in return?

Tears in the dark.

He'd been enraged when Billery had demanded a kiss from Minerva. And yet the man had simply wanted a moment—a salacious one, it was true. Harrison had taken Minerva's whole life.

She loved Abby and James and he had taken advantage of that.

Was all this true? Or was his mind doing what minds did in the night…indulging in worry regardless if it was warranted or not?

Was he imagining a problem when one didn't exist?

There was only one way to find out.

Tossing off the blankets, he got out of bed. He crossed the room and opened the door which joined the children's chambers to this one to go and check on them.

Their room was cooling off, so he added a log to the fire, then came back to add one in this chamber's.

Minerva seemed to be asleep, with her eyes closed and her breathing slow. She hadn't stirred while he was walking about.

Even if she was asleep he must speak with her. If there was something he'd done to cause those dried tear tracks on her cheeks he had to know what it was. If there was something he could do to keep them from falling again, he needed to know that, too.

He sat down on the bed, near her feet.

'Min, are you awake?'

She rose up on her elbows, blinked her round, dark-lashed eyes at him. 'I was trying not to be.' Slowly, she sat up fully. 'Is it the children?'

'No, I've just checked on them. They are well.'

'What is it, then? Are you ill?'

'It's nothing like that.' *Not exactly.*

'It must be something or you wouldn't be sitting on my bed.'

'You were crying, Min. Tell me why you're unhappy. Do you miss London after all?' This last was the worst, and he hated to say it but knew he must. 'If you wish to return I won't prevent you.'

She got out of bed. Her sleeping gown swayed softly about her. Her hair lay over her shoulder in a single braid. It caught the light of the flames in the hearth. The blue-black glimmer of it was all he could look at.

If he sat on his hands she'd probably wonder why. He would simply have to ignore the itch in his fingers, reminding him that despite the decision he'd made regarding the carnal aspect of their marriage he was still a man.

'How can you think that? Only a few hours ago I told you it was good to be home.'

'Since you were crying, I thought perhaps you were homesick.'

'There are many reasons women cry. Perhaps it was because I'm so glad to be home that I was overcome with the joy of it.'

He didn't know women well enough to be certain if that was true.

Drawing the curtain wider, she indicated that he should return to his side of the room.

'What will make me happy is getting back to sleep. The day begins early here.'

He stood up and crossed back to his side of the room.

What could he do but accept what she said? And then lie awake praying that her tears would not begin again.

Chapter Eight

By morning Minerva's outlook had improved. Wasn't it strange that troubling thoughts of the night could right themselves with the rising sun?

Today the sun shone brightly, so they decided to have lunch on the beach. Soon the days would grow too cold for such outings. It would be good to play on the shore while they could.

Walking along the beach, with warm sand squishing between her toes and the sun on her face, she was grateful to feel life returning to normal again.

It had been confusing to have her heart go off balance, even if only for a short time.

Poor Harrison had taken her tears to heart last night. Hopefully he'd accepted what she'd told him about women crying for any number of reasons. It was true after all.

The last thing she wanted him to know was the

truth—that for an instant last night she'd hoped he was going to kiss her.

Instead of a kiss she'd been informed he was going to make quick work of completing her chamber.

What a let-down.

To go from feeling embraced to feeling rejected in the space of a heartbeat had been disconcerting. It had left her emotions exposed, vulnerable.

Naturally she'd been reduced to tears.

Waves pounded, crashed and rushed onshore, the same as they did every day. Seagulls dashed in and out after the tide. And always the children laughed… Life was as normal as it had been before she'd briefly lost her reason.

But mercy me... She did look forward to having her own chamber and a bit of privacy at the end of each day.

'Watch me chase the waves, Mama-Min!' Abby dashed towards the receding tide. 'Scared it away!'

Off she ran again and again, stamping and splashing after the waves.

Further down the shore Harrison and James walked together. She squinted after them, then sighed.

James was copying Harrison's walk. For the first time the child had a man to emulate. The tilt of his head, the set of his shoulders… He might have been Harrison's shadow.

They were near the cave when they turned around and walked back in her direction. Big man, little man… It was one of the most endearing things she had ever seen.

When she thought back to the sad, frightened children they'd been when they'd arrived at the orphanage and then saw them now, she was incredibly grateful.

And this change had occurred because one man had given up the life he'd planned for himself.

Harrison was a natural father. Abby and James were the proof. He deserved to have a dozen sons and daughters.

Perhaps in time?

But no. He'd made his feelings on that clear from the beginning.

He would be no less a brilliant father to the children he had because of it.

And she would be their grateful mother. If the longing for more children came upon her, she would simply cherish the ones she had all the more.

'I've already told you…the cave is dangerous, son,' she heard Harrison saying. 'You mustn't go near it.'

'Magic caves don't hurt anyone.' James seemed convinced of this for some reason.

'It's just a common cave—and this one could.'

Looking at the boy's expression, Minerva wasn't convinced he was really listening.

What had she been doing daydreaming about other children when they had their hands full with the ones they had?

* * *

The voices of the builders Harrison had employed came to him as he led the team from the stables to the paddock.

Good. They were a timely lot and there was quite a bit to do.

He latched the paddock gate and then went back into the stables. This was going to be a fine day.

He snatched up his nail bag and slung it over his shoulder. Equipped for work, he hurried out to greet the men.

By the time he'd reached the house Minerva was already leading them inside.

Restoring the cottage with his own hands had been his dream—however, dreams had a way of changing. It would be no less his home for having shared the construction with others.

What he was building now was a family, which was a far more important endeavour.

However, he did plan on working alongside them. For as much as he enjoyed building he was a novice, and he looked forward to what he could learn.

Coming inside the house, he saw the children sitting at the dining table. Minerva thought it was time James learned his letters.

Abby insisted upon 'learning' too, so she sat beside her brother, making scribbles on her chalkboard.

Voices drifted down from the chamber Minerva would occupy.

Going upstairs, he saw Minerva directing one of the workers on where to add a door.

'Being able to enter the children's room from mine without going into the corridor will be convenient,' she told a husky fellow.

Three others listened, their smiles indicating that they wanted nothing more than to make Minerva's life easier.

Last week it had seemed a wise decision to hurry the construction for Minerva's chamber.

Last week his emotions regarding the chaste state of their marriage had been disturbed.

Now that his relationship with Minerva had returned to normal, he found he wasn't in such a hurry to lose her company at bedtime.

He looked forward to the evenings, and then to the end of the day, when he and his wife spent quiet time talking over their day.

Naturally, he knew they couldn't continue as they were, and yet he was going to badly miss those times.

Walking about the chamber now, giving instructions on how the new and larger window was to be placed and what colours the walls would be painted, she looked happy.

Oddly, he was not.

Still, it would be some time before the chamber was ready for her to move into. He hadn't even purchased the window yet…

It had been a long, busy day. Minerva had washed the clothes, taught James to write his name, and made sure the building crew had enough to eat.

By the time she'd fed her family their dinner, bathed the children in the tub in the small room off the kitchen and then tucked them into bed, she was exhausted.

Perhaps employing a maid to help out *would* be in order…

She settled into her chair beside the hearth, thinking she would bring the subject up with Harrison as soon as she could keep her eyes open long enough to do it.

The wind was up, howling about the eaves and huffing against the windows.

She closed her eyes…heard the front door open.

A rush of cold wind washed in.

Harrison would be back from settling the horses for the night.

No doubt he was as weary as she was, having worked all day with the builders.

Moments later she heard footsteps walking on the upper floor. He must be checking on the children. He did it every evening—often more than once.

Weary, but feeling wonderful, she thought to

indulge in a short doze before going up. The fire was warm, the day was done, so why not?

Something brushed her hair, which roused her but not to full wakefulness. Her mother, perhaps.

The chair across from her creaked. Harrison sighed, settling in it.

She must have fallen asleep again, because all at once she was being lifted from the chair.

'Come along, Sleeping Beauty,' Harrison whispered. 'Time for bed.'

Looping her arms around his neck, she snuggled her head on his shoulder. She ought to inform him that she could walk up the stairs on her own.

Only, she didn't want to.

'You're so strong,' she murmured into his neck.

'And you're not really awake. So I will not take to heart what you're saying.'

She *was* awake.

'I like you a great deal,' she whispered.

'And I like you too…a great deal.'

The bedroom door squeaked when he opened it.

The mattress gave when he set her gently upon it.

When he started taking off her shoes, she rubbed her eyes, pretending to wake up.

'How did I get here? Last I knew, I was sleeping in the chair.'

'You must have been exhausted not to wake when I carried you up.'

'I only hope I didn't talk in my sleep.'

He shook his head, pushed his glasses higher

up his nose with one finger—a gesture she was becoming fond of.

'Mumbling only. Nothing that I understood.'

It wasn't right to tease him, but it was a great deal of fun.

'We should get to sleep.'

With a yawn she opened the first four buttons of her dress. Not so many that she was indecent, but just enough to be rewarded by his half-choked gasp.

After he stepped behind the curtain she heard the thump of his clothes hitting the floor, the creak of bedsprings when he got into bed.

'Goodnight, Min.'

'Goodnight, Harrison.' She smiled at him across the dim room. 'I really do like you a great deal.'

'You minx—you were awake all along!'

'Mostly awake.'

'I like you a great deal too—but you already know that now.'

When she fell asleep, it was with a smile.

After three days of construction, Harrison realised he was getting in the way of the builders rather than helping them. The patience the men displayed at his many questions was likely feigned.

That afternoon he turned his attention towards the clocks he'd been neglecting. Three broken ones set on his work table, awaiting his attention. If clocks could actually await anything…

But if any inanimate object could, he supposed it would be a timepiece.

With the weather having turned uncommonly warm he'd rather be outside—but, again, he didn't wish to be an annoyance to the fellows he'd employed.

From the open window he heard the children laughing and running about. To his mind it was like music.

Glancing through the curtain, he saw Minerva hanging laundry on the line to dry, while Abby and James chased the kittens.

In London his wife wouldn't be doing such a menial chore. A niggle of guilt ate at him. He shook it off, refused to let it shadow his mind. Minerva had told him she was happy with her life here. He must believe her.

She did like him 'a great deal', after all. She'd admitted it. And he liked her a great deal too.

If she was unhappy she wouldn't be singing while hanging his shirts on the line.

Life with Minerva was as bright, as warm and as happy as sunshine on the cliff.

When had he ever seen a woman lovelier than his wife?

Somehow he couldn't take his eyes off her as she bent to take a wet garment out of the basket, snapped it with a wiggle and a jiggle, and then reached high to pin it to the line.

Dip, snap, wiggle, reach...

He was trying very hard to ignore the jiggle, because even though she was his wife, what was jiggling was forbidden between them.

For the good of the family.

The very last thing he wished for was an impassioned marriage. The nature of that beast led to betrayal, disappointment and heartbreak. He had seen it, lived it, so he knew it could happen.

This day, though, was too fine to dwell on distressing thoughts.

Besides, Min liked him a great deal…

Given a choice between paying a social call in London or hanging laundry to dry in the sunshine, Minerva would choose the latter every time.

If she lifted her gaze from her task she would see Abby and James at play, with miles of clear sky and sparkling ocean in the background.

However, if she were in London, taking tea, and she lifted her gaze she would see ladies posturing, each trying to look prettier and more accomplished than the lady beside her. And all for the sake of the marriage hunt.

No, thank you very much.

'Where are you two?' she called, because they had wandered from her line of vision.

'Over here!' James called back, his voice coming from around the corner of the house.

Close enough. 'Don't wander far.'

'We won't!'

No? Then why did his voice sound further away? Not too far, though. The fence would keep them from going where they should not.

Her thoughts returned to Harrison. So did her eyes. She could see him behind a window curtain, seated at his desk, his head bent towards something he was repairing.

He'd told her he liked her. There wasn't much more a woman could ask for, was there?

A declaration of true friendship might not be as exciting as a declaration of true love, but it was fulfilling, nonetheless.

All of a sudden she was aware of silence where children's laughter had been a moment ago.

She dropped the gown she held back into the basket, glancing about.

'James!' she called. 'Abby!'

She dashed around the corner of the house. Why, the little rascals had sneaked off…

Her heart gave a great hard thud. The gate in the new fence was open, swaying in the breeze.

She ran towards the window of the room where Harrison worked. Shoving the curtain aside, she leaned her head in. 'The children have wandered off. I think they've gone down to the beach.'

Dropping the small wooden cuckoo bird he held, he slid backwards in the chair. He climbed out of the window, one long leg after the other.

'We told them not to go beyond the gate,' he said grimly.

'I'm sure they've not gone far. I saw them only moments ago…right here in the garden.'

He arched a brow at her. 'They are quick, aren't they?'

He caught her hand. They dashed across the grass, through the swaying gate, then down the path to the beach.

There the children were, walking along the sand and going north.

'James!' Harrison's deep voice pierced the afternoon. 'Abby!'

Looking as guilty as pups with tails tucked between their legs, they turned.

'Now what do we do?' Minerva asked.

This was the first time they'd ever faced disciplining the children.

'How did your father handle it?'

'When I was little I knew how to charm my way out of trouble.'

'I shall be on my guard,' he said with a smile, and they picked their way along the shore.

'How did your father discipline you?' she asked.

'He didn't. He never paid enough attention to me to care what I did. Apparently we're going to learn how to do this together, then.' He straightened his shoulders, narrowed his gaze. 'We will not be swayed by charm.'

'Or tears.'

'You were guilty of that tactic too, I gather?'

'Be careful—it's highly effective.'

Within a few moments they stood face to face with the miscreants.

'You were forbidden to come down here without me or your mother.'

'But Mama-Min was busy and a kitten had wandered down here,' James said plaintively.

'I see.' Minerva gave the children the severest look she could manage, but she had stood in their place before, so she had some compassion for their plight. 'Then we shall search for it together. Which way did it go?'

James glanced about, frowning. 'Don't know.'

'Do you know, Abby?' Harrison asked.

'Kitten up there.' Abby pointed up to the cliff.

James kicked at the sand with the side of his shoe.

'Where were you going, son? Tell me the truth.' Harrison placed his large hand on James's shoulder.

'For a walk.'

'To bad cave.'

'Abby!' James cried.

'Come up to the house. Your mother and I will decide what's to be done.'

It frightened Minerva that James had ignored their order not to visit the cave. It looked safe now, with the weather fine and the tide low, but she had seen it when a storm blew in.

Gazing at Harrison while they made their way up to the house, she knew that he was worried too.

* * *

Harrison stood at the dining room window, gazing at the night. A fat full moon reflected on the crests of the waves, making them glow, and moonlight illuminated the land and the sand below.

It had been a long time since he'd gone for a night swim.

Perhaps he ought to. It would be easy to see his footing going down.

The water would be cold, but bracing, just the way he liked it.

'You did a good job of meting out their punishment,' he heard Minerva say from her chair by the fireplace.

'You'd think I sentenced them to an awful fate. But thank you for warning me about the tears.' He glanced back at her over his shoulder. 'I wouldn't have withstood them otherwise.'

'I didn't expect it to be James shedding tears, though.'

'He's very attached to those kittens, and a week without playing with them must seem like for ever to him.'

'I only hope he's learned a lesson,' she said. 'I know I have.'

'It isn't the easiest thing to discipline children, is it?'

'Or to keep track of them. One moment of inattention and they run off.'

He had a feeling she blamed herself for what had happened, which wasn't right.

'You're a brilliant mother. Never doubt it. No one can be on guard every moment.'

Minerva's skirt rustled when she rose. 'I suppose not.'

She joined him at the window. 'That is a beautiful sight.'

'Anyone would think that cave was magical seen in this light.'

They couldn't see the cave from the window, but it was easy to imagine what it looked like.

'I'm going up to bed. Being a mother is exhausting.' She squeezed his elbow, then walked out of the room.

He couldn't argue with that—only she didn't look exhausted, she looked lovely.

He should not be watching her walking out of the room. Or at least not watching her the way he was doing…taking delight in the way her skirt swayed with the roll of her hips.

With a grunt, he shifted his gaze back to the window.

Ah, what was that? Far out something large glided on the surface of the water, then disappeared. From up here he couldn't tell what it was. But he wanted to be like it.

Why shouldn't he go for a swim? Everyone was in bed, which meant he had some time to himself.

* * *

Minerva undressed, but didn't get into bed right away. Moonlight filtered through the window curtain, reminding her of how beautiful it had looked a moment ago, shining on the water.

Wearing only her shift, she stretched. What a wonderful sensation to be free of her undergarments. It made her feel lighter, freer.

She leaned against the window frame, moved the curtain aside and gazed out.

A movement caught her eye.

Oh… Harrison. Apparently he wished to have a closer look at the night's beauty…to stand in it and let it wrap around him.

She could see him fairly well in the moonlight. The cliff wasn't so far away that she could not see his silhouette, if not every detail of his figure.

He stood for a time with his hands on his hips, glancing this way and that. Then he drew his shirt off over his head.

It wasn't terribly cold, but she thought it was probably too chilly to be shirtless.

Then he bent and pulled off his shoes, one then the other. Next, he stepped out of his trousers, and tossed them on top of his shoes. And then…*oh, my*…he shucked out of his drawers.

His sense of freedom must be exhilarating.

Imagine standing in the open and not wearing a stitch!

Naked, he lifted his arms towards the moon, appearing to reach for it.

It might not be right to watch him during this private moment, but how could she not? Even if she did turn away from the window she would still see him in her mind's eye, so what was the point of looking away?

It was nearly magical, seeing him this way, with his limbs cast in moon shimmers. She could only imagine what it must feel like to have nature's hand upon her. Light and liberated. He must feel like a part of the night.

Joy in motion was what he seemed like as he dashed down the path. She saw him burst upon the beach with a leap and a hop. Probably a shout too, but of course she couldn't hear him from here.

Her eyes were working just fine, though. And the moon shed just enough light for her to see the beach. Not as well as on the cliff, but well enough.

She had never seen a naked man before. Statues and artistic drawings didn't count. A nude man in the flesh was a world beyond that.

And, while she had been fascinated by many things in her life, this made her feel unsettled. In a pleasant way, though.

Although she couldn't make out details clearly, she could see how long, lean and fit he was.

Running along the shore, he kicked up water. Then he waded into the waves…slowly, with his arms raised, as if he wished to get everything wet but his hands.

In a normal marriage it would be commonplace for husbands and wives to see each other without clothing.

Minerva's marriage was far from normal.

Seeing Harrison glide across the surface of the water, his muscular back and bare bottom glistening, was not commonplace.

The longer she looked at him the more uncomfortable she became. But she wasn't really betraying his privacy. For one thing at this distance she had to really strain to see him…which she was doing, she had to admit. For another thing this was her home, her window, and she had every right to look out of it.

The longer she stood there, the less she wanted the chaste marriage he desired.

But she gave herself a good mental shake, and then a physical one.

Having gone off balance once before, she was determined not to do so again. It was far too unsettling.

Chapter Nine

Harrison sat on a stool at his work table. James sat on the stool beside him.

Rain hit the window hard as he explained how the cuckoo bird knew when to pop out of the clock.

It was a lucky thing he'd indulged in his late-night swim when he had. The weather had turned colder this morning, and now a storm was blowing in off the ocean.

Earlier today it had been thrilling, standing at the front window with the children and watching while the clouds crept ominously across the water towards the shore.

He'd made sure to point out to them how large the waves were. How the cave would be filling with water.

'The waves must be huge if we can hear them all the way up here in the house,' he'd said, making sure to emphasise that.

When the storm had come upon them it had

been fierce. But the wilder it was outside the cosier it was in the cottage.

The builders had arrived early this morning, before the storm had hit. The sound of hammering and sawing went on merrily overhead. Although looking at the turn the weather had taken, he thought they might need to spend the night.

Looking up from the work table, he saw Minerva in her chair by the fireplace with Abby curled into her, sound asleep.

A letter had come for Minerva with the morning post. Hopefully the postman had made it back to St Austell before the storm, otherwise it would be a miserable muddy trip.

Later he would need to venture out to feed the animals, but that was later.

For now, he would teach his son how rewarding it was to take a broken timepiece and make it tick again. Also, how the bird in the clock knew when to come out and call.

After a while, he heard the crackle of paper being unfolded. Minerva must be reading her letter.

'Would you like a cup of tea to go with that letter?' he asked.

'I would, thank you.'

Having lived alone for a time, he knew how to brew a good pot of tea and was rather proud of the skill. A typical baron would only know how to ring for one.

Coming back with a cup of tea in each hand, he set one on the table beside Minerva.

Since James had left the work table and gone to the window to watch the storm, he sat in the chair across from her.

The scent of tea twirled out of both cups.

Whack, whack, whack, went the hammers.

Tap, tap, tap, went the rain.

There was no place in the world he would rather be than here in this moment.

He watched Minerva while she read the letter, which was from her sister-in-law, Evie. Sometimes she smiled, other times she laughed quietly…and then she sighed, closed her eyes.

'Is something wrong?' he asked, although judging by her soft smile there was nothing to be worried about.

'Oh, no! Quite the opposite.' She pressed the letter to her heart. 'Evie says all is well. William and Elizabeth came for a visit and have now returned to the farm. We only just missed seeing them, it seems.'

'In spring we will pay a visit to Wilton Farm.'

'The children will love playing with the lambs and the dogs…there are plenty of both.'

'What else does Evie say?'

'I shall read it to you. You will be able to hear her joy in her own words.'

'I'd like that.'

She sipped her tea before she started.

'Well, then, I'll begin right here…' She tapped the page with her finger. '"Praise the Good Lord I am finished with the baby making me sick and sleepy all the time. It now seems it will all be worthwhile. More than worthwhile. I've been feeling little Miss or Mr Grant moving about for the last week. It's a busy child, for certain. I adore it already. And last night the most marvellous thing happened. Thomas and I were in bed, just talking before we fell asleep…"'

Just like he and Min did! For some reason that made him feel good.

'"We were looking up at the ceiling and Thomas had his hand resting on my belly. Our babe gave him a good kick in the palm. We laughed so hard. Minnie. It's the most amazing thing one can ever feel. I cannot wait until you—"'

There was clearly more to it, but Minerva folded the letter and tucked it into her bodice pocket.

'As you can tell, they're very happy.'

So was Minerva—he could see it in her eyes. That, and something else…

Not sadness, he didn't believe, but was it regret?

She had always indicated that the children they had were enough.

'I wonder, Min, do you regret not having—?'

'Of course not,' she answered, too quickly. She lifted Abby's plump, limp hand and kissed it. 'What more could I possibly want?'

Her own child to quicken within her? Was that

what was behind her smile? Was that why she'd been crying the other night?

What if it was? His conscience gave him a kick. He couldn't give her another child. The act of begetting one would involve so much more than a casual getting to the point of the matter, so to speak. He couldn't indulge in such intimacy with her without yanking his heart out of his chest and handing it over to her.

That, he knew, would be madness.

Except that she already had his heart…just not in that way.

All of a sudden the hammers upstairs ceased. The men must be taking a break.

'It doesn't appear they'll be able to go home tonight,' she said.

If regret for not having a child of her own saddened her, it didn't show. Perhaps she didn't feel it, either. It might be his conscience imagining what was on her mind.

'We shall make a party of it tonight.' She gave him a bright smile which put his fears at ease. 'The builders will be our first guests.'

'Will there be room for all five of them?' He glanced about, not sure. 'And enough food?'

'We have plenty of bread, a ham and a wheel of cheese. And eggs. For sleeping we can make them pallets on the floor. The fire should keep them warm.' She slid a sidelong glance at him.

'The weather was so much warmer last night, don't you think?'

Luckily for him, it had been. It might be a long time before the opportunity arose for another night swim.

'Last night they could have washed off the day's work with a nice moonlit swim,' she added.

'If they liked cold water.'

Why was she looking at him that way? As if she had a secret she wanted to reveal, but was going to let him guess it instead?

He was certain she knew nothing of his night-time swim. She'd already retired before he'd gone out.

'What are you really talking about, Minerva?'

'I envied you last night. You looked as happy as a porpoise. I nearly came down to join you.'

So she had seen him! In that case, it truly would be a long time before he indulged in another private swim… He wondered if last night might have been the last one.

Her coming down to join him would never happen, of course.

Just because he was resolved not to be intimate with her, it didn't mean he had unlimited restraint.

'I thought you were asleep. I assumed my indulgence was private.'

'Might I point out that you were standing in the open, which isn't private at all?'

'I beg your pardon, then. I hope I didn't offend you.'

Her eyes looked bright and merry. She covered her mouth as if she were hiding a giggle. 'Oh, I wasn't offended.'

'I see that… But you really shouldn't have watched me, you know.'

'If you didn't wish to be seen, you should have kept your clothes on.'

She bit her lip, clearly trying not to smile, but her eyes gave it away.

What was it about the situation that troubled him so much? It wasn't as if she'd raced out of the house to seduce him.

Perhaps part of it was his pride. He shouldn't care what she'd thought of seeing him naked. Although any man would be vain enough to wonder what his wife thought of him. Had she been pleased? Or disappointed?

Never mind. He couldn't think about nudity and Minerva at the same time. Trouble would only follow…

And how much could she have seen in the dark, really? Not enough to make a judgement.

'Do you want to know something I like quite well about you, Harrison?'

Probably not. She had seen all of him, after all!

'Those interesting lines…right there between your brows. They grow deep and expressive when you frown.'

She reached her hand across the distance between their chairs. She touched him above the frame of his glasses, where they crossed his nose.

'You, my friend, have nothing to frown about. You have a very fine form.'

'How good of you to say so.'

His ego was appeased, he had to admit. However, the opportunity for her to see his 'fine form' again was not going to come. His mind was set.

But a thought struck him—there and gone in a flash. *What a shame*, it suggested.

Not so much a shame when it would leave his family vulnerable if he became distracted. No temptation could lead him to do that.

'Don't let your tea grow cold.' He nodded at her mug. 'When the weather clears,' he added, 'we will go to town. Spend a week there so we will not be in the builders' way.'

'That sounds wonderful. I'll begin a list of what we need.'

Just like that the subject was changed. It was as if she'd never mentioned his naked swim—as if she'd already dismissed it from her mind, as easily as butter melted into hot bread.

For all that he tried to, it was unlikely *he* would dismiss it from his mind. Not tonight or for many nights to come.

The storm pummelled the coast for two days and then blew away, leaving sunny skies and muddy roads.

It was another day and a half before Minerva bundled the children into the carriage for their trip to Saint Austell.

They still intended to stay for several days, in order to allow the builders to work without the family underfoot.

Minerva was glad for the short break, because she intended to do plenty of shopping.

It was a couple of hours before sunset when they arrived at the hotel. After being greeted warmly by the doorman they entered the lobby.

'What's that thing?' James asked.

'It's an elevator, son. A bird cage elevator made by Elisha Otis's company.'

No doubt it was called a bird cage because that was what it resembled. A large, ornate birdcage.

While they watched, it carried the operator and his passenger right up the wall to the third floor.

The car, being open to the lobby, would give a fascinating view of plush sofas and potted plants.

It was hard to know who was more fascinated by the elevator—father or son.

By the time they'd checked into their room there was no time for anything but a short walk with the children before dinner.

The hotel was located across from the harbour. From their third-floor window there was an expansive view.

But what she loved most about the hotel was

that one only needed to step out through the front door to find shops of every kind.

All the way here Harrison and James had talked about going to the clock shop. Harrison was anxious to add a few pieces to his collection. And Minerva had promised Abby a new dress…or three.

Once dinner was finished, they took the elevator to their suite of rooms.

Abby and James were beside themselves, having never ridden in one before. They waved their arms as if they were birds, flying up and up. James vowed he wanted to do nothing else on the visit but ride up and down in it.

Hopefully the operator was a patient soul.

What Minerva wanted was to go for a walk in the hotel garden. She'd caught a glimpse of it through a set of glass doors when they'd first come in. It promised to be a magical place.

'What a beautiful suite.' She noted that their bags had already been brought up. Living in London, there had been little need for her ever to stay in a hotel. 'I think we'll have a wonderful week in St Austell.'

The children would, for certain. Spotting the large bed in the chamber Harrison had indicated would be theirs, they dashed for it, jumping madly up and down on it.

She put a stop to it, of course—after looking the other way just for a moment. What she really wanted was to join them. It was a shame to outgrow such fun…worse to be obligated to call a halt to it. But heads could be bumped…a fall could cause a broken limb.

Minerva meant to enjoy every moment of their time here. Especially the nights. Once they returned to Cockleshell Cottage she would be sleeping in her own chamber…which was for the best, naturally.

Oh, but for now she would enjoy the remaining nights of falling asleep knowing her husband was only in the next bed, an arm's reach away. Not that either one of them would be reaching for the other, but it was a comfort knowing he was close by.

Later in the evening, with the children asleep, she and Harrison sat in a pair of chairs in the bay window that overlooked the street and the harbour.

With the shops closed there weren't many people on the street, and only the occasional carriage passed below the window. But there were a few ships docked. By lantern-light they watched some men rolling pallets up gangplanks.

'I wonder what they're taking aboard.'

'China clay. It's what kept the town going after the mine ran out of tin.'

'I'm glad for the clay, then. St Austell is so lovely. I am grateful we have it fairly close to home.'

They talked of this and that…nothing terribly important. Except that it was. The fact that they spoke so easily with one another about little everyday matters made her feel that they really were friends.

She liked having a friend to call her own…to share a name with. Being wed, they were bound for the rest of their lives, and she was glad of it.

Had she married as her father had wished, she might be bound to a man who was appropriate to society but not a friend with whom she could sit and chat about common daily events.

Said man might want a child with her, of course… But never mind that. She was content with what she had…content enough, at any rate. After all, one didn't need to be completely content in order to be happy.

Drowsy, she yawned twice. Harrison countered with three. They retired to their room.

Harrison fell asleep quickly, but she lay awake, listening to the comforting sound of his even breathing across the small room.

It was easy to reflect upon things in the dark. It came to her that there wasn't much in her life she would change.

Watching the strong profile of her husband's nose, the soft line of his lips in slumber, she sighed.

Perhaps there were one or two things she would change…

Thoughts for another time perhaps…or perhaps not at all.

Despite the fact that the children had a dozen new choices for breakfast, they chose their usual.

Toast, jam and clotted cream. They had finished eating before she and Harrison had even made a choice, which meant they had to wait impatiently for them to finish.

Their plan for the morning was first to visit the ships at dock. James was eager to see a sailor… perhaps hear a bit of crusty language. Abby hoped to see a rat.

Minerva couldn't imagine why and chose not to ask.

Hopefully they would not encounter either a sailor with crusty language or a rat.

After their visit to the docks they were going to go shopping. After that, lunch and a nap. It sounded a perfect day, which Minerva was going to cap off with an evening walk in the hotel garden.

The outing began splendidly. At the docks they heard sailors singing, not cursing, while going about their work. Rats were probably present, but they didn't show themselves.

Something else did show itself, though.

'What is this?' Harrison exclaimed.

'Puppies!' Spotting one with its nose pressed against the shop window, Abby clasped her father's hand and tugged him towards the door. 'Want one, Uncle-Papa!'

After spending half an hour in the shop they left without a dog, but with 'maybes' being spoken of.

Coming out of the pet shop, Minerva passed close to a woman pushing a pram, catching sight of a baby bundled in blue blankets and sucking madly at its small fist.

A shadow dimmed her joy in the outing, but she banished it by watching Abby skipping a step ahead while singing a song about puppies.

They visited other shops, purchasing what she needed to make her chamber at home a lovely one. But for all the pretty things she bought, there was one thing she could never buy. Her husband's comforting presence in it. All the dainty frills in the world wouldn't make up for that.

She couldn't say she did not adore the bedframe, the chairs, and the bedding that looked like a spring meadow. It was only…if she were to be completely honest with herself…she adored Harrison more.

In a chaste, friendly way.

She might even have believed what she'd told herself if Harrison hadn't bent in that instant, picked up Abby and lifted her over his head, making the child giggle.

Her husband had the best heart of any man she knew. And he was strong…so very manly. Her heart tip-tapped, because she now knew exactly what those lean, flexing muscles looked like underneath his clothes.

Abby giggled. James bounced about on his toes, demanding to have the fun his sister was having. No doubt he would lift James as effortlessly as he had Abby.

To distract herself from forbidden longing, she concentrated on admiring a pot of flowers hanging from a lamppost. Then she made a comment on a dog being walked on a jewelled leash on the dock side of the street.

As she'd hoped, her comment involved the whole family in a discussion of which pup they might choose—if they got one.

The rest of the day passed pleasantly—except that it began to drizzle, which would prevent her visit to the garden. Well, tomorrow night would do as well…

Later, with the children sleeping, she and Harrison were once again in their chairs, talking over the events of the day.

Harrison seemed subdued.

'Is something wrong?' she asked.

'Ah, it's nothing you need to be troubled about. Down by the docks I heard a couple arguing. They had a child with them, and it brought back bad memories.'

'I'm sorry, Harrison. Would it help to speak about it?'

He shook his head, as if he didn't wish to, but then he did.

'My mother told me once that in the beginning she and my father were very much in love. My father was her whole world and she was his. But after a time I suppose it wasn't enough. They began to argue violently. And then they did all they could to hurt each other in other ways. You already know what they were.'

'I can only imagine how awful it must have been for you.'

Clearly it had been. She could see that it affected him deeply, even after all these years.

He thumped backwards in his chair, crossed his arms over his chest, and shook his head.

'So you can understand why I don't wish to… fall in love…so to speak. The risks…' His voice trailed off.

Moving from her chair, she knelt in front of him, touched his tense hands, soothed them with her fingers.

'Don't be afraid that will happen to us. We won't betray one another. We're great friends and always will be.'

Catching both of her hands, he brought them to his lips. He kissed her fingers.

'I wonder if you'll ever feel you have given up too much for our unconventional marriage.'

If she were to be completely honest, she couldn't say for certain that she'd never wonder. Never imagine how their life together might have been if not for the demons of his past.

Not that any of that was his fault.

'I'm happy with what we have. I have said so before.'

And that was the truth…for now.

He stood. With a hand under her elbow he lifted

her from her knees. And then he drew her in, wrapping his arms about her in a hug.

'I've never cared for anyone the way I care for you, Min.'

It was not terribly unusual for friends to exchange hugs. She had hugged Evie and Elizabeth many times.

And yet only an idiot would compare the two.

Her husband was a friend, yes, but of a very different sort—even if he didn't recognise the fact. He was masculine all over…which she had good reason to know.

She leaned into him, gave him comfort in the way he needed it. Trying not to think how much more she could give him if things were different.

Then he kissed the top of her head, dropped his arms from about her.

'If we wish to keep up with the children tomorrow we should get some sleep.'

How, she wondered, was she ever to keep up with her confused emotions about the man she'd married?

'I only hope we don't spend the whole day in the elevator,' she said lightly, so he wouldn't suspect that she was conflicted about what they had and what she was beginning to want from him.

She walked towards the bedchamber, gazed at him from the doorway, then smiled. 'Give me ten minutes to change and then you may come in.'

If he entered too soon—before she was in her

sleeping gown in her own bed, with the covers up to her chin—well, she couldn't be held accountable for where her confusion might lead.

Once she had her own chamber at the cottage she would surely no longer be troubled by the maelstrom of emotions going on in her heart.

Last night's drizzle had ended, leaving the day sunny, if cool.

This morning the family had spent a quarter of an hour in the elevator, while the children pretended to be flying. The adventure would have lasted longer, except that they had also been anxious to visit the pet shop again.

No doubt the elevator operator had been glad to see them move on with their day.

They'd spent nearly a half-hour visiting the puppies, only finally convincing Abby and James to leave by offering a few more 'maybes'.

The window of the shop they'd stopped in front of now displayed frilly dresses and finely tailored suits for little boys.

'Perhaps James and I shall sit on the bench near the docks and watch the ships,' Harrison suggested.

'Me and Mama-Min go here!' Abby tugged her hand, as eager as Minerva was to go inside and browse the pretty garments for sale.

'Look at that pretty bonnet,' Minerva said as

they entered the shop. 'It would look just right with your brown eyes.'

'I has brown eyes?'

'Indeed you do, miss. Big round, beautiful, brown eyes.'

'Wike dis dress,' she declared, her eye colour seemingly forgotten.

And so their shopping began. They went through all the dresses from the front of the shop to the back. Having intended to purchase three dresses for Abby, Minerva ended up choosing five.

While they were being packaged, she spotted a display of infant gowns.

They were delicate, and so adorable. She couldn't purchase one for a babe of her own, but she could buy one for Evie's baby.

'Which one of these do you like Abby?'

'For a dolly?'

'No, for a baby. Your Aunt Evie has a baby in her tummy, and once it's grown enough to be born it will need a gown.'

'What is born?'

'That means when the baby comes out to see us.'

'Yellow.' Abby poked her finger at a lacy hem.

Minerva picked it up, turned it front to back, then hugged it to her heart. What would it feel like with an infant in it? Warm, tender…so very, very fulfilling.

She sighed, folded the small gown over her arm,

then traced her fingers across the tiny buttons. Well, then, she would enjoy seeing Evie's baby wear it.

'Mama-Min has baby, too?' Abby touched Minerva's stomach, looking puzzled.

'No, Mama-Min has Abby.'

With that, she swept the child up and nuzzled her cheek, thanking the good Lord for the path her life had taken.

And, really, who knew what else her future held?

Hearts could change.

Even if they didn't, Minerva was beyond grateful for the little girl now plastering kisses all over her cheek.

A pair of fellows could only watch ships bob on the water for so long before it grew tiresome.

'What do you say we ask the ladies if they've finished shopping and want to join us for ice cream?' Harrison asked James.

'I say yes!'

Hand in hand, they crossed the street. How could he ever have imagined he would enjoy the feel of a small fist nestled trustingly in his own?

But he did. Somewhere along the way Abby and James had changed from an obligation to a delight. He couldn't imagine them not being in his life.

At one time he'd thought his life was perfect.

He'd wanted nothing more than to be left alone. This was no longer true.

When he and James entered the shop a bell tinkled. He spotted Minerva and Abby at the back, where an assistant was busy wrapping small dresses in paper.

Minerva was holding up a lacy infant gown, turning it from front to back. Tenderly, she hugged it to her chest, closed her eyes.

What was she feeling?

That she wanted a child of her own?

If so, what kind of husband was he to deny her that?

She'd assured him that Abby and James were enough for her...more than once. But was there an empty space in her soul that a child of her own body should fill?

He'd thought he knew her well. Perhaps not as well as he ought to.

She and Abby exchanged words which he couldn't hear.

Abby touched the front of Minerva's skirt, gazing at her.

All at once Min scooped Abby up. Abby smacked kisses on her mother's cheeks.

His two ladies laughed and smiled. He was relieved to see it.

What would he do if his wife wanted a child with him? Refuse her and live with her sadness?

Give in and as a result fall in love with her? Jeopardise what they already had?

When he joined her at the counter Minerva had handed the infant gown to the assistant and asked her to add it to the rest.

What could this mean?

'Aunt Evie has a baby in her tummy,' Abby announced.

Oh! Of course. Minerva hadn't been dreaming of a child of her own at all—she'd been thinking of a niece or nephew. He ought to have known better.

'We give it a pwesent.'

'I'm sure the baby will look sweet in it,' he said.

'Mama-Min doesn't have a baby in her tummy.'

Minerva glanced at him, then quickly away. There had definitely been something in her expression. Regret?

He would have felt more reassured if she'd laughed at Abby's announcement, but she hadn't. Rather she turned her attention to the assistant, asking to see clothes for little boys.

'But we're going for ice cream!' James protested.

Minerva arched a brow at James. 'The quicker we find you new clothes, the quicker we will have ice cream.'

'But Uncle-Papa said—'

'We shall do what your Mama-Min says and then we'll have ice cream.'

They worked well together as parents, he thought,

not without pride. And with a great deal of affection, too.

Without Minerva there would be no family. He owed her a great deal. But a child would be shamed by bearing the Elmstone name, as he had been.

No, he had determined that was something he'd never do. He would not stray from that decision.

'What flavours shall we have today, I wonder?' Minerva said when they finally came out of the shop.

Her smile was so bright and cheerful he thought he must have misinterpreted what she'd been thinking while holding the infant's gown.

Chapter Ten

Minerva glanced out of the window. The sky over St Austell this evening was clear, but there was a bank of storm clouds threatening on the horizon.

She couldn't risk missing some time in the garden again tonight.

'Would you mind putting the children to bed?' she asked. 'I want to go into the garden before the weather turns.'

This wasn't something barons usually did, yet she didn't feel wrong asking it of him. She knew he wouldn't take offence.

Harrison Tremayne was a remarkable man in many ways.

Uppermost, he was a wonderful father. Not distant, as some were. When he touched the children it was with affection. When a challenge was presented, he disciplined them firmly but with gentleness.

She couldn't imagine where this wisdom or his devotion to them had come from.

It was surprising, given the example of fatherhood he'd had growing up.

She loved him for it…loved the father he was, she meant. She couldn't risk loving *him*, woman to man, even if she wished to. He didn't want her to love him that way.

'Enjoy your time,' he said.

In case all the things she'd just thought about him weren't enough, he also had an engaging smile. It always went straight to her heart.

'Thank you. I won't be long.'

The garden turned out to be as captivating as she'd thought, even though it was no longer lush with summer greenery.

Lanterns glowed along paths and illuminated trees which were already half bare. Benches lined the curved garden path.

Spotting an appealing-looking one, she sat down. She seemed to be the only guest seeking the peace of the garden tonight. Possibly because of the storm whistling in from offshore.

Not that she minded a whit. She was cosy in her warm coat and wearing a hat which covered her ears. Her hands were warm even without mittens, since her pockets were deep and soft.

Only two more days until they returned home, and she was glad of it. While their time here had been a great treat, it was not as fulfilling as everyday living at Cockleshell Cottage.

Her chamber would be finished and ready to

decorate. She was glad of this too—more than she was not.

What a beautiful room it would be once she made it her own. It would even still be connected to Harrison's chamber, in a sense. By leaving the doors to the children's room open it would seem like one huge chamber. That was how she was going to think of it.

It was interesting how quickly she'd become used to sleeping with another person so close by…

The garden was doing its magic. A sense of peacefulness crept over her, making her relax in a way she hadn't been able to all day.

Closing her eyes, she felt her breathing become even…slow. Her mind wandered from one pleasant image to another.

Puppies in the pet shop…which one would the children choose once the 'maybe' turned into a 'yes'?

How sweet Abby would look in her frocks.

Her mind drifted to an image of an infant wearing the yellow gown… Evie's new baby…wouldn't it look sweet too?

She sighed, her heart swelling, as she imagined how good it would feel when she could hold her niece or nephew in her arms, breathe in her favourite scent once again.

Next, her drifting mind wandered to a mental image of Harrison holding the baby. Ahh, that was sweet too. He'd told her he hadn't held a baby before. He would be good at it, though. She could imagine him cradling the tiny girl or boy in his strong lean arms…cooing at it.

A raindrop hit her nose. Since it was only one, she remained where she was, content and dreamy.

Easily she drifted back to the image of Harrison holding a baby in his arms.

Her blissfully dozy mind decided it was nearly a crime he didn't have one of his own. Of his own body, she meant—because he did, in fact, have two lovely children already.

But not an heir. He might say he didn't want one, but she thought he might be making an awful mistake.

The better she knew him the more she believed it. In spite of how he felt about his family line ending with him, he was an amazing father.

Maybe, as his wife, it was up to her to point out that he might change his line for the better, not end it.

As far as his concern about a child being scorned by society went, it hardly mattered since they lived away from London. Here they would be able to raise their children with so much love that if any instance occurred when they were looked at slyly, they would have a sense of worth which would protect them from the sting.

She opened her eyes, because her thoughts were no longer wandering but focused.

The more she considered this, the more she thought it was what he needed to hear.

It was time to speak her mind on the subject.

He wouldn't be happy to hear it. Not at first. But once he had time to consider what she said, he'd change his mind. Surely he would.

Hearing steps on the path, she looked over and saw the very man occupying her thoughts coming towards her.

'I was becoming concerned. You've been out here for a long time.'

Had she been? It hadn't seemed that long to her. But she had been caught up in important thinking.

'You haven't left the children alone?'

'No. They are asleep, and one of the hotel staff is sitting with them.'

Good, then.

'It is inviting out here, don't you think?' She patted the bench beside her.

'If by "inviting" you mean cold and about to rain, then I suppose it is.'

'By "inviting" I mean peaceful.'

He sat down. As if of one mind, they slid close together on the bench. It seemed natural for them to do so. They really were becoming close, and—

'Would you mind being peaceful upstairs, where it's warm? Your nose is turning red in the cold,' he muttered.

'Soon… First I have something to say to you—a matter to present. Afterwards, do let's go up.'

'Is it a quick matter? I don't like shivering out here when we could discuss the matter somewhere warm.'

'Very well, we can walk and talk at the same time.'

She stood up. It might be better this way, since movement would help cover her nervousness.

'I think you're an excellent father,' she said, coming to the point quickly before she lost her courage.

'Thank you. And you are an excellent mother, Min. The children seem happy, so we must be succeeding.'

Of all the comments he could have made, none could have been better to help her begin what she had to say. If this wasn't the time to speak what was on her mind, there wouldn't be a better one.

'As to that, parenthood is what I wish to speak to you about…specifically, us being parents.'

Half a dozen raindrops spattered on the path, dotted the lenses of his spectacles.

Quickening their pace, he drew her towards the patio doors.

'Wait one moment, Harrison. Let me say this before we go inside.'

'Say it quickly, Min, or we'll get drenched. I think that we've established we admire one another as parents.'

More rain landed on their heads, growing heavier by the second.

'You ought to have a child of your own.'

Taking off his glasses, he wiped them on his trouser leg, then put them back on his nose.

She held her breath. It might be that he wanted to see more clearly, or he might be taking a second to digest what she'd just blurted out.

'You know my feelings on that. The Elmstone title ends with me. I will not see it curse another generation by having an heir.'

Spinning neatly on the heel of his shoe, he hurried towards the door, keeping several paces ahead of her.

Oh, dear…she ought to have phrased that better.

Half running, she caught up, tugged on his sleeve.

'A child of yours would never be a curse…and you would never let anyone act as if it were.'

They'd reached the patio doors. He drew one open, then went in after her.

They walked across the lobby towards the elevator, silent. The storm from outside seemed have taken hold of his disposition. This conversation was doomed to die a cold, silent death.

The elevator operator had apparently retired for the night. Harrison opened the door. They stepped inside. Running one long finger across the controls, he looked at them this way and that. Then he pushed a lever.

Whirling, clicking sounds issued from underneath and they began to rise.

He was silent, looking down at the lobby, which had the illusion of growing smaller as they rose.

'We need to discuss what I just told you,' she said.

He didn't look up, but studied the tips of his damp shoes. 'We had an understanding, Minerva. For the wellbeing of the family we would be friends and no more than that. Are you suggesting we go back on it?'

'That isn't what I'm suggesting. What I'm saying is that the world will not be worse off simply because you have an heir; it will be better. I think we can accomplish the deed and still remain friendly.'

The elevator had reached the third floor, but he didn't open the door.

'Accomplish the deed?' he asked, incredulous.

She couldn't possibly understand what she was saying.

'Yes, you know... A man and a woman come together briefly, and if they are lucky the joining results in a child.'

He felt punched...in the gut...in the head... No, in the heart. Did she think him so cold that he could lie with her and be that unfeeling about it? That his heart would play no part in the matter whatsoever?

He was not his father...nor his brother.

Besides, his heart was already too involved with

her. What he needed was to distance himself, not grow closer.

Did she actually believe she could lie with him and not involve her heart? Or his?

She touched his face, her fingertips cold on his cheek. 'I have been clumsy in explaining.'

Not clumsy—she had been direct. But she was ignorant of what went on between a man and a woman.

He had been angry at her seemingly callous suggestion, until he'd realised that as a protected daughter of society she was not likely to know about the passion which usually came with being intimate.

However, this was Minerva—and, given her highly curious mind, she probably did understand the basics of a 'joining'.

What she wouldn't understand was how lying together would so drastically change what they now had. Apparently she thought the begetting of a child was akin emotionally to a handshake or a hug.

'You don't realise what you are suggesting, Minerva.'

'I do realise it.'

Clearly he wasn't going to convince her with words. He must show her.

But not in their suite.

It would be madness to prove his point there. Much too dangerous. There were risks involved in this lesson. Teaching her anywhere near a bed would likely end in disaster.

'So, then, you believe we could do what we need to in order to have a child and just remain as we are afterwards?'

'Of course we can. Harrison, you are the dearest friend I have ever had.'

'We shall see...'

He touched her mouth with his thumb, pressing down slightly, delighting in the plush texture of her lips even though he didn't wish to delight in it. But his point must be made clear, even if he had to take a risk. He drew his finger down her chin...a slow, deliberate path to the delicate hollow of her throat.

While an elevator was not precisely the place to demonstrate the sexual draw between a man and a woman, it was the safest place to keep him from getting carried away.

The cage, while open in design, was private enough for his purposes this high up. Hopefully this late in the evening there would be no interruptions. He had an important point to press upon his innocent wife.

Continuing with his finger, he circled the top button of her blouse, and thumbed it open.

'I don't understand what you are doing,' she whispered breathlessly. 'If you have changed your mind and want an heir this might not be the best place for it.'

'I'm not doing that. What I am doing is showing you just how dear a friend I can be to you.'

He felt her shiver as he drew his finger up her neck, tracing the delicate shell of her ear.

'My, that is friendly...' Her sigh was warm on his wrist and he suddenly feared he was making a mistake. A large mistake which he would not be able to retract.

But, mistake or not, this was a pleasant lesson and no denying the fact.

He would be wise to proceed carefully here. The problem being, the more he touched her the less wise he felt.

'How about this?' He bent and put his lips where his finger had been, at the spot on her throat where her pulse beat rapidly. 'Is this friendly?'

'I would say so, yes.'

It had been a misstep to release that one button, because all he could think of now was freeing them all.

His hands were itching, to the point where he felt he must do something with them or...

But they were in an elevator, he reminded himself.

He plucked the pins from her hair, watched the dark mass tumble slowly down her back, over one shoulder and across the bodice of her blouse. He sifted the strands, savouring the sudden hitch in her breathing. He felt her heartbeat racing against his knuckles.

A buzzer sounded three storeys below, indicating someone was summoning the elevator car to the lobby.

Not yet. Whoever was down there should take the stairs if they didn't wish to wait.

He meant to kiss his wife thoroughly—to make her understand the consequences of crossing the line they had so wisely established.

He hesitated…watching her lips…mentally licking his. There was a question in her gaze. Her smile challenged him to answer it.

All at once he wasn't sure of anything. Who was teaching this lesson, and who was learning it?

There was only this… He would have her kiss.

All of a sudden it didn't matter what his motive was, only that it happened—that he took the heat arching from her to himself and stoked it even higher.

His intent could not have been clearer. She gasped softly. Warm breath skimmed his mouth. He dipped his head, parted his lips and placed them on hers, and then… Then the essence of his Min rushed in, filling all the dark places in his soul.

Completely undone, there was nothing left to do but give himself away.

Which had not been the point of this.

Where his body was hard and tense, hers was soft, giving. They fitted together as if, against all reason, each of them had been born for the other.

He'd meant to teach her what passion was, the power of it and where it might lead, but instead…

In a heartbeat, in the heated whisper of a sigh, he questioned everything he'd ever believed.

Could he have been so wrong about what made for a secure, successful marriage?

The buzzer went again—three times in quick order. Still he did not open the door and release the car.

He kissed her again, more deeply than before, revelling in her quivering response. Then, reluctantly, he set his wife and her sweet lips away from him.

'Ah, Min…don't you see the risk for us now?'

Please let her say she did. Because all of a sudden he was shaky about it himself.

He wished she would say something—not simply look at him with wide round eyes.

What was going on behind her half-frowning, half-smiling expression?

Perhaps the kiss had meant nothing to her and he need not worry that she wanted to take it any further. But no, he knew she'd been as subsumed by it as he had.

'I understand the risk to you, if you don't release this car. Whoever is down there will soon climb the stairs and challenge you to fisticuffs.'

What? That was what she was thinking about? While he exposed his heart, she was thinking of the person needing to use the elevator?

He opened the door, then stepped out after her.

The way he felt, a round of fisticuffs might be what he needed to clear his head.

He was certain this woman had kissed him back with the same fervour he'd kissed her with.

There was no mistaking passion given and received…multiplied and then—

Left hanging, as if it hadn't happened.

They stepped into their suite. He closed the door behind them.

'I'll stay out here while you prepare for bed,' he said grimly.

'No need. I'm going to sit with the children for a while. I didn't kiss them before they went to sleep.'

He followed her to their room, leaned against the door frame.

Minerva sat on Abby's bed, brushing a web of fine blonde hair away from her cheek. She leaned down to place a goodnight kiss on her forehead.

Rising, she walked around to the other side of the bed, bent to kiss James's forehead. 'Goodnight, my little man,' she whispered.

Passing Harrison in the doorway on her way out, she paused, looking up at him. 'I do understand what just happened.'

'Do you, Minerva? Truly? Because I'm not entirely sure that I do.'

She touched his arm, nodded. 'Look into your heart and you will see.'

Hadn't he always done that? It was only in the

last few moments that he'd been knocked off balance…had received a glimpse of something else. Something that frightened him.

All he could hope was that in the morning all would be right in his mind again. Daylight would set everything in proper order.

He crossed to the window, stared out. It was raining hard. Out in the harbour he could barely make out the shapes of the ships. They were no more than a blur, with halos of bobbing light.

Listening to what must be a skirt and petticoats hitting the floor, he suddenly felt rather like those vessels. A blur. His thoughts no more than bobbing pinpoints of confusion.

'You may come in now,' Minerva called.

He heard the bed shift as she turned to face the wall and give him his privacy, as had been their custom before he'd put up the curtain.

What was the point of it, though, when she had already seen all he had to offer while he'd been swimming naked in the sea?

Seen and not wanted, apparently.

It was for the best, he admitted. Not terribly flattering, but for the best.

'We still haven't made a decision about an addition to our family,' she said. 'I think we should do it before tomorrow.'

He took off his shirt, shed his trousers. In spite of the past few moments, was she really inviting him to 'do the deed' tonight?

'I'm not ready for that… I cannot say I ever will—'

'How many more times can we tell the children "maybe" without giving them a yes or no about the puppy?'

His shoulders sagged—whether in relief or disappointment, at this point he didn't know. Probably because it was a dizzying combination of both.

'Ah, yes, the puppy…what do you think about it?'

'We don't yet have a dog. I think we need one.'

'Let's sleep on it and give them an answer tomorrow.'

He got into bed. She turned around again, her hair a dark wave washed across the white pillowcase.

'If you wish—but you do understand that to children "maybe" is the same thing as yes?'

'"Maybe" means the decision will be made at another time.'

She laughed. It was one of the best sounds he'd ever heard. It was as if all the tension between them had suddenly dissolved and they were themselves again.

More than ever he was convinced that the marriage they had was wonderful as it was. For it to become something else was tempting…but no. Even if Minerva was right about a child of his growing up to be honourable, not subject to feeling shamed—and he was not yet wholly convinced she was correct—he wouldn't take the risk of everything falling apart as it had for his parents.

'It means yes. "Maybe" is simply a way of giving parents time to get used to giving in to what the children want.'

'So, will we get to choose which pup we want?'

'We shall see,' she said.

'Is that the same as "maybe"?'

She laughed again.

He fell asleep holding the sound of it in his heart.

Chapter Eleven

The next morning Minerva was the first to awaken. She did not get out of bed, but stared at the ceiling in an attempt to gather her scattered wits.

Last night had left her flustered.

Before she set a foot out of bed she needed to step into her role of mother. Into her role of wife—whatever that role was.

She'd thought she understood it but here she lay, once more off-balance where her husband was concerned.

No, not once more…more than ever.

For all that she'd made light of what had happened between them in the elevator, she'd been irrevocably changed by it.

Harrison's intention had been to teach her a lesson—which he had done.

He would be stunned to know the lesson she'd learned wasn't the one he'd thought he was teaching.

While his touches and those marvellous kisses

had pointed out that what was between them would change if they became man and wife in truth, they had also made her realise that she truly did wish for that kind of marriage.

To Harrison's way of thinking, it would put the friendship they shared at risk. She could understand why he felt that way. His parents had given him a miserable example of love within marriage.

To her way of thinking, love within marriage would only strengthen what they already shared.

She wanted that. To be wed without it was to have only half a marriage.

Evie had tried to tell her as much.

Harrison stretched under his blanket. His endearing long toes popped out of the end, as usual.

Sitting up in bed, she swung her legs over the side. Elbows on knees and chin on open palms, she watched him come slowly awake.

There was nothing unlovable about this man. The more she looked at him, the less off-balance she felt.

I love you, she whispered at him, but without sound.

And right there everything off-kilter within her came back into balance.

Good, then. Now all she had to do was carry on as if, in spite of the kiss and all that had gone with it, she was still no more than his great friend.

For a while...but not for ever.

What she needed was time to show him how

being in love would not ruin but would enhance what they already had.

Luckily, she had time. Their vows to each other had been for ever.

He blinked his eyes, reached for his glasses and put them on. He looked over at her.

'Good morning, Minerva.'

'Good morning, my friend.'

Tomorrow they would be going home. She would plot against his fear once they got there.

For now she would relax and enjoy the rest of this holiday with the family she loved.

'That one, do you think?' she said quietly to Harrison while they watched the children stroking the puppies.

'Maybe…' He arched a dark brow at her, gave her that flat smile, curved at the tips.

She jabbed him in the ribs with her elbow, smiling to make it clear she'd got his jest.

'Or maybe the little black and white one?' he suggested.

'Both of them…maybe? We have two children after all.'

She laughed. So did he, unaware that in her own mind she'd added the rider, *two for now.*

'Come along, now, children,' Harrison called. 'We'll visit them again before we leave tomorrow.'

'We get ice cream?' Abby dashed across to clasp his hand, looking hopefully up at him.

'Soon. First we'll go to the antiques shop.'

James, holding Harrison by his other hand, gave a happy hop. 'I'm going to find the Ruby Fairy Watch.'

'You will need to look closely, son. No one's seen it in many years, remember.'

'James find it,' Abby declared, seeming quite certain he would.

So out of the pet shop they went, off on a treasure hunt.

The children's anticipation was high.

She felt herself rise to the adventure.

'Anything can happen in an antiques shop with timepieces everywhere one looks,' Harrison declared.

Abby shimmied down, wriggling out of Harrison's arms as soon as they entered the shop.

'I find fairy, Uncle-Papa.'

She dashed about, peeking under a chair and then going up on her toes to peer on top of a table.

'Where *is* you, fairy?'

James sent his sister a frown. 'Not a fairy. Her magic watch.'

The shop sold all sorts of antiques. Minerva was standing in front of a display case containing jewellery.

He should give her something pretty.

The thought whispered through his brain and

he didn't like what it suggested. A bauble as a substitute for his love?

Surely not. A necklace or earrings would simply express his appreciation for all she did to make them a family.

Standing beside her, he pretended to be looking at clocks—but what he really wanted was to know if anything in the case had caught her eye.

There was an emerald bracelet which was exquisite. He would purchase that. It matched her eyes.

'I should buy the whole case,' he muttered quietly.

Not quietly enough, because Minerva and the shopkeeper both glanced at the huge case full of clocks happily ticking away, behind the counter.

'Not that case,' he clarified.

Minerva looked relieved...the shopkeeper disappointed.

'May I see the emerald bracelet, sir?' The more he looked at it the more he thought it was meant for his wife.

Taking it out of the case, the shopkeeper draped it artfully across Harrison's palm.

Deep, glimmering green winked in the stones. Taking Minerva's hand, Harrison circled the bracelet around her wrist and fastened the clasp.

'Do you like it?'

'It's stunning.' She lifted it to a beam of sunshine streaking through the window.

Suddenly stricken, he noticed that Baroness Elmstone did not have the hands of a pampered lady. The hand he gazed at was the hand of a woman who pampered other people.

On their wedding day they'd been soft…as smooth and unlined as her position warranted.

She deserved so much more than a smattering of emeralds.

What she deserved was to be cherished, appreciated and loved.

He did cherish her, and he greatly appreciated her. He even loved her in his own way.

The question in his mind was, how long would she be satisfied with the sort of love he offered? The love of a friend and the love of a husband were markedly different.

'Are those earrings a match to the bracelet?' he asked the man.

'Yes, sir, there's a set of three. The bracelet, the earrings, and here…look at the necklace.'

'It is beautiful,' Minerva said. 'All three pieces are. But you don't need to indulge me.'

He did. The question was, why? Was it simply to please her? Or was this an attempt to appease his guilt over the business of not allowing her to give him an heir?

'Wrap them all up for me, please.'

Whatever his reason was, she'd look lovely in emeralds.

'I'll wear the bracelet now,' she said, then went

up on her toes and kissed his cheek. 'Thank you. They're lovely and I adore them.'

As long as she was happy, he supposed his deeper motives didn't matter. His intention had been to please her and it seemed he had.

'James is about to stare a hole through that case, trying to find that watch,' Minerva said.

'It really would be magic if he did.'

Minerva hurried over to Abby, snatching her away from the window display she seemed intent upon climbing into.

'Don't see fairy,' she complained.

'Perhaps she's gone outside. Shall we look there? If I were a fairy I would be hiding among the pretty autumn leaves.'

The bell on the door jingled as they went out. He and James carried on with their quest of seeking out interesting timepieces. One never knew what one might come across.

Harrison had his nose all but buried in the broken workings of a tall grandfather clock when James cried out.

'Here it is! I've found it!'

Dashing across the small shop, James snatched Harrison's sleeve, tugging him towards the case.

Whatever James thought he'd seen, it could not be the Ruby Fairy Watch. People who knew about it had been looking for it for years without success.

He did hate to disappoint the child. He would suggest something else for him to search for.

James tapped one finger on the glass, imitating a busy little woodpecker. 'There it is. See? It's the swans, just like you said.'

'And with a ruby in their beaks?' Harrison bent to peer in the case. 'It must have the ruby, son, or it's not the Ruby Fairy Watch.'

'It does!'

It did?

Harrison took off his glasses, cleaned the lenses, and set the glasses back high on his nose. He studied the watch, taking in each detail of the engraving.

As incredible as it seemed, right before his disbelieving eyes was the very watch that had become a legend. It matched the drawing he had studied in every detail.

'How did you acquire this, sir? And how much will you take for it?' Harrison asked the shopkeeper.

'A fellow came in with a box...your emeralds came from it, too. He was selling his late aunt's belongings. He's an honest man, and I've bought from him before, so you need not worry they're stolen. I'm very careful what goods I acquire.'

'It's the Ruby Fairy Watch and it's magic,' James informed the man.

'Magic, you say? It must be worth a great deal, then.'

James nodded, his hair flying madly about. 'Whoever has it gets their dearest wish granted.'

'That is very fine, young man. Do you think your father will buy you such a wonder?'

Half dancing on his toes, James glanced up, his expression balanced between hopeful and agonised.

'I am anxious to purchase it, naturally,' said Harrison. 'But you must know before you sell it that it is an extremely rare piece and has not been seen in many years.'

'The seller did say the box was in the darkest corner of an attic, under years' worth of discarded items. He might not have found it at all had he not sold his aunt's house and been required to clear it out.'

'I would love to add it to my collection, if you're willing to let it go.'

'Well, sir, I'm in the business of letting things go. I will sell it to you with my blessing. I hope it makes all this young man's wishes come true.'

Leaving with the treasure, and a doll for Abby, he could scarcely believe their luck.

Even though he'd now had several minutes to let the notion that they had found the treasure sink in, it still seemed like a dream.

Abby tucked her doll between her arm and her side while she ate vanilla ice cream. James stared intently at Harrison's coat pocket, where he'd put the box containing the Ruby Fairy Watch.

All the way from the antiques shop to the ice

cream shop Minerva had thought the pair of them walked on air rather than the pavement. After all the conversations he and James had had about the watch, she couldn't quite believe they had actually found it.

'We shall find a very special place for the watch when we get home, son,' Harrison said.

Looking between them, she couldn't decide which of them had the wider grin.

'Get el'vator for home?' Abby asked.

'I'm sorry, Abby, we cannot have one of those,' Harrison answered with an indulgent smile.

'I wish for a puppy,' James declared. 'I wish it on the watch.'

'Me wish it too!'

'Maybe...' Minerva said.

'We shall see.'

Harrison gave her the wink that always made her feel silly inside.

All at once they heard a child crying. Coming around the corner, a boy about James's age was being tugged along by a person who appeared to be his nanny.

'Mama!' he sobbed. 'I want my mama!'

'Come along, you young scoundrel. Your father will not be happy to know you've misbehaved again.'

'His mama in Heaven?' Abby asked, hugging her doll to her cheek.

Abby's question made James bite his lip, blinking his eyes rapidly. Harrison hugged his shoulder.

'Shall we let him touch the watch so his mama will come back?'

The tremble in James's voice cut Minerva to the heart. Neither of the children spoke much about the past, but that didn't mean they never thought of it.

'I imagine he's only crying because he will be in trouble with his father,' Harrison said. 'I don't think touching the watch will help.'

'Me and Abby don't need to cry any more. We can wish and wish to always have you and Mama-Min.'

Minerva glanced quickly at Harrison, her heart swelling in her throat.

He looked at her with the same choking emotion.

'James, son…' Harrison gathered the boy onto his lap and hugged him. 'The watch is a fine thing to have, but even without it you'll always have me and Mama-Min.'

'And a puppy,' Abby declared.

'It's so good to be home!' Harrison announced.

Hearing the joy in his voice as he turned the carriage onto Cockleshell Lane put a smile on Minerva's face too.

Looking at the roof peaks, seeing smoke curling out of the pair of chimneys and hearing the front door creaking out a welcome…it was very good indeed to be home.

Nearly a week ago they'd departed for St Austell to the sound of hammering. Now here they were, returning to the same.

'I wonder how much progress they've made,' she said.

'Without us underfoot, I expect they've accomplished a great deal.'

'May we take Jolly down to the beach, Uncle-Papa?'

'Here, pup.' Harrison lifted the small black and white dog from James's lap, setting him on the ground. 'It's too late for that now. It would be good for him to romp around the garden for a bit, though.'

Having been confined to the carriage for a couple of hours, the newest addition to their family would need to dash and leap as much as the children needed to.

'I'll stay out here with them if you wish to go inside,' she said.

That, it seemed, was all the encouragement Harrison needed to sprint across the yard and up the steps.

The pup ran in circles, yapping. Abby and James ran in circles after him, clapping and copying his high-pitched barks.

They had named him Jolly because, after they'd

presented several names to the dog, he'd wagged his tail at that one.

Given that the dog wagged his tail constantly, he might have been named Sky or Wheel or any number of things!

Jolly was a good name, though, and it suited Minerva's mood.

Home and comfort…a sense of wellbeing wrapped around her. She'd felt something like it once before when they'd returned from London. This homecoming was different, though. This time she had an even greater sense of belonging. Sights, sounds and smells were familiar rather than still new.

This was home.

The little ones running about the garden were her children.

The man in the house, industriously exploring the renovations, was her husband.

In nearly every way she was content.

And in that one way that she was not?

She sighed, pursing her lips. Evie had told her not to close her eyes to the possibility of having the sort of love she had in her marriage, as William and Elizabeth also had. In the moment she had not understood what Evie meant. Now that she was in love, it all made sense.

To her it did. Apparently to her husband it did not.

That was a rather large obstacle.

Soon the sun would set and they'd need to go inside. But just for a moment she closed her eyes, listened to seabirds crying while they settled in for the night. To Jolly barking, probably not ready to settle for the night. And the children laughing… That was the dearest sound of home.

The sound of a window scraping open came from upstairs.

'Min! Your chamber is finished!'

Harrison's voice was another sound of home. It caught at her heart in a way she'd never expected it would.

How could it be that only a short time ago they'd been strangers?

Given how she felt about him now, it hardly seemed possible.

'Bring the children! Come and see.'

How many more nights did she have before she moved into her new chamber? Her purchases were due to arrive tomorrow. She could go slowly with the decorating, but there wasn't much point in putting the move off.

Perhaps moving would even work in her favour. Harrison might miss her…wish to share a room with her again. She certainly intended to do what she could to that end.

When she thought about it, she had to smile. Looked at in a hopeful way, what seemed an obstacle might end up being a great deal of fun.

She waved to Harrison, letting him know they were coming inside.

The children hesitated to give up their romp, but once she made a game of it by calling for a race they dashed eagerly inside.

Banging, slamming sounds of construction came from the kitchen. Before going up, she peeked around the kitchen door.

The kitchen was now bright and inviting.

'This is lovely,' she told the men when they stopped work to greet her.

'Almost finished, my lady. You'll have your house back in no time at all.'

Before leaving St Austell Harrison had interviewed a cook and a maid. That was wonderful, of course, and yet life here would be different once they arrived.

No longer would it be only the four of them.

And yet in the end it would be for the best.

Almost. With other people in residence Harrison would probably not indulge in moonlight swims. She would miss that.

'Thank you for everything, gentlemen. And for lighting the fireplaces. It was a welcome sight.'

She hurried up the stairs, anxious to see her room…nearly.

'Are you hungry?' Minerva asked Harrison as he carried a pail of steaming water from the huge kettle in the kitchen to the bathtub.

He was, of course, given what a long, busy day it had been.

But what kind of hungry was she referring to?

She was standing beside the tub wearing a robe, loosely secured by a tie, and her nightgown, with a towel slung over her arm… He did wonder if she was speaking of food.

If she *was* referring innocently to food, then his mind was wandering of its own accord, with no encouragement from his wife.

'Thank you for taking the furniture up to my chamber. It was very strong of you.'

Strong of him? That was a strange turn of phrase.

'Dutiful, do you mean? Since I am your husband, it's only natural that I should do it.'

'Dutiful, then.'

She gave him the oddest smile. He wasn't used to seeing one like it from her.

'A husband's duty is never done, I suppose,' she said. 'Can I get you a slice of pie? I am sensible of my duty as your wife. I wouldn't wish to deny satisfying your hunger.'

He wouldn't be standing here wondering what was really being discussed had the furniture delivery not been delayed by a day.

He would have had help carrying it all upstairs. But since the builders had finished their work and gone home, the labour had fallen to him.

So she thought him strong. And she wanted to… to serve him pie?

'I'll get it. You have worked as hard as I today, and you did it with a puppy rushing outside at every turn.' He dumped the last pail of hot water in the tub. 'Better take your bath before the water cools.'

'Thank you…the steamy water is going to be a great treat.'

Steamy? She might have simply called it water. *Steamy* suggested—

Never mind that. He was probably wrong about it anyway.

She was walking past him with an enchanting sway his eyes couldn't look away from, and she loosened the tie of her robe, casting a glance at him over her shoulder.

'Close the door behind you, will you, Harrison? There will be a draught otherwise.'

He felt a draught—and it blew right through his sense of good reason.

Minerva had taken baths in the tub many times, so why was he staring at the closed door as if this was the first time?

It might be because she was splashing and singing. It seemed she was enjoying it more than usual.

Finding the pie, he sliced a piece and leaned his hip against the new kitchen table, slowly nibbling. It was blackberry pie…lush, juicy and delicious.

That was a rather descriptive way of thinking

of the pie. It was good pie, though, and he was enjoying it in poetic terms. There really was nothing else to be read into it.

Who didn't enjoy a poetic pie?

Now she was humming.

He heard the sound of dripping water, which must be falling from the washcloth onto…

He gave himself a mental shake. He couldn't imagine why her day's work being washed away should sound so enticing. Why it should capture his imagination as it was doing.

What a lie, he told himself. He knew exactly why it had captured his imagination.

He had opened a door in that hotel elevator, so to speak. He hadn't meant to, but now… Well, images paraded in his mind no matter how he tried to prevent them.

This was the first night Minerva would sleep in her own chamber—maybe that had something to do with it.

He was going to miss seeing her at night. He would miss hearing the splash of water in the basin when she refreshed herself before bed… miss watching her silhouette on the curtain. Even the sound of her blankets rustling in the night had become something of a lullaby.

He could never have guessed how it would feel to have another person so close by in the night.

Not just another person. His lovely and loving Min.

The sound of sloshing and dripping water indicated that she'd stood up, finished with her bath.

He thought he heard the towel, briskly rubbing her skin dry, but it might be his imagination.

It was more vivid than he'd ever realised.

Either way, he finished the rest of the pie in a single bite, then went into the parlour to sit by the fire.

Now that Minerva had a chamber of her own, would she perhaps join him in here to discuss the day's events, like they'd used to in their chamber, or would she sit by the hearth in her own room?

Gazing out of the window at the bank of fog sliding across the cliff towards the house, he imagined it would be a dreary evening if she didn't come.

In that instant six cuckoo birds came chirruping out of their clocks. Over the noise, he heard her footsteps approaching.

Oh… Good, then.

She padded into the room barefoot, again wearing her nightgown and robe.

All of a sudden he wasn't sure how comfortable this was going to be. For him, at any rate.

Chapter Twelve

Chances were her husband might be scandalised at her coming into the parlour wearing her night-clothes. Truly, though, he must be familiar with what she slept in, given that they shared a bed-chamber…well, they used to share one.

However, having just finished her bath, she wasn't going to dress again. That would be foolish. Besides, although she knew very little about subtle seduction, she did think it would be easier done barefoot and in her nightclothes.

'I love it when the fog comes in at night. It makes everything so cosy inside,' she said, while settling back into her customary chair, giving the process an uncustomary wriggle and a sigh.

'It will make taking the pup outside in the night chillier.'

Digging about in her stitching bag, she glanced up at him. 'You'll let me know how he does in the morning?'

'Will I?'

His brow wrinkled in the way she found utterly charming.

'How else am I to know?'

'It is fair, I admit. You tended to him all day. What is it that you're doing?'

'Needlework.'

'You hate needlework.'

'Usually.' She shrugged the robe off her shoulders. 'It's warm in here, don't you think?'

'I hadn't thought so, no.'

She hadn't thought so either—in fact there was a bit of a chill. But if she wished to convince her husband that a change in their marriage would be a good thing, she must put some effort into it.

Wait, though, Harrison was giving her a singular look. *Well, my goodness.* It wasn't so cool in here after all. With one unguarded glance he'd warmed her nicely.

'Why are you doing something you dislike?' he asked.

'This is a special project. One I will actually enjoy, I think.' She withdrew a handful of colourful skeins of thread. 'Red, blue or green? Oh, maybe yellow? Here is lavender, though.'

'I suppose it depends upon what you're stitching.'

Lovely—he wasn't looking at the colours of the thread but at the blush she felt flushing her skin.

'There's one thing that our home is missing.'

She hesitated to say what it was in the hope that his mind would suggest it. If it didn't, her seduction was missing the mark.

His blank stare of confusion indicated he hadn't made the connection.

'A framed stitching over the front door. *Home Sweet Home.* Every proper home should have one.'

'Red, then.'

She let her robe slip lower. As she'd hoped, his gaze followed it. The way his eyes rested upon her so intimately made her mind fuzzy.

Not so off the mark, then.

'Red?'

'Thread…for the embroidery,' he said.

'Silly me—of course for the embroidery. That's what we were discussing.'

Until she'd got lost in her longing for things he resisted giving her.

Suddenly, he stood up. 'It's been a tiring day, my dear. If I'm to be on puppy duty tonight, I will bid you goodnight now.'

This was disappointing. All she'd revealed to him were her bare toes and a slip of shoulder—not that she quite knew how to bare anything without bumbling it. She was not by nature a seductress.

'Sleep well in your new chamber.'

He paused beside her chair. He dipped his head, his mouth descending as if he meant to kiss her.

More than likely he didn't mean to. And yet what if he did?

Her nerves leapt in anticipation of another kiss.

If he did kiss her again it would be because he wanted to. The first time it had been to illustrate the dangers of kissing…of the misery it could bring.

She must be a miserable student, then. The only thing she'd learned was that a second kiss would be delightfully delicious.

And another kiss might mean that he'd learned kissing her was a good thing.

Perhaps he'd come round to her way of thinking.

Even as his breath skimmed her nose, her mouth, she wondered if changing his mind could be this easy.

And yet he was so close that his masculine scent filled her. How could he not want what she did?

His fingers stroked the line of her chin…then turned it.

He kissed her. On the cheek. Solidly on the cheek.

'Goodnight, Min.' He walked quickly towards the hall.

'Goodnight, Harrison,' she replied, far too cheerfully.

With a jab, she made the first stitch on the word 'home'.

It wasn't only tending to Jolly which kept Harrison awake.

It was the silence of his chamber.

It echoed from corner to corner in a way it hadn't done before Minerva had shared it with him.

He'd slept alone all his life. What was so different now?

His wife.

He missed her.

Lying on his mattress, restless, he found his thoughts had only one place to go. To the moment a few hours ago when he'd nearly kissed her.

For a second time!

The first time he'd done it had been to teach her a lesson about the risk of giving in to passion. What had he meant by it this time?

Nothing except to indulge. She'd looked so beautiful, needle in hand, ready to stitch something pretty for their home. She had been the very picture of domesticity…except that she had been plying that sharp little needle only half clothed.

The one and only motive he'd had for kissing her this time had been because he desired it… desired *her*.

He had come within a breath of going against what he considered wise and prudent. Luckily he'd come to his senses in time to redirect the kiss to her cheek.

Small paws pattered across the floor. Jolly must have heard him flopping to and fro on the mattress.

It wasn't time for Jolly to go outside again, so no doubt the puppy was lonely and wanted company.

'Come, then.' Harrison got out of bed, picked Jolly up. 'Let's check on the children.'

With the pup tucked in the crook of his elbow, he walked through the doorway joining the rooms.

'You've worn them out, it appears.'

The door to Minerva's chamber was open. He went to it, leaned against the jamb.

It looked as if Jolly had worn her out too. She lay in the pose he was used to seeing her sleep in, with one hand curled between her cheek and the pillow.

Perhaps if he stood here long enough he could soak in the sight of her, carry it back to his too-silent chamber and manage to fall asleep with her image in his mind. It would be a poor substitute for seeing her with his eyes, but this sleeping arrangement was for the best.

Even so, he stood watching her sleep, or perhaps dream. If she was dreaming, what was she dreaming about?

He yawned, blinking his eyes.

What was that?

He rubbed his eyes to clear his vision. It did no good, since what he saw was in his imagination, not before his eyes. It was difficult to look away from a thing that was in one's mind, he discovered.

And the image that resisted being rubbed away was a picture of him in her bed, spooning her against his chest, belly and thighs. He imagined he'd been whispering in her ear, and she was smiling in response.

What had he said? The fantasy hadn't revealed that. He had an idea, of course.

Going against what he held to be right, he was sure he'd asked her to share the intimacy to be found within the marriage bed.

Would it be so awful? he wondered, approaching her bed for real.

How sweet was that one funny corkscrew of hair that always popped out from the rest at her temple… No matter what Minerva was doing, that curl was constant. If he gave in to temptation and made love to her, it would look exactly the same before as after.

What an odd symbol of constancy. But the point was, she would still be who she was and he would be who *he* was.

What if he took the risk and they became lovers? It might not ruin their friendship. She'd assured him it wouldn't.

It was temping to get in beside her and find out—to see if she would smile at him as she had in his vision.

His long-held belief that passion and friendship didn't make lasting companions seemed to be shredding while he stood there.

Jolly whined, scrambling to get out of his arms.

Minerva turned on her back, opening her eyes.

She looked up at him, her gaze dreamy and unfocused.

'Can't sleep?' she mumbled. 'Me neither.'

No? She'd given an excellent impression of it.

'Jolly woke me,' he said.

'Mmm...' She closed her eyes and turned away from him, then went back to sleep.

The curve of her hip made a lovely mound under the blanket.

Dashed imagination! It made him question everything he'd ever believed about marriage.

Minerva, his alive and vibrant wife, was giving him pause. Calling him to examine everything he'd once thought to be right.

Harrison stared at his mother's bedchamber door, feeling evil pulsing on the other side of it. The wood throbbed as if it had a heartbeat. Even a child knew this could not be...haunted wood, evil behind a door. He tried to run away but his short legs were stuck in something. Mud lay thick and cold all over the floor. Mother would be angry when she discovered it.

Something dripped off the doorknob. It might be water or it might be blood...

He'd never stayed dreaming long enough to find out. In his dream, as soon as Father went into a rage at Mother, the evil thing shook the door and he'd wake in a sweat, shaking, glad the argument hadn't been real...not this time.

This time, however, the dream didn't let go of him.

His bare feet were stuck in the mud. His hand was reaching for the doorknob even though he tried to yank it back.

He cried out when the door swung open and he was sucked into his mother's chamber.

There was a storm in the chamber—lightning but no thunder, wind with nothing blowing.

In a flash of light he saw the slow burn of his mother's anger. In the next flash he saw Father's flaming tantrum.

The diamond on Mother's wedding ring glowed bigger and brighter with each strike of lightning. Then it burst, sending sharp shards all over the room. One of them cut his cheek. He felt the dampness of blood but no pain.

The storm stopped.

Father whirled away like a puff of smoke.

Mother lay upon her bed, wet, draped in seaweed and a tattered wedding veil.

He knew she was dead, but she sat up and spoke to him.

'There you are. I waited and waited for you to come to me.'

'I was scared, Mama.'

'Afraid of your own mother? Come closer, boy.'

She beckoned him with a long finger that looked like bones.

'But, Mama.' He didn't believe this was his

mother. 'There was blood on the doorknob, and tears.'

'Don't be like your father, you nasty child.'

All right...maybe this was his mother. That was exactly what she'd call him if she wasn't dead.

'I have something to tell you, son. Come closer so you'll hear me.'

He didn't want to! But when he tried to run backwards, he went forward instead.

Cold bones clutched his small arm, squeezed.

'If you don't wish to end up in this bed of despair like I have, never fall in love. It is a folly which will ruin you.'

When she said 'ruin' it sounded like a howl.

'Tell me you will not. Vow it to me... Do it now.'

He tried to argue but his mouth seemed to be glued shut.

'Kiss my cheek, my boy, so I will know you promise.'

He struggled against the bones which drew him closer to her dead cheek, to the jaws that clacked, clacked, clacked.

He tried to scream with his sealed mouth. No one would hear him and he would...

'There now…'

A calming voice, a gentle hand on his shoulder intruded and shattered the bones binding him to the nightmare.

'It's only a dream.'

Breathing hard, drenched in sweat, he opened his eyes.

Min sat on the bed next to him. She patted his hand.

Sitting up, he tried to shake off the leftover terror the dream had left behind.

He knew the nightmare wasn't real life, but the emotions it had caused were horridly vivid.

It was going to take some time to go back to sleep.

'Are you all right? I heard you cry out from my chamber.'

'Better now.' *Somewhat.* At least his heart was no longer trying to break out of his chest.

'Would you like me to stay for a while?'

'Thank you, but no. I meant to wake up anyway, and take the dog outside.'

The bed creaked when she stood up. She squeezed his shoulder. 'I can go with you if you like.'

'There's no need. It was only a dream. I am recovered now.'

'Goodnight, then.'

'Goodnight, Minerva.'

She walked out of his room, through the children's chamber and into her own.

Plucking Jolly off the floor, he went downstairs.

Fog still hugged everything, thick and milky, so he didn't go far.

While the pup sniffed the grass he thought about the dream.

What did it mean?

Nothing in it had actually happened in real life. His parents had both perished when the ship they were on went down in a storm.

And even though his mother had been dead in the dream, he didn't think it was about her death. Rather, it was a reminder—a grim image of how love gone wrong had ruined his family.

Had his mother come to his dream to warn him?

He thought that unlikely.

It had been his own common sense asserting itself.

Earlier in the evening he'd come close to kissing his wife again. He'd been within a breath of allowing emotion to lead the way in his marriage. But no more.

Tonight's dream had awoken him to the reality of what made for a satisfactory life.

A successful marriage was one anchored in mutual understanding…in peaceful relations.

There was a price to be paid for a chaste union, no mistake about it. And yet the security of his family was worth any cost.

Minerva walked along the path towards the stables, carrying a bag containing her stitching supplies. When she'd passed the kitchen delicious scents had drifted out from the window, which was cracked open an inch. She could still only half believe she'd smelled bread in the oven…something savoury simmering in a new pot on the new stove.

The cook and the maid had arrived yesterday—to the great delight of everyone. Especially the children. At present they were in the kitchen, watching Cook make scones.

For the first time in a great while Minerva was alone. She wasn't sure she liked it.

A brisk wind whooshed in off the ocean. She drew her cloak closer around her. 'Come along, Jolly. Let's visit Harrison.'

The dog had been banned from the kitchen, so she wasn't completely without company.

Ordinarily, this time of day would find her tending to one chore or another. Now that there was a maid to perform most of them, Minerva was left to embroider.

'I'd rather hang laundry, if you wish to know the truth, Jolly. After I finish this stitching I will retire my needle.'

The stable door was not latched, so it thumped in the breeze.

The pup spotted Harrison before she did, and dashed into a stall.

Following Jolly's happy yips, she found her husband replacing dirty straw with clean. With his shirt half out of his trousers and his hair a tousled mess, he looked nothing like a gentleman of society.

He glanced up from his industrious sweeping. 'Good afternoon, Minerva.'

'If by "good", you mean somewhat dull, then it is perfect.'

Even if she'd had a dozen pursuits to keep her busy, it would not have been perfect.

Ever since his nightmare three nights ago Harrison had not called her Min.

Something had changed. He was polite, and as considerate as he always, but also distant. The warmth and the humour he'd used to have when he smiled at her was no longer there.

She felt the loss acutely, since his affection for the children was as obvious as ever.

'Don't you appreciate having free time, like you did in London?' he asked.

'I paid social calls in London—or received them. All day long. It wasn't "free time".'

He gave his attention to the broom. *Swish, swish, swish.* It must be more entertaining than she was.

'Perhaps I shall pay a call on the seal I saw lounging on the rocks by the cave.'

'It appears you need something new to occupy your time.'

'That's precisely what I've been thinking.'

A small, sweet baby to love and care for. That would keep her busy. But apparently loving her husband was going to be a one-sided affair that would keep her busy no longer than a wink.

She opened her mouth to speak her mind about it. Her efforts at seduction had fallen short, and she needed him to understand what could be between them if he would but allow it.

'You have a budding talent for cooking,' he said, before she could. 'I'm certain Mrs Beasley would be happy to instruct you.'

'You only think I have a talent for it because you were hungry. All I did was keep you from starving until our neighbour arrived with dinner.'

There was nothing to say about that, since he knew very well she was a miserable cook.

'Since I have no one else to give my attention to, I shall give it to you.'

'Here? In the stall?'

'On that barrel just beyond.'

While Jolly scampered about after the broom, she sat on the overturned barrel, then brought out her embroidery.

She drew the thread in and out, out and in… And all the while she wondered how what was between them had gone from being affectionate to… not cold, she didn't think, but not intimate either.

If she were to set aside her stitching, rise from the barrel and then dash into the stall and kiss him, would he turn her away with an absurd declaration about friendship being the best path forward?

'Tell me about your dream,' she said instead.

It had been after the nightmare that he'd changed towards her. If he spoke about it she might get an understanding of what had made him withdraw from her.

'It was nothing. In fact I've had it in various forms since I was a boy.'

'It didn't seem like nothing.'

No one cried out in their sleep and awoke in terror over nothing.

'I assure you it was. What do you suppose Mrs Beasley is preparing for dinner?'

He raised his brows at her in a tricky attempt to draw the conversation away from his dream.

It gave her heart pause, because he'd never been anything but honest and forthright with her. He wasn't by nature a tricky man. Or so she had believed.

'I don't know, but it smells wonderful.'

She'd answered casually about dinner, but all the while she wondered how she might get past the wall he was building between them.

He swept…she stitched.

Completing the word 'Home', she held it up for him to admire.

'It looks so good I shall ask you to do one which reads "Stable Sweet Stable".' The quick tug in his smile gave her a glimpse of the man who was fun and affectionate…but it was there and gone in a heartbeat.

Although he was only feet away, she missed him. It had only been a few days since he withdrew from her, but they'd been long, dull days.

'Very well, I will—since I have nothing better to occupy my time.' She added a great sigh.

She ought to be forthright, to blow down his wall by boldly telling him she wanted what Evie had.

What she should do was tell him she loved him, and then let him lead the way in what came after.

But, not trusting he would lead them the right way, she held her tongue and poked her needle into the embroidery.

Chapter Thirteen

'Show me the Ruby Fairy Watch again, Uncle-Papa!'

This would be the third time today, but Harrison couldn't refuse. Especially since he enjoyed admiring it as much as the boy did.

Retrieving a key from the desk drawer, he unlocked the glass cabinet where the watch was kept. He lifted it from the display hook, then handed it to James.

Minerva worked quietly on her stitching. Too quietly.

She didn't seem herself lately.

It was his fault.

She had offered herself to him, heart and body. So much so that she was willing to have his child.

And what had he done but run from her as if a bee had stung his rear?

Now he didn't know where he stood with her. Friend? Foe? Or had she finally become indifferent to him?

He did know where they ought to stand. As friends and parents. As solid anchors for their family, which would not be blown off course by the whims of passion.

'What would you ask the watch for, James? What would be your wish?' he asked.

At least he and James had grown close. He and Abby as well. Each day he loved them more.

'I will save my magic wish.'

Minerva looked up at that. 'Why would you save it? Anyway, I thought you used it to wish for a puppy?'

'That was a normal wish—not a magic one,' he said importantly.

Abby was patiently teaching the puppy to sit.

'We no need Uncle-Papa…no need Mama-Min.'

'You don't need us?' Harrison arched his brows at Minerva and she arched a look back at him. For that second they connected again—were who they'd always been.

'We has you awready.'

'Indeed you do.'

'You wish for baby, Mama-Min?' asked Abby.

'I have you and James. What else could I want?'

Minerva glanced at Harrison, and then away. She was happy with her family—he knew she was.

He also knew she wanted more.

She deserved more.

Seeing her suppress the wish of her heart slammed him in the gut.

She'd given up so much when she married him. More than he had.

In the beginning this sort of marriage was what they'd both said they wanted. Now everything was different.

Wisdom was not different, though. What made for a safe family had been the same then as it was now.

'What do you think, children?' Minerva lifted her project, turning it for them all to see. 'Only one more word to add.'

'Can you write my name on it?' James asked.

'Write Abby too!'

'I will stitch all our names on it.'

In spite of how things were at the moment, asking Minerva Grant to marry him had been the best thing he'd ever done. They wouldn't be a family were it not for her.

The best thing he'd ever done, yes, but also the riskiest. He couldn't allow himself to love his wife—not in the way he thought she wished for.

She didn't truly understand how families were ruined by allowing oneself to be vulnerable to naked passion.

It damaged children. He wasn't certain he would ever be healed of the wounds of his past.

Minerva was the best person he knew, and yet still he wouldn't hand over his heart to her because he feared so greatly to do it.

Perhaps his mother really was reaching out from the grave and clutching him with her bony hand…

It was late when Minerva tiptoed downstairs—the wee hours, perhaps.

One would think with so many clocks in the house she'd know the time to the second.

Entering the dark parlour, she heard them ticking merrily away.

Having finished the stitching, she was anxious to put it on the wall so her family would see it when they awoke.

There were several nails in the wall, all of them with clocks attached. Since she didn't wish to wake anyone with hammering, she removed the clock within her reach and placed 'Home Sweet Home' in its spot.

Standing back, she curled her hands on her hips, studying her work this way and that.

This might be the best project she'd ever completed. It should be, though, should it not? Having been made with affection and not resentment. And she had stitched each of their names with great love.

There was still room left for another name. She'd left a blank space with the same love with which she had stitched the rest.

No doubt she was foolish to imagine a child which did not and might never exist. And yet she still somehow held out hope that her relationship with Harrison would change...would one day lead to her embroidering that final name.

In the dim light, she traced each name with her fingertip. Then the empty spot.

'Goodnight, little stranger,' she murmured.

Turning about, she realised she wasn't alone. Harrison lounged in a chair within the bay of the window.

'It looks perfect there.' He stood up and joined her in front of the embroidery. 'I thought I heard you talking to someone?'

She could say it was the dog, but the pup was asleep in the chair Harrison had only just risen from.

'To myself,' she answered honestly.

She couldn't tell him what she'd said, of course. Only admit that she had spoken to herself.

But Abby had spoken of Minerva's wish, and bless her dear little heart for it. 'Out of the mouths of babes...' seemed truer than ever.

'What are you doing down here so late?' she asked.

Ordinarily he fell asleep quickly and deeply. Perhaps he'd had a return of his nightmare. He might feel better if he talked to her about it, but since he refused to do so there was little she could do to help.

'By the looks of things out there, I think a storm is coming. An unusually big one,' he said.

'It seems clear to me. Look at all the stars.'

'It's a feeling, mostly.'

'One cannot predict bad weather by simply having a feeling,' she pointed out. 'There needs to be one cloud at least.'

'Something's coming. But let me walk you back upstairs.'

'That sounds vague. Anything could be coming. A visitor, or a letter…possibly a mouse.'

'Mouse?'

'They are skilled at getting into very small places, you know.'

'I hope our cook doesn't leave if she sees one.'

This was silly talk, but it felt easy and wonderful. She had missed it over the past couple of days.

Mounting the stairs, she felt his fingers brush hers, almost as if he'd meant to hold her hand but then thought better of it.

It would have been better had he not considered it.

At least if he hadn't she would know for certain how he felt about the state of their marriage.

Now she was confused…again.

Wind blew hard all the next day.

Standing beside the parlour window and gazing out, Minerva watched the stacks of clouds out over the ocean grow blacker. Stabs of lightning lent them a menacing greenish appearance.

It seemed that Harrison's feeling of 'something' coming had been right.

And judging by the way the wind blew, it wouldn't be long before it was upon them.

She didn't know what was to be done about it except to secure the stables, latch the shutters over the windows in the house, then sit tight through it.

Hearing the front door open, she hurried into the hall.

Harrison's hair was blown around so it looked like a mop. He gripped his glasses in his fingers, nodded at her. 'We are as secure as we can make ourselves.'

'The house has been here a long time. Surely it's weathered worse than this,' she said hopefully.

'I hope so. Oh, there is a carriage outside.'

'What?' She hurried back to the parlour to look for herself.

There really was a carriage.

She rushed back to the hall, where Harrison already had his hand on the door latch.

'I wonder what they want?' she said, peering past his shoulder at the small conveyance. 'Why have they come out in this weather?'

They had never entertained guests before. Luckily, she had been trained from childhood to entertain unexpected arrivals.

Harrison opened the door to a young couple, clinging to one another to keep from being blown off the porch. Once inside, with the door closed, they continued to hold on to each other.

'Welcome to Cockleshell Cottage,' Harrison

said. 'I am Harrison Tremayne, Baron Elmstone. This is my wife Minerva.'

'I am George Moore, my lord. May I introduce my wife Tillie?'

George Moore cast his wife a clearly smitten glance while Harrison and Minerva went through the process of greeting and welcoming their guests.

But *why* did they have guests? They weren't expecting anyone.

Minerva invited them to sit in the parlour while she went to ask Mrs Beasley to prepare tea and serve some of the scones the children had helped make. And to ask Clara, the new maid, to prepare Minerva's chamber for them, since clearly they were not going to be able to leave.

As busy as she was, she did have a chance to wonder how her husband would feel about having her back in his bedroom. She was pretty certain he wouldn't be thrilled.

On her way back to the parlour she met Harrison and Mr Moore, who were going back outside to settle the team and the carriage in the stables.

'Tea will be here by the time the men return,' she said to Tillie Moore, and then sat down in her usual chair, which was across from the sofa occupied by her guest.

'Thank you—tea sounds just the thing.' The other woman folded her hands in her lap, glanced about. 'I'm so sorry that we must impose on you, my lady, but the weather was clear when we left St Austell.'

'Is that where you live?' Minerva asked, because until the men returned they would have to engage in polite, getting-to-know-you conversation—not the reason for their visit.

This was quite a challenge, since Minerva was beyond curious to know.

At last Harrison and Mr Moore returned, looking as if they had been carried in by the wind and not their feet.

Abby, James and Jolly trotted into the parlour after them.

George Moore took the seat beside his wife. They sat shoulder to shoulder, hands clasped. Minerva thought that a whisper of air would not be able to pass between them.

Jolly sniffed Mr Moore's trouser leg, and James sat down on the rug and proceeded to tell them all about the magic cave on the beach.

A great slap of rain hit the window all of a sudden, drawing everyone's attention to the glass.

It was a relief to see that the panes held, in their brave, sturdy frames.

'It seems you arrived not a moment too soon,' Harrison said.

James and Abby dashed to the window and peered out.

'Is the cave filled with seawater now, Uncle-Papa?' James asked.

'I am certain it is, son.'

Mr Moore glanced about the room, his gaze taking in Harrison's collection of clocks. Naturally the conversation went that way. It seemed that both Mr and Mrs Moore were as enamoured of timepieces as her husband was.

Minerva watched the visitors admiring the clocks, thinking that they were very much in love with one another.

They would be—naturally. In the course of their casual conversation, before the men had returned, Minerva had discovered from Mrs Moore that they were newlyweds, honeymooning in Saint Austell.

And now perhaps at Cockleshell Cottage. Who knew how long the storm would go on?

After a few more moments of admiring the clocks, George got to the point of their visit.

After a long, loving glance at his wife, and after kissing her on the cheek, he told them what it was.

'I wish to purchase a timepiece from you, my lord. When my wife and I were in the antiques shop in St Austell I was told that it's one you recently bought.'

It was hardly a surprise that the visit concerned clocks.

'I have purchased a few recently.' Harrison's face and voice were alight with joy to be discussing something so dear to him. 'Which one?'

'The most special of them all,' Tillie said. 'My husband and I have been searching for it since we became betrothed, and now that we are wed…' Tillie ducked her head, blushed.

'I promised it to my bride as a wedding gift. You can imagine our dismay when I found we'd missed it by such a short time.'

'All of them are special. Which of them are you interested in?'

'Why, the Ruby Fairy Watch!' Tillie hugged George closer, if such a feat were even possible.

James spun away from watching the bolts of lightning stab the sea. They were still far enough out that they couldn't hear thunder, or perhaps the heavy rain was drowning out the sound.

However, there was a great deal of thunder in her son's expression. James's mouth had dropped, and his hands were clenched into fists, small but fierce.

'We have a special request to make of it.' Tillie's face could not blaze any hotter.

'Of a private nature,' George added.

Minerva was certain their wish was for a child. What else would a newlywed couple want? Very clearly they already had all the love they needed for a happy marriage. No doubt a child would soon be on the way, wishing on a watch notwithstanding.

A prick of envy was the last thing she wanted to feel.

Who was Minerva Grant? Not the woman she had been when she wed. Now that she was Minerva Tremayne, Baroness Elmstone, everything had changed.

Sadly, Harrison was the same man he'd always been, with the same wants and non-desires.

It was wrong to be envious of Tillie Moore, and yet she wanted the kind of marriage her guest had…she coveted it without shame. Well, nearly without shame. Coveting usually led to all sorts of trouble…

'I cannot sell you that watch. I'm sorry. It has a special meaning to me and my son. But perhaps you would like to see it?'

'Oh, yes! Maybe holding it will be enough to—'

Apparently it *was* possible for Tillie's cheeks to grow redder. The blushing bride might burst into flame if she knew what Minerva was thinking. That it wasn't holding a watch with a legend attached which would get her with child. Oh, no, it was holding a man with something else attached.

Wasn't that the most inappropriate thought she'd ever entertained? And the most uncharitable?

Tillie must know a great deal more than Minerva did about intimacy between a man and a woman. It was hardly Tillie's fault that her husband wanted all of her and Minerva's husband did not.

Harrison unlocked the case and removed the watch. He slipped the key in his pocket, then carried the treasure reverently to show it off to its admirers.

James pressed close to George, as if fearing he might dash off into the storm with the treasure.

'I wonder how many wishes have been granted by it?' Tillie said, sounding wistful.

'We got Jolly!'

A fact which the lady would be aware of, since Jolly suddenly made a leap and snatched at the scone she had been reaching for.

'Jolly, no!' James cried, and then chased the dog about the room.

The watch was unlikely to have granted any wishes. If it had the power to do so, Minerva would no longer be dreaming of her husband's love—she would already be aglow with it.

Standing suddenly, Minerva crossed to the window, picked up Abby.

If she never shared that sort of love with Harrison...if she never had a child... Well, so be it. She had two children whom she loved desperately.

It would be wrong to long for what she didn't have at the cost of not cherishing what she did.

'Would you like to hold the watch for a while, son, before I put it back in the case?'

Harrison's question came just in time. Another moment more and James might have plucked it from George Moore's hand.

After Minerva had managed to set aside her prickly envy, the afternoon became delightful. She found the company of her guests enjoyable.

It was dark outside when Mrs Beasley announced that dinner was ready.

Well, really, Minerva thought, watching the Moores walk into the dining room, arm in arm, seeing George give a quick kiss to Tillie's cheek, and then Tillie going up on her toes to give him one back, they would turn the darkness light and dispel the storm.

Again, she wondered who she had become. More than that, could she continue to pretend she hadn't changed? That she didn't want what she wanted?

It was difficult not to when the image of what she desired sat across the dinner table from her.

Was Harrison aware of the difference between the Moores' marriage and theirs?

If so, it didn't show.

She knew the understanding she'd had with Harrison before they'd wed was no longer enough for her.

What she didn't know was what to do about it.

How were she and Harrison to have their 'Home Sweet Home' without love to bind them?

Their guests had retired early for the night. It was obvious why. They wished for no one's company but their own.

Harrison sat in his chair, watching Minerva at the window while she stared at the rainwater distorting the view.

'I don't suppose you see it clearing?'

'No. Only water on the window.'

She turned to look at him, her arms clasped about her middle.

They ought to retire, like their guests had… Only not precisely like their guests had, he admitted.

There was only the one bed in his chamber now. A bed he didn't dare share with Minerva.

'I will spend the night down here,' he said.

'If you wish.'

Minerva spun about on her heel. She didn't wish him goodnight. Did not smile warmly at him.

He wasn't used to this treatment from her. Ever since dinner she'd not seemed herself.

He tried to sleep, but could not. The chair wasn't fit for anything but a nap.

But that was not the thing keeping him awake.

Clocks ticked. Wind blew. Rain slammed against the window.

In the end he must have drifted off, in spite of his anxiety.

He woke to the noise of shuffling skirts.

Minerva stood by the window, gazing out. The storm was as bad as ever, but the darkness had begun to lift with the coming of morning.

He rubbed his hand across his face. 'You're up early, Minerva. What time is it?'

'Six.'

From the kitchen he could hear Mrs Beasley going quietly about her morning duties.

Minerva must not have slept well either.

He'd seen the way she'd observed the Moores all evening…noticed the expression in her eyes when she'd watched them climb the stairs. There had been no hiding her longing to have the kind of marriage they had.

But Minerva wouldn't look at them that way if she understood what was in store for them. While she envied them, he feared for them. It was only a matter of time before they paid a very high price for giving all of themselves to each other.

With a great sigh Minerva turned, sat down in her chair.

He heard a soft shuffle in the hallway. But when he turned to look he didn't see anyone. Only Jolly, sniffing about.

Thoughts must be swirling in her mind, because she bit her lip. Clearly she wanted to say something, but hesitated to do so.

Having an idea of what it was, he hoped she would not.

Some words were better left unsaid.

If there was one thing he dreaded, it was disputes between husbands and wives. It was all too easy for a common argument to explode into rage.

'What are you thinking, Min?'

'Two things.' She held his gaze across the short distance between their chairs.

'The first, then? What is it?'

'I do not wish for you to call me Min.'

That shook him.

His dearest friend was slipping away. He wouldn't be able to hold on to her. This just went to show what happened when friendship got muddled with love and passion. Emotions became too intense. Disillusioned love killed marriage.

'Tell me the second one,' he said, heartsick over the turn he felt their relationship was taking. He had resisted every temptation in order for this not to happen, and it had happened anyway.

'I want to know what you think of Tillie and George.'

'I like them…'

He knew he must say the rest of it, even though he knew it would end in—

Damn it! Minerva needed to know what was in store for their guests. Him and Minerva too, if he gave her what she wanted.

'But I think they're going to end up miserable. They don't understand what makes for a strong marriage. Once the passion wears off—and it will—they will end up hating each other.'

Minerva stood up, gripped her skirt in blanched fists. 'That, Harrison Tremayne, is extremely cynical. You don't know that's what will happen!'

He stood too. 'I do know it! How many families do you think I've seen ruined by infidelity?'

His voice was raised in the very passion he

sought to avoid. If he didn't control it, he would wake the whole house.

'Plainly enough of them to warp your mind.' She poked him in the chest with her finger to get his attention, in case she didn't already have it. 'You're not the only one to see what marriage can be like. My parents, my brothers and their wives—they are proof that intimacy can hold people together. There's no hope of happiness without it.'

'We were happy.'

Surely she knew they had been?

'Only until I fell in love with you!' Her hands shook…her lips trembled. 'How am I supposed to do this now? I cannot leave the children, and yet living so close to you…it's breaking my heart.'

'You shouldn't have fallen in love with me, Minerva. I told you what would come of it.'

'In the beginning I agreed with you. Not now. Now I know better. You are wrong!'

Backing away from him, she pressed her hand to her bosom. She was blocking him out of her heart.

'Don't you see that the very distance you believe will save us is what will eventually ruin us? You don't withhold yourself from the children. Why do you do it to me?'

She turned, ran into the hall.

He heard a crash, then her footsteps running up the stairs.

Following her, he spotted the framed embroidery she had stitched with such love.

Love for them all.

Love for him.

Now it lay on the floor, with the print of her shoe in the centre of it.

Was she right? Had fear kept him from the one thing he truly wanted?

His parents had ruined his childhood. Was he now going to allow them to ruin the rest of his life as well?

It felt as if his mother's skeletal hand still had a hold on him…

He had only just straightened up and somewhat gathered his emotions when he heard a cry.

Minerva had reappeared in the hall, her eyes wide in alarm.

'Have you seen James?' she panted.

'No.' He grasped her arms, steadying her, because she looked pale and about to fall to her knees.

'He isn't in his room and the Ruby Fairy Watch is gone.'

Oh, no, he'd forgotten to lock the case! The key was still in his pocket.

'Do you think he overheard us arguing and ran away?' Tears gathered in the corners of her eyes.

He very well might have.

Harrison recalled the noise he'd heard.

'He must have done.'

It was all Harrison could do not to feel sick…or to shout…to feel like a helpless boy again.

'Do you think he's gone to the cave?'

'I think it's likely.'

Where else would a boy who believed in magic go to make a wish to save his family?

'I'll just ask Mrs Beasley to listen out for Abby and to wake Mr Moore.' Minerva ran back to the kitchen.

Then, not bothering with coats, they tore outside.

Minerva stumbled on the slick porch steps. He grabbed her elbow.

'Wait for me here.'

Rain hit them hard, obscuring their way down to the beach.

He heard Minerva's footsteps running behind him.

'I can't see him!' Minerva cried when they were halfway down the path.

Waves pounded the shore with the force of a fabled Leviathan slamming its tail on the sand.

Moment by moment the ocean gobbled more of the shoreline.

A small boy would be helpless against this.

'I'm going ahead,' he shouted. 'Wait here for George, then send him after me.'

In the middle of everything, the fear and the danger, a thought came to him.

It wasn't love that had ruined the Tremayne family. It was the loss of love that had done it.

Minerva would not wait there. She followed Harrison down the path to the beach—what was left of it. The tide was high and the storm whipped the waves, making them seem like great jaws eating the sand.

Picking her way along the path, she had to watch every step. The way was treacherous. She fell behind Harrison, who had already made it to the slip of beach which remained.

Nature's force made her tremble—and so did her fear for James. He was only seven years old. The sea was ancient, wild in a way she'd never seen before.

Harrison was now nothing more than a blurry figure in the rain, struggling against the swirling water already rushing over his ankles.

But where was her son?

The ocean seemed a living thing, a monster which had snatched up her child and swallowed him whole. Dragged him into the great, cold darkness.

It was too much…

She couldn't breathe, thinking of it.

She slid against wet grass going down, ignoring the stones gouging her thighs.

She was still ten feet up from the beach when a movement caught her eye.

James clung to the side of the huge rock near the cave, where the seals liked to lounge in the sunshine. Water crept up the side and would soon cover it.

She screamed for Harrison, but he didn't turn.

Reaching the beach, she ran after him. Surf dragged at her skirt, tangled around her legs and slowed her down.

Still Harrison didn't hear her screaming.

Waves came—and came again. She was going to be swept out to sea before she could alert him to where James was.

A movement on the cliff caught her attention. George Moore. He spotted her. She pointed frantically towards the rock.

George shouted. His voice was deep, and loud enough for Harrison to hear. He gestured madly towards the rock.

The rock was not terribly far from where Harrison was, but it might as well be miles. The tide crept steadily higher, hindering his progress.

James was struggling too. Water lashed about his slim shoulders as he tried to climb to the top of the rock.

Oh, but he was so small. How would he manage to hold on? Surely it was impossible.

Deepening water forced her back to where the sand met the wall of the cliff. There was nothing she could do to help.

Footsteps splashed, coming from behind her. George ran past.

She knew the men would do what they could to save James…give up their lives if it came to it. Seeing them press on, she realised there was no denying the risk they took.

With her back now pressed against the cliff, she did her best not to tremble for James…and for the men trying to save his life.

She kicked at her skirt. It had grown too wet, too heavy. It was now her enemy as much as the surf was.

Loosening the waist, she stepped out of it, then tossed it at an incoming wave.

But getting rid of the skirt might not help her survive the spot she now found herself in—which was with a slippery wall behind her and a great angry ocean rising in front of her.

There was nothing she could do for any of them.

No, that wasn't true. She could pray.

Looking towards the rock, she saw Harrison dive into the surf, fighting the crests of the waves which tried to keep him from reaching it.

George was closer to her than to the rock, so he wouldn't be able to do any more than she could.

Something subtle caught her attention—a change in the sound of the water, perhaps.

She glanced out to see a massive tower of a wave cresting. She couldn't climb, and there was no time to run back to the path. Not for her or for George.

She could not look at what was coming or she would lose control, begin to scream when she needed to pray.

Looking back at the rock, she asked for deliverance.

The wave advanced. It sounded as if it was breathing. Still she didn't look at it, but kept her prayers and her attention on Harrison and James.

But there! The great swell had lifted Harrison and carried him towards the rock. He latched onto a crevice, and hand over hand he made it to James, slung an arm about him.

George cast a desperate glance at her.

The last thought she had was how sad this would be for Tillie…

Chapter Fourteen

'Tea!' a voice shouted, and it sounded a great distance away.

Was there tea and shouting in Heaven? And shivering? She was so cold. Who would have expected Paradise to be so uncomfortable?

It was all her fault she was here. The fact must be faced. Had she not argued with her husband in a way which James could overhear, he wouldn't have run off. Harrison had tried to warn her that passion led to anger, and she'd refused to believe him.

She hoped that when Harrison remarried he would choose a lady who'd love the children as much as Minerva did. And please let her be a woman who would love him less than she did.

'Minerva?'

Oh, no!

'You're here, too? What about James?' She peered at Harrison blearily, one eye cracked open a bare slit.

'He's here.'

'George?'

She didn't know how he could have avoided dying any more than the rest of them.

'Right over there…drying out by the fire.'

It would be a comfort for Tillie to know he was drying out, but of course there was no way to let her know.

She wept then. One more thing she hadn't thought happened in Paradise. 'What will Abby do without us?'

'Without us? Why would she be without us?'

While things were still fuzzy, and nothing seemed quite real, it must be worse for Harrison, given he didn't understand what had happened.

'Because we are dead and she is not. There is a great distance between us.'

Weight shifted on her bed. A small knee pressed her hip.

It was odd that she was in bed and everyone else was moving about.

'Here I is, Mama-Min!' Abby hugged her tight.

'We aren't dead, at all.'

James? She sat up. Her head ached and her nose itched with dried salt water.

She glanced about. This was Harrison's chamber and she was on his bed. George really was drying out by the fire.

But… James! Alive and looking unharmed! She gasped, grabbed him in a great, tight hug.

'Ouch!'

'Here is the tea.' Tillie hurried across the room, placing the cup in Minerva's hands with great care. Probably because they were trembling.

'I don't understand... How are we not...?'

Harrison steadied the cup and lifted it for her to sip. His brows lifted in the way they did when he was confused.

'Dead, I mean?'

'I don't understand it either, Minerva.' Harrison took the cup from her fingers, setting it on the bedside table. 'I knew I wasn't going to make it to James in time. There was no way it was possible. I saw him losing his grip on the rock. But then a wave lifted me up, pushed me to where he was—to the very place where I could grab him. Then another wave hit us and carried us to the cave entrance...high up, though, where there is a ledge. I pushed James up to the top, and Tillie was waiting to draw him the rest of the way up the cliff. I came out after him.'

'But George and me...?'

Harrison waved George over. 'He can explain it better.'

George crossed the room. Harrison gave up his chair to allow him to sit beside her.

'I cannot explain it at all, my lady. A miracle is the only thing I can think of. We both knew we weren't going to survive that wave.'

'I thought we hadn't. When I woke up here, I assumed it was…*there*.' She pointed up.

George shrugged, shook his head.

'After that wave hit I was under deep water. I knew you had to be too. Then I got knocked against something. It stuck out of the cliff. A root is my best guess. I latched onto it, because the current was wild and twisting me out of control. Next thing I knew, you'd bumped into me. I let go of the branch and held on to you with both arms. We twisted madly up and down. The wave slammed us against the sand, then it drew us up, and then we were tumbling. I didn't know if we were getting carried out to sea or towards the rocks.'

'Thank you for not letting go of me.'

'We did have help at the end,' he said.

A glance at Tillie's beaming smile told Minerva she thought her husband was a great hero. Minerva thought so too.

'I thought we would drown, rolling and hitting the sand over and over. I had no idea where we were—near land or out to sea. I was only half conscious when I felt something grab the back of my trousers, and then all of a sudden I could breathe again. I couldn't see for a second, and I felt you being prised from my grip. I fought to keep hold of you. Then I heard your husband saying he had us. I managed to walk out of the surf, but he carried you.'

'Well, he is very strong. But, George, you didn't

let go of me—even to save your own life. I am for ever grateful.'

'Oh, I couldn't have faced Tillie if I had let you go.'

Then she looked at Harrison, noticing, now, how done in he seemed.

Even in his exhaustion she believed he'd do it all over again right now if his family was in danger.

He might not know he loved her, but he certainly acted as if he did. She would make do with that from now on.

Mrs Beasley came in then. 'Her Ladyship's bath is ready.'

'Bath? Now? I don't think—'

Harrison reached over George's shoulder, plucked something from her hair. He dangled a piece of seaweed in front of her nose.

Well, perhaps she should.

She turned to get out of bed, but Harrison swept her up in his arms.

'Tillie, would you mind tending to the children for the day?'

'I would adore it.'

'What are you doing?' Minerva asked.

'Taking you downstairs.'

'Yes, but why are you doing it? Put me down. I'm not injured.'

Plainly he was not convinced. 'We have something to discuss. I cannot do it while you are shivering.'

He tightened his arm around her back. Long fingers curled about her thighs, gripping her through her chemise.

To anchor her to him? In case she decided to scramble away?

All of a sudden she wasn't shivering quite as much as she had been. And it was only fair to admit the shivers she'd felt hadn't exactly been caused by a chill.

Being held close to Harrison's heartbeat was a snug place to be. She was content to have his solid, lean muscles under her legs and encircling her back. They flexed with his steps, making her feel as if she was light as a feather—which she was not.

He carried her downstairs, through the kitchen and into the room behind.

Now was her chance to breathe in the scent of his neck, where a salty dampness rose from his shirt collar. For this one moment she would cherish the heat of his breath, moistly puffing against her hair.

Since he didn't want the sort of marriage she did, it was unlikely she'd ever be this close to him again.

And even though he wouldn't be able to give her all of himself, she was willing to take what he could give.

She'd been content with that in the beginning, and she would learn to be again.

After entering the bathing room, Harrison

closed the door with the heel of his shoe. He set her down, slid the lock closed.

The water steaming up from the tub was a pure invitation. What bliss it would be to slide into it. The sooner Harrison left her alone, the sooner she could get to it.

Given that he'd locked the door, he probably intended to stay and discuss the disagreement they'd had before James had fled. Point out to her that that was what came of being in love.

Not that she believed it—but she could see how what had happened might have reinforced his point of view.

There was a chair beside the tub, with a towel draped across the back.

'You should sit,' she said.

'I intend to.'

But he did not. He simply looked at her, in an unreadable way.

He had been through a great deal more than she had—getting James to safety and then coming back to rescue her and George.

'Sit in the tub, I mean.'

'I intend to do that, too.'

He still made no move to sit anywhere.

'Well, one of us ought to get in before it cools off.'

She walked to the door, sliding the bolt open, ready to go out.

He covered her hand and slid it back. 'We need to talk, Minerva.'

Steam rose off the water, resembling wispy fingers inviting her to indulge. Crossing to the tub, she trailed her fingertip in the tame, heated water.

'Yes, you're correct…we do.'

She shook the droplets from her fingers. His expression shifted. Still she didn't understand what was behind it. Only knew that she had not seen one like it on his face before.

Not quite.

When he'd kissed her in the elevator, she'd seen a flash of something similar.

'Turn around,' he said.

What? Very well. It probably would be easier to speak without looking at him.

'I'm sorry I told you that I loved you,' she said. 'I know it was the last thing you wished to hear from me.'

Something tickled her neck. His fingers?

'What are you doing?'

'Unbuttoning your blouse.'

Why was he doing that? It made no sense.

'Those buttons are wicked little things, I will warn you.' Confused, she was reduced to babbling. In that moment, who really cared about buttons?

Plainly dealing with buttons was not as annoying a chore to him as it was to her. Of course he had the advantage of looking at them, while she'd always had to do it by reaching behind her.

Now her thoughts were babbling, as well as her spoken words.

Why was she giving so much thought to his easy way with her buttons when she ought to be wondering why he was unbuttoning them at all?

'Is there something else you wish to say?' he asked.

'One thing.'

If only she could recall what it was when he was plucking at her buttons so leisurely.

His fingers made hot streaks on her skin as he drew the blouse back from her shoulders.

It almost seemed as if he was trying to seduce her.

Why would he be doing that?

Was he, for some reason, giving in to what he thought she'd all but demanded of him?

He slid the blouse off her arms, dropping it beside the tub, and then turned her by the shoulders to face him.

His gaze slipped down her body. Before it occurred to her that her shift was too thin to protect her modesty, he snapped his eyes back to her face.

But what was that? In that quick glance she'd seen something unguarded cross his eyes.

Desire?

Surely not. Harrison Tremayne spurned that emotion.

Since she did not, she reacted to the mysterious message glittering behind his eyes in a way which could only be called…tantalising…secretly and delightfully tantalising.

But was she only seeing what she wished to see?

Surely not—because what she saw right now was seduction.

But was he doing it purely to appease her?

She wouldn't respond to any obligatory desire. It could not be true desire if it was forced.

'What is the one thing you want to say to me, Minerva?'

If only he would look past her…or at the floor…or the chair.

With real desire or forced, his eyes held hers, giving her an all-over flush. If the curl at her temple had had the ability to do so, it would have gone limp.

She stiffened her emotional backbone because… What was he about? The last thing she was going to accept was pity love.

Best to get it said and then put it behind them, once and for all.

'That in the future I promise to do my best not to tell you I love you,' she said.

He gave her the smile she loved best. The one he used when he was trying not to smile but couldn't help it. What was the man about?

'Get in the tub, Min.'

She backed towards it, frowning all the way. Because…was he offering false desire behind that smile?

She stepped into the tub—shift and all.

The swirl of warm water around her shins was

delightful. She sighed and slid happily down into it—despite her confusion over this man whose smile had now grown into a grin. A great, broad grin which undid her.

He sat down on the chair, picking up a cup from the floor. Scooping it full of water, he dribbled it over her hair, then her face.

She plucked the cup from his fingers. 'There's no need for you to pretend to have any feelings for me.' The truth must be stated.

'Good, then.'

Being this close to hot water, the lenses of Harrison's glasses had fogged up. It was just as well, since she didn't wish to see the look of relief brightening his eyes at knowing he no longer needed to give her a passion-filled gaze.

'You may leave me now,' she said.

He anchored his arms over his chest, stretched out his long legs and crossed them at the ankle—as if he meant to stay until the water grew cold.

With another long, languid look, he took her in…curl to toenails. She felt exposed. Her soul more than her body. She couldn't recall her soul ever being exposed before. It was disconcerting because… well, by refusing to love her, he would never expose his soul to her in return.

She tugged the towel from between Harrison's back and the chair, gave it a snap, then spread it over herself.

* * *

'You may stop looking at me that way now,' she told him.

'What way do you mean?'

Glancing at him from under half-lowered lids, she seemed to suggest he was dim for not already knowing.

'With false passion.' She adjusted the towel higher, looking down and then sliding it back to where it had been before.

If she thought it to be false, she was mistaken. And it was his fault. He was going to set that right if he could.

'So we may carry on with our marriage as it was,' she said.

No, they could not.

All his life he had been mistaken about love and what resulted from it. Now he was going to take great delight in discovering just how wrong he had been.

An hour ago, death had nearly taken Minerva from him. Nothing he'd ever experienced before had shaken him like looking at a future without her had done.

False passion?

It was his past indifference which had been false.

By covering herself with the towel she had been making a point of putting distance between them. But his wife wasn't the only one with a point to make.

Slowly, deliberately, he reached into the bath and drew the towel out. It hit the floor with a wet smack.

'If you wish us to remain friendly, you should put that back. I told you I would do my best not to admit that I love you, but you must help me a bit, don't you think?' she protested.

'When I said there were things we must discuss, the "we" meant I have things to say as well.'

'Speak quickly, then, before the water cools.'

Drawing her long dark hair over her shoulders, she covered herself once again…somewhat.

He left her hair where it was. Perhaps once he'd had his say, then…

'Given how close we came to losing James,' she prompted, 'you now have a new understanding of how important family is? Is that it?'

Facing death did make a man see life more clearly. She was correct. There was nothing like thinking his family had been lost to him to bring home the point.

Also, he now saw that everything he'd believed about marriage was wrong. Romantic love *did* matter. It was all that mattered.

Life was meant for loving his wife with all his heart and for every moment they were alive.

'And because of it,' she went on, 'perhaps you

have changed your mind and now want an heir. Don't worry. I won't shirk my duty.'

The hot water had turned her skin as pink as rose petals.

He pulled his shirt off over his head, and quickly stripped off everything else.

'What are you doing?'

'Make room. I have something to tell you too, Min.'

'There's not much room to make.'

She did move over, though, and he folded himself into the space across from her.

'So, then…am I to assume you wish to beget an heir now? Right at this moment?' she asked huskily, eying his naked body with delight.

He grinned. 'It's not an heir I want. It's you.'

'Me?'

'I love you, Min. So, yes. I want you very badly.'

She cocked her head at him. His heart tumbled a dozen different ways in love. Why had he wasted so much time avoiding something so wonderful?

'You don't believe in love, Harrison.'

'I didn't. Now I do.'

He was no Don Juan when it came to words. She was going to need convincing of another sort.

'Turn around and lean back against me. I need more room for my legs.'

On her knees, she twisted, then lowered herself back into her spot. Water slid over her skin, giving it the look of glass… It was not cold like glass was, though.

'That's better. Thank you.'

Laying his arms on the sides of the tub, he gripped it hard. He would not speak to her with intimate touches yet. Sincere words, if awkward, would have to do until he spoke his heart and she believed him.

She moved forward an inch, so she wasn't quite touching him.

'You know better than anyone that I didn't believe in it…not this sort of love, anyway.'

Long and wavy, her wet hair draped over her back, glimmering softly in the dim light of the one lamp. He focused his attention on the loops and whirls sticking to her skin.

'Facing death has given you a sudden revelation?' she asked.

And why wouldn't she be sceptical?

'Yes and no, Min. When I knew I loved you it wasn't a revelation…more an innate understanding of what had been there all along. An unveiling, you might say.'

His profession of love was met with silence. Water dripped from her hair…plopped in the bathwater.

His heart pounded madly. Surely she must hear it.

What was he to do if she refused to believe his change of heart?

Only hours ago he'd denied her—had been willing to let her believe he would never love her.

'I am a great fool. You know that.' He touched her hair, smoothed the strands between his fingers. 'But won't you forgive me?'

It seemed for ever before she answered.

She shrugged, glancing at him over her shoulder. 'You did save my child's life, so I probably should.'

She smiled.

Suddenly life felt wonderful in a way it never had.

Were it not for Minerva, he might never have understood just how deeply his parents had wounded him.

But love healed. It did not destroy.

She pivoted as much as possible in the small space.

He touched her cheek, traced the forgiveness offered in her smile.

Life clicked into place.

His past was no longer something that weakened him. Instead, to his surprise, he found it strengthened him.

But that was wrong. It wasn't his past giving him strength. It was his wife. It was the love she had freely given him, no matter how stubbornly, how foolishly, he'd refused it.

Until now.

'I love you, Minerva. In every way a man can love a woman, I love you.'

She gave a great relieved sigh. 'Oh, thank goodness. I told you I wouldn't say I love you again, but honestly, it would have been impossible.'

Turning, she leaned back, snuggled against his chest. 'I love you too. In every way a woman can love a man.'

Free now to do it, he moved his arms from the sides of the tub and wrapped them about his Min. He rested his chin on her wet shoulder, just feeling her breathe. He was so relieved and grateful he thought his heart would burst.

'You need a shave.'

He moved her hair to one side, rubbing his bristles against her neck. She had the loveliest neck, with the softest skin. From now on he intended to kiss it as often as the chance presented itself.

As it did now. So he did.

'A shave? That is all I need? You, my dear, have nothing to wear to go back upstairs.'

'We could just stay where we are until everyone goes to bed,' she suggested.

'It's not yet noon. And I've had enough cold water for a lifetime. And since there's no room for me to do what will keep us warm…'

Minerva stood up, stepped out of the tub, drew her shift down, wriggled it off, then walked out of the wet circle it had made on the floor.

If the bath water had cooled while they were in

it, he couldn't tell. Simmering sights and steamy thoughts were the order of the moment. Even an iceberg would melt if it came between them, he thought hazily.

Then she snatched up his shirt and shrugged it on.

Covered to mid-thigh, she was more seductive than anything he had ever seen or imagined.

As impossible as it seemed, this alluring woman was his wife.

Seeing her like this reminded him yet again of what an idiot he'd been to blind himself to this part of marriage for so long.

He would kick himself, were such a feat possible, because it had taken a hard stare-down with death in order for him to recognise the truth.

'You are bewitching, Lady Elmstone.'

Her smile enchanted him as much as seeing her slowly, enticingly, buttoning the shirt from bottom to top.

'We should hurry upstairs before you change your mind.'

Her smile was a tease, an invitation.

Excellent.

He stood, stepped out of the tub, then snatched up his trousers. He drew one leg to his knee. Then nearly choked because she was giving him the same intense perusal he'd given her.

While he'd sown a certain amount of youthful

oats, being naked in front of her seemed new and exciting all at once.

Minerva had her hand on the door lock. He caught her fingers, drawing them to his mouth for a kiss.

Given that the only towel was in a soaking heap on the floor, both he and Min must stay damp under his clothes.

He drew her in for a kiss. Lamplight glistened on her neck and on his arm.

'I won't change my mind, Min,' he murmured close to her lips. 'Never.'

Her sigh was soft. It skittered over his skin… sizzled.

Then words failed him. His mind went blank except for one thought.

'You have such a sweet round bottom.'

'Yours is firm.' She gave it a squeeze to illustrate that.

While this wasn't the first time he'd kissed his wife, it was the first time he'd done so feeling like a full-blooded husband.

Several moments later he opened the door, peeked around. Not spotting anyone, nor hearing Cook pottering in the kitchen, he tiptoed out, waving for Minerva to follow.

Coming out of the room, she caught his hand, keeping watch behind while he watched in front.

'I never thought marriage would be such an adventure,' she whispered. 'I wonder where everyone is.'

'Out of the way, it seems. The children are playing with Tillie and George outside, perhaps.'

Casting a glance over his shoulder at his wife hurrying behind him, her legs bare as eggs, he thought that adventure took many forms. Sneaking through the house was only one. Once they reached the bedroom…

He grinned. Adventure wasn't a word he'd ever equated with marriage, either.

Love was a miracle. That was all he could think.

Another miracle, since how else was he to explain how any of them had survived the ocean?

Pausing at the door leading from the corridor to the hall, he listened.

'I can't hear anything.' Minerva's voice sounded soft, hopeful. 'No, wait… They're in the parlour.'

'Sounds like it. Be ready to dash into the cupboard if someone comes out.'

'Truly? That sounds inviting.'

She was right. It did… Still, it was their chamber he was intent on reaching undetected.

Halfway across the hall Minerva stopped, wriggling her fingers out of his grip.

'Home Sweet Home' was still on the floor. With all that had happened, no one had noticed it.

She picked it up, dusted the footprint off with the tail of his shirt—which, obligingly, rose up her hip.

'I was in a temper when I did that,' she whispered apologetically. Quietly, she placed it back on the nail, straightened it.

'I can't believe how close I came to missing it,' he whispered.

'It wouldn't have been your fault if you'd stepped on it.'

'Let's go.'

He placed his hand at the small of her back and urged her to hurry up the stairs. Once inside the room, he stood behind her, drew her close, her bare legs against his trousers, the borrowed shirt against his back.

'I didn't mean I can't believe I missed stepping on the embroidery. I meant I can't believe home is what I nearly missed. The sweet part of it.'

Turning in his arms, she drew his face down and gave him a quick kiss, happy in nature rather than sensual.

'My half of your clothing is damp. If I get shivery will you take it off me?'

'Seems to me you are shivering now.'

'Home Sweet Home', indeed.

Minerva dressed for the morning, not certain she had ever seen a prettier one.

Sunshine streamed through the chamber window and stabbed a ray at Harrison, who grabbed the edge of the blanket at his shoulder, dragging it with him when he turned over.

He'd had a busy night. She ought to let him sleep in so he could have a busy night again tonight.

She would need to wake him in a moment, though. George and Tillie were returning to St Austell this morning, to finish their honeymoon.

The mattress gave when she sat on the bed, but Harrison still didn't wake up.

What had become of the Ruby Fairy Watch? Given everything else, she hadn't thought of it until now.

But that was something for later. Right now she needed to awaken her sleepy man. It was a good thing she was already dressed, otherwise…

Visions of last night flitted across her mind like silky butterflies, alighting on one delicious memory, then fluttering with delight to the next.

Harrison's lashes twitched in his sleep. She ran her fingertip along one dark curve. She had never touched anyone's lashes before. Interesting how they were soft and bristly all at once…

Her victim's chest rose with a deep breath, but he remained asleep.

Very well.

She blew into his ear.

Nothing. Not from him. But her heart had gone soft…softer than it already was. Never in her life had she imagined marriage being so wonderful that you could puff into someone's ear and not feel odd about doing it.

She finally understood fully what Evie had been trying to tell her before she wed…about the pleasure to be had between a man and a woman.

Now Minerva had found that treasure. Not only last night but this morning, in the joy of everyday moments. Such as which way of waking her man would be the most fun?

A tickle? But where? Earlobe? Rib? Hmmm… He'd thought her bottom was a lovely place to tickle, so fair play and all that…

Slowly, stealthily, she reached under the blanket, felt the heat pulsing from one unsuspecting nether cheek.

All at once the bedclothes erupted. She found herself tossed onto her back, with Harrison looming over her, one large hand tucked underneath her. Had it not been for the layers of skirts and underclothes between her and his flexing fingers, she would already be the victim of his tickling.

'You're awake!'

'If I must be.'

He rolled off her, then sat up on the edge of the bed and rubbed his hand across his face.

'You must.'

Rolling off the mattress, she reached out her hand to encourage him the rest of the way out of bed.

He groaned, rose, and then wrapped her in a hug.

She felt him investigating the fabric at the back of her skirt.

Twirling away, she reminded him, 'George and Tillie are leaving today. We must bid them good-bye.'

'Very well,' he said, walking to the wardrobe. 'And there are the children to see to. I don't suppose we can let them dash about unsupervised except for the poor Moores.'

'Even supervised they're a challenge.'

'So we've discovered. I am grateful every second that there are the two of us to keep up with the two of them.' He opened the wardrobe and yanked out a clean pair of trousers. With one leg shoved in, he cast a wink over his shoulder. 'Although I expect that will change in future.'

'How will we manage being outnumbered?'

'Something will come to us.'

There was a teasing quality to his smile. No doubt he meant it to be secretly seductive.

Although, after last night, really there weren't any secrets left between them.

Dressed now, he crossed he room, gave her a kiss on the forehead. 'Have I told you I love you yet this morning?'

'Yes, you murmured it in your sleep.'

'Did I? Must have been dreaming about…' He arched a wicked brow and patted her bottom.

'Let's go down and have breakfast with the Moores before they leave.'

'I'll miss them. We should call on them the next time we go to London.'

'Will you hate it terribly when we go back?' she asked.

He stopped midway down the stairs, appearing to think it over.

'No, I don't believe I will.' He did not continue down but laid his arm about her shoulder. 'You asked me about the nightmare… I never answered you.'

'You don't have to.'

'I do need to, Min—only not all of it, as it's exceedingly unpleasant. It's enough to know that it has to do with my parents behind their closed chamber door, and the evil between them. The last time I had it—when you woke me up—the door to their bedroom finally opened. In the past, I've always woken up before it did.'

'From what I could see, it was terrifying.'

'Yes, but last night I had a different dream. I dreamed I was in front of the door again. But I was a man in this one and not a terrified boy. And there was peace beyond the door. I knew you were in there this time, so I didn't hesitate to open it. There you were, sitting on the bed, as happy as I've ever seen you. You were telling me to come over and meet our… Well, it was twins.'

'Girls or boys?'

'The dream didn't reveal that.'

'Twins make sense… Why should I be different from my brothers in that? Did the dream reveal how long we have to get ready for them?'

'I think that's probably up to us.'

'Ah, soon, then.'

Heads bent towards each other, they laughed all the way to the hall.

'Oh! I nearly forgot to ask… What happened to the fairy watch?'

'All I know is that James took it with him to the cave.' Harrison shrugged. 'He didn't have it afterwards. I think it's fair to say we've seen the last of it.'

'I hope James isn't too upset.'

Which, she thought, was a rather large hope.

Harrison stood on the cliff, his arm slung over Minerva's shoulder. They watched their children dashing about the meadow between the house and the stable, Jolly barking after them.

Down below, the Moores were taking a final morning walk along the shore.

To look at the beach now, one would never guess that yesterday had happened—not the bad part at least. Brilliant autumn sunshine and a blue sky with a single cloud shaped like a dragon drifting tamely across it made it hard to believe.

Unless one had lived it and nearly died in it.

And yet the storm was gone and here they were. It might take him a few days to go back down to the beach and feel comfortable, but he would do it.

One day soon he was going to dance on the shore with his wife. Under the stars or under the sun—it didn't matter. Baron and Baroness Elmstone were going to dance. Life held more reasons to celebrate than he would ever have imagined.

George and Tillie began their walk up to the cliff.

When they reached it, Minerva hurried to give her new friends a hug.

A blessing had come from the loss of that watch. At least that was what legend would say…probably James too.

He hadn't spent any time with his son since last night, so he didn't know if he was upset about the watch. If he was, it wasn't apparent.

Harrison waved the children over so they could say goodbye to the Moores. The whole family was going to miss them.

After hugs, good wishes and promises to visit one another often, they all walked towards the Moores' carriage.

'Ah, James.' George reached into his pocket. 'We found something down on the beach which belongs to you. It was tangled up in a piece of wood that had got washed up on the shore. Tillie spotted it reflecting the sunshine.'

Grinning, George drew a chain out of his pocket. At the end of it dangled the Ruby Fairy Watch.

James whooped, leapt to take it. But then he shook his head, took a step back.

'No, sir, you found it, so it's yours. And I no longer need it.'

'I shall pay you for it, then. Name your price, young man.'

'You have paid me already.' James sidled sideways, hugging Minerva's skirts.

By saving his mother's life. That was what James meant.

James hadn't been sheltered from what had happened yesterday. How could he have been, having lived through it?

Harrison's heart swelled with pride in his son's understanding. But he refrained from bending down to hug him.

Since the child was behaving as a man, he was due that respect.

George must think so too. He extended his hand to James. Large palm swallowed small fingers in a handshake.

'Thank you, James,' Tillie said. She did bend to give him a hug. 'If you're ever in need of a magic wish you may borrow it back in an instant.'

'I won't be.'

George shifted the watch from hand to hand, his attention on James's earnest little face.

'The thing is, the watch has taken rather a beating. It isn't working. If you and your father would be so kind as to repair it for us, we'd be very grateful.'

All child again, James snatched the watch, hopping about with it.

'I fix it too!' Abby chased her brother, trying to wrest it from him.

Against the swell of a building argument between the children the Moores drove away, with promises to return soon to pick up the watch.

It was Jolly who ended up with the watch in the end, snatching it neatly off the grass when James dropped it.

After a short pursuit, Harrison caught the dog. The Ruby Fairy Watch was rescued from disaster for the second time since yesterday.

Holding it to the sunshine, he watched the gold glimmer, the ruby winking. Perhaps it *was* magic. Who was he to say it was not?

The Tremayne family had certainly been blessed while it was in their possession.

'Shall we sit on the cliff and watch the ocean before lunch?' Minerva asked.

'Scary…' Abby shook her head.

Minerva scooped her up, snuggled her against her heart. 'That is exactly why we should sit there. We need to get to know it the way it was before.'

So they sat side by side, Abby on Minerva's lap and James on Harrison's.

'Look there!' Harrison pointed a finger to the rock near the cave. 'The seal has come back to sunbathe.'

'I can hear it barking!'

James leapt up, but kept hold of Harrison's hand.

It was going to take some time to get over what happened, but they would—the four of them together.

'Son, I have a question for you.'

'I know, Papa. I will not go back to the cave, no matter what.'

Papa? Not Uncle-Papa?

'Good. You are a smart boy to learn from your mistakes. But my question is, why did you tell Mr Moore you no longer needed the magic wish?'

'Because I don't. It's already come true.'

Abby kissed Minerva's cheek.

James let go of his hand, dashed to his mother and kissed her other cheek.

'I wished for me and Abby to get a family again, and my wish came true.'

'Me too,' Abby insisted.

'You couldn't make a wish, Abby. I found the watch.'

While the discussion went round and round, Harrison caught Minerva's eye. Her smile was a kiss.

The magic of the fairy watch notwithstanding, his life was a blessing.

He shot the kiss back to her with his smile. No… with his heart.

Minerva Grant Tremayne was his magic.

Rivenhall, June 29th, 1893

'Where's the elephants, Mama?' Abby asked, looking fearfully disappointed. 'I can't see elephants.'

'Grandfather was not able to get elephants. But

we have pink poodles. Piccadilly Circus has neither of those,' Minerva said, stroking her daughter's straight blond hair.

'I want to go to Piccadilly Circus.'

She glanced at Harrison across the pair of prams where their twin sons peered over the sides, clearly wishing they were able to climb out and romp about with the rest of the children.

'But it's not truly a circus, Abby. And there are no elephants there,' Harrison explained. 'It's only a place where some roads meet. Your grandfather's circus is much better.'

Today in Piccadilly Circus a statue was being unveiled to honour the Earl of Shaftesbury and his charitable acts towards the children of London.

Since they didn't wish to take all the Rivenhall children to Piccadilly Circus, yet they did want to honour the event, Minerva's father had decided to hold a celebration here in the garden, where the children could run about and be free.

In the spirit of the event he had also purchased a statue for the garden, which would be unveiled to coincide with the one in honour of Lord Shaftesbury.

The statue itself was a great secret. No one knew what it was. It was large, though. The canvas cover draped over the limb of a tree fell all the way to the ground.

Minerva thought her father had done a marvellous job in transforming the garden into a circus. Colourful streamers hung from trees. There was an organ player, as well as hired clowns. The Rivenhall circus even had three rings. One ring held tables laden with delicious food. Another ring was for the poodles, who all knew their tricks. The third ring was for the pair of ponies her father had rented to give the children rides.

And there were so many children, dashing merrily about. All her father's grandchildren were here, as well as the staff and the children from London Cradle.

Nothing, he had insisted, could be more appropriate to honour Lord Shaftesbury than to invite orphans.

'Need an elephant. Can we go to a *real* circus, Papa? Where ladies swing way up high.'

'How do you know they do that?' Minerva asked.

'Grandfather told me. It must be great fun.'

Heaven help them. Harrison cast her a glance. She grimaced in answer. *Please do not let her want to swing from a trapeze.*

Although not hers by blood, Abby was too much like Minerva for her own comfort. Father seemed to delight in the fact. He enjoyed pointing out to Abby every bit of mischief her mother had ever got into.

'I'm going to ride a pony.' Abby dashed off and stood in the queue of children already waiting.

'How many children are here, do you think?'

Minerva asked, watching James run about with his cousins and a couple of other boys.

'There are our four, and I cannot tell how many others.' Harrison glanced around with an indulgent smile, patting his sons' matching curly heads. He gave her his funny flat smile. 'The question is… are there too many or not enough?'

'There can never be too many, if you are asking in general. But if you mean for us… Don't even think of it until these two are steadier on their feet.'

Why did he have to grin at her like that? For a man who at one time had been happy living by himself, he now seemed dedicated to filling every room of Cockleshell Cottage…a home which now had many rooms and the potential to build even more.

Glancing to her left, where her sisters-in-law were watching the children playing, she did have to smile at all the prams.

There were Minerva's two. Then Evie had one and Elizabeth had two—one containing a baby and the other a toddler…and a dog. Its snout popped over the edge of the toddler's pram.

Her father wandered by, grinning. He bent over Evie's pram, cooed at the baby girl in it.

'You have gone to a great deal of trouble to make the children happy, Father,' Minerva pointed out. 'It cannot have been an easy task, making it all come together.'

Harrison rounded the prams and stood beside her, snaking his arm about her waist.

Well, when had 'easy' ever equalled 'happy'?

For her, taking a risk by wedding a stranger had equalled happy.

It had proved true for her brothers as well as for her.

None of them had taken the wise, easy path, but look where those paths had led!

To the family now growing both in joy and in numbers.

'It is nothing. Children should be happy. This honours Lord Shaftesbury's memory every bit as much as the celebration in Piccadilly Circus does.' Father scratched his chin, smiled broadly. 'How many of them are ours? I've lost count.'

He had not lost count. He dearly loved adding them all up.

'Ten, is it not?' He answered his own question. Then he grinned at his son-in-law. 'And how many more to come?'

Harrison slid her the wink he very well knew she could not resist, in a clear invitation to increase the family numbers.

There was no doubt whose side Father was on.

'Good man,' her father declared. 'Keep up the fine work.'

'Father, Abby is disappointed there is no elephant,' she said, in order to turn this conversation in another direction.

'Oh?' Father picked up both of her boys, one in each arm. He kissed their cheeks, then put them back, both in one pram. 'Shall we all take a trip to a real circus, my boys? I bet you would like to watch those trapeze artists. It's only a shame your mother retired her trapeze gown...'

Arching a brow at her, he went to join the children waiting for pony rides.

Harrison shrugged, squeezed her tighter and kissed her cheek. 'Well, it does seem he has finally forgiven you.'

'I imagine so. In the end, I did marry.'

'Not a man he would have chosen for you.'

'He knew all along that whoever I wed would never be his choice. But Father has come to adore you. You know that, don't you?'

'All it took was giving him four more grandchildren. How much will he approve of me if I deliver him a few more?'

'Well, it isn't you who'll be delivering them, is it? And I think Father likes you well enough already.'

A couple entered the yard through the garden gate. They too pushed a pram.

'Tillie!' Minerva exclaimed. 'Oh, George, it's so good to see you both.'

After hugs and greetings, Tillie bent over to pick up her newborn daughter from the blankets of the pram.

This was the first time Minerva had seen the baby. 'She is wonderful. May I hold her?'

Taking the baby, she sniffed the top of her head. Oh, but she smelled amazing. Her young sons had already lost that unique scent newborn babies had.

'This is such a magical thing your father is doing,' George said, glancing about.

'He cares very much for children,' she pointed out, even though it was obvious.

So did Harrison Tremayne. He cared for children more than any man she had ever met. And society was beginning to take notice. In time, she believed the name of Elmstone would become a very well-respected one.

'Several of these children are in need of homes, George,' Tillie said, shooting her husband a hopeful smile.

Minerva placed the baby back in her blankets. The Moores hurried away to join the fun.

A trumpet announced that Father had walked over to the statue and was ready to unveil it.

Everyone gathered around the tree to watch.

'In honour of children...of all ages,' he said, and then swung the canvas cover out of the tree.

The statue was a replica of the tree in the front of the house. There was a swing flying high and a pair of children seated on it, a girl and a boy. It might have looked innocent enough—except that on the tree trunk hung a bronze trapeze gown.

Her father looked at her, gave her a great grin

and a wink. For all time she would be reminded of her youthful transgression and where, in the end, it had led.

She grinned back at her father, and nodded to let him know she understood. Pardon, love and humour—all in one bronze piece of art.

'It is lovely, Min.' Harrison nudged her in the side. 'Your father has a great sense of humour under his viscountly demeanour. I believe you take after him as much as you do your mother.'

'The statue is his way of pointing it out,' she said, feeling a tear sting her eye.

'Do you know that some people are saying the statue in honour of Lord Shaftesbury is naked?' Harrison raised his brows at her.

'They say it is in the name of art.'

'I like naked in the name of...' Dipping his mouth close to her ear, he whispered, 'Minerva Tremayne.'

He finished his scandalous whisper with a nip on her ear.

'What sort of thing is that to say in public?'

'Whispering in the Rivenhall garden isn't exactly in public. There is a difference.'

She gave him a quick kiss on the cheek. 'A delightful difference—although I am scandalised at how you react to such a statue in Piccadilly Circus.'

'It's you I'm reacting to. Seeing you hold Tillie's baby gave me...ideas.'

'As long as they stay ideas for now.'

The man was distracting…breathing in her ear the way he was. Did he not notice how two of the children they had were beginning to poke and pull at one another?

'Min, I've had another dream.'

'Tell me you were not staring at a door?'

'I was.'

'Tell me, then, that you didn't open it.'

'I did. As quickly as I could.'

Would there ever be a time when she did not succumb to his smile?

She hoped not—with all her heart.

'And?'

'Congratulations, Min. It's a girl.'

She was light-headed all at once. Harrison must have sensed it because he caught her around the waist.

'It's only one this time, though.'

She held on tight, until the ground felt solid underneath her again. Another child? Well, didn't she just live to make Father happy?

'When?'

'The dream didn't say.'

He touched her chin, lifting it for a long, lingering kiss.

'Soon, then.'

And then she kissed him back, to make sure it would be.

* * * * *

MILLS & BOON®

Coming next month

LORD MARTIN'S SCANDALOUS BLUESTOCKING
Elizabeth Rolls

He was going to kiss her.

Her pulse kicked up, every nerve dancing under her skin.

Once before, just the once, he had kissed her. In the gig as they drove out to Isleworth on the day he had given her the betrothal ring. Only once, and now he was going to kiss her again.

On the cheek.

She didn't want a chaste peck on the cheek. She couldn't have what she did want – but she could have more than a kiss on the cheek. Even if they were standing on a public street outside a tavern.

With his lips a breath away from her cheek she turned, oh so slightly, and their lips met. Worlds stilled, his mouth on hers unmoving… Time shimmered in stasis – then a sound, half sigh, half groan, broke from him and his lips moved in the sweetest of dances, a large gloved hand cradling her cheek as she caught the rhythm and the kiss deepened. For a heart shaking moment that encompassed an all-too-short eternity every planet, star and moon aligned. Everything danced together for one brief measure. Then, as sweetly and gently as it had begun, it was over.

He stepped back, his hand lingering on her cheek and jaw.

"Kit, I'm sorry. I should not –"

"You didn't."

Slowly she lifted her hand to trace with one gloved finger the edge of his lower lip. "I did. If I can't have what I once wanted, at least I could have that."

Continue reading
LORD MARTIN'S SCANDALOUS BLUESTOCKING
Elizabeth Rolls

Available next month
www.millsandboon.co.uk